NAUSICAÄ

Of The Valley Of The Wind

7

HAYAO MIYAZAKI

Nausicaä of the Valley of the Wind
Volume 7

STORY & ART BY HAYAO MIYAZAKI

Translation /Matt Thorn
Translation Assist — Studio Ghibli Library Edition /Kaori Inoue & Joe Yamazaki
Touch-up Art & Lettering /Walden Wong
Design /Izumi Evers
Editor — 1st Edition /Annette Roman
Editor — Studio Ghibli Library Edition /Elizabeth Kawasaki

Kaze no Tani no Nausicaä [Nausicaä of the Valley of the Wind]
Illustrations and Story by Hayao Miyazaki

First published in Japan by Tokuma Shoten Co., Ltd.

Printed in Canada

Published by VIZ Media, LLC
P.O. Box 77010
San Francisco, CA 94107

Studio Ghibli Library Edition

10 9 8 7 6 5 4

First printing, August 2004
Fourth printing, July 2012
First English edition, August 1997

www.viz.com

"MASTER OF THE CRYPT"!? WHO IS THAT?

ANSWER ME, NAMULITH. WHAT DO YOU MEAN, "THINGS ALWAYS TURN OUT AS THE MASTER OF THE CRYPT SAYS THEY WILL?"
HEE, HEE, UNH-H-H ...
ゴオーゴオーン

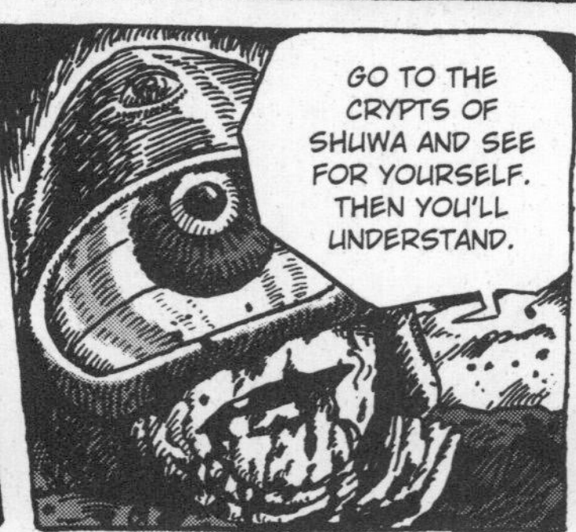
GO TO THE CRYPTS OF SHUWA AND SEE FOR YOURSELF. THEN YOU'LL UNDERSTAND.

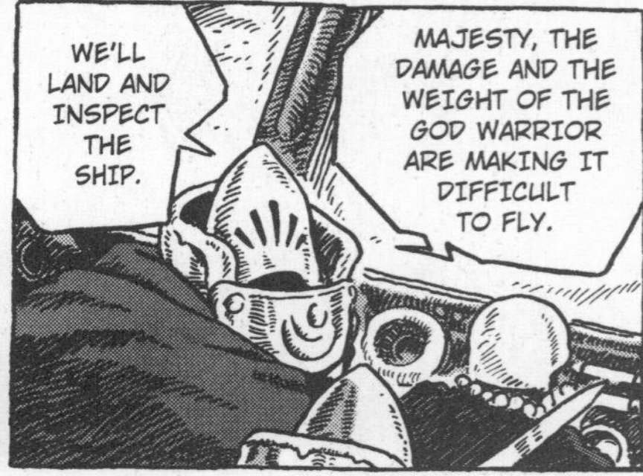
MAJESTY, THE DAMAGE AND THE WEIGHT OF THE GOD WARRIOR ARE MAKING IT DIFFICULT TO FLY.
WE'LL LAND AND INSPECT THE SHIP.

グイ

KUSHANA, BLOW MY HEAD OFF FOR ME.
ゴボ
THIS HEEDRA BODY OF MINE MAY BE IMMORTAL, BUT THE PAIN IS THE SAME AS ANY HUMAN BODY.

HEH, HEH. DAMN, THE PAIN IS UNBEARABLE.
ピクッピクッ

ブチ
ドロ

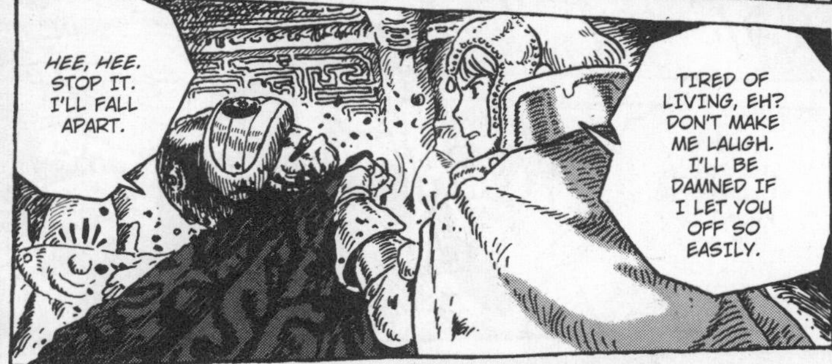
HEE, HEE. STOP IT. I'LL FALL APART.
TIRED OF LIVING, EH? DON'T MAKE ME LAUGH. I'LL BE DAMNED IF I LET YOU OFF SO EASILY.

SOME WIFE YOU ARE.
WHOOPS. NOW THERE'S NOTHING LEFT BUT MY HEAD.

ズル
バタバタ

WHAT'S THAT!? BRING US CLOSER!
オオー

WE'RE GOING TO SEE THE END OF WHAT YOU STARTED.
COME WITH ME.
I'M BEGGING YOU, KUSHANA-- KILL ME.

バタ
バタ

IT'S KUSHANA!!
THAT'S HER, ALL RIGHT! THE LITTLE VIXEN'S STILL ALIVE!!
ゴーーン
ゴーーン

WHAT'S SHE DOING STANDING IN FRONT OF THE GOD WARRIOR LIKE THAT!?

ウオオオオーー…ン

オオオ

カアーァ
DON'T SHOOT!! THEY'RE MY FRIENDS!
オオオオオ
ギュン
NO !!
NO !!
YOW !!
THAT'S RIGHT. YOU MADE SURE THAT SHOT DIDN'T HIT THEM. THAT'S A GOOD BOY.
MAMA'S FRIENDS ?
FRIENDS ...

ARE THEY MAMA'S ENEMIES? SHOULD I KILL THEM?

WHERE IS MAMA'S ENEMY?
I WANT TO FIGHT FOR YOU, MAMA.

I DON'T LIKE IT HERE. I WANT TO LEAVE.

HE'S FRUSTRATED... LIKE A CHILD WHO'S HAD HIS TOY TAKEN AWAY.

THOSE PEOPLE ARE MY FRIENDS, TOO. THERE'S A GOOD BOY. THERE AREN'T ANY ENEMIES.

MAMA'S ENEMIES ARE NOT HERE. I CAN'T KILL HERE.
ゴオーン
ゴオーン
WHERE ARE MAMA'S ENEMIES? I DON'T LIKE IT HERE.

パクッ
ズズーン
WAH! THERE HE GOES AGAIN. THAT MONSTER'S OUT OF ITS MIND.
シュー
シュー
シュー

HEE HEE! WHAT A SIGHT.

THIS THING'S A REJECT. IT CAN'T EVEN CONTROL ITS OWN POWER.
JUST THE COMPANION FOR A GIRL WHO WOULD BE A GOD, DON'T YOU THINK?

UNH ...

SOME WIFE-- TOSSING AWAY HER HUSBAND'S HEAD.

HEY!

THAT'S YOUR CHILD, GIRL. TAKE HIM TO HEAVEN OR HELL, WHER-EVER YOU PLEASE.

TELL ME WHAT I HAVE TO DO TO DESTROY THAT THING FOR GOOD!!
CAN YOU HEAR ME, NAUSICAÄ !?

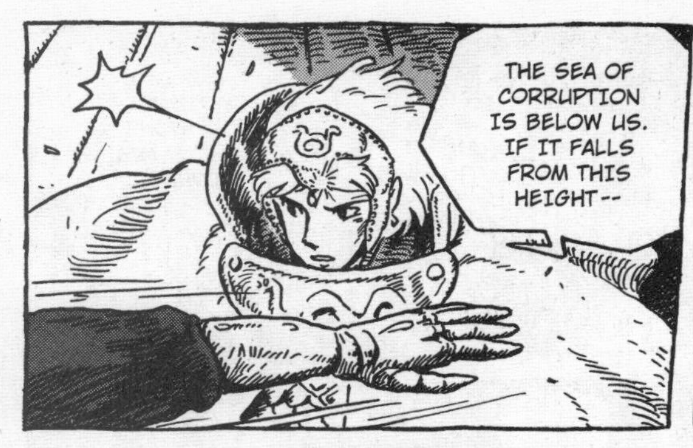
THE SEA OF CORRUPTION IS BELOW US. IF IT FALLS FROM THIS HEIGHT--

IF THERE'S NO OTHER WAY, I CAN BLOW UP THIS ENTIRE SHIP RIGHT NOW!!
WE CAN'T LET THIS MONSTER LOOSE ON THE WORLD!
バタ
バタ

HA, HA, HA. NAUSICAÄ'S THE ONE WHO USED FIRE FIRST!
ピョコ

WE HAVE NO CHOICE BUT TO LEAVE THIS TO NAUSICAÄ. FIRE WON'T WORK ON THAT THING.

LORD YUPA.
QUIET.

THIS CHILD IS LIKE A NEWBORN BABY.
I'M GOING TO GO WITH HIM TO SHUWA.

MASTER YUPA! KUSHANA!
NAUSICAÄ.

THIS CHILD IS MY CHILD. TOGETHER WE'RE GOING TO SEAL THE DOORS OF THE CRYPTS.

TO SHUWA !?

THE ENGINE'S OVERHEATING!! IT WON'T HOLD ANY LONGER!
BRING HER HIGHNESS INSIDE IMMEDIATELY!! WE'LL DESCEND!
YOU CAN FLY, CAN'T YOU? LET'S GO. TO THE WESTERN LANDS.
FLY ... WEST ...
I'LL GUIDE YOU. LET'S GO. TOGETHER.
GO... GO WITH MAMA. FLY...
WESTERN ... LANDS ...

HEE HEE. INCREDIBLE.

ジン
ジン
ジジジ
ジーン

CLAD IN LIGHT, THEY FILLED THE SKY... GREAT WARRIOR GODS, BEARING DEATH...

THIS IS THE RING OF LIGHT THE BOOK OF EXTINCTION WRITES OF!

DOES IT THINK IT'S SOME KIND OF GOD!?
WHAT TH--!? THE DAMNED THING'S GIVING OFF SOME KIND OF LIGHT.
ウォォー
MAJESTY! INSIDE, QUICKLY!!
NAUSICAÄ! TAKE THIS!!
パッ
THANK YOU !!
I'LL HEAD FOR SHUWA, TOO! WE'LL MEET AGAIN THERE!!

カァッ
SO THIS IS WHAT THE OLD BOOKS MEANT BY "TWISTING SPACE!!"
OUCH! THAT DAMNED LIGHT BLEW ME RIGHT OFF THE DECK.
AND JUST WHEN THINGS WERE GETTING INTERESTING. I GUESS THIS IS THE END...
スッ

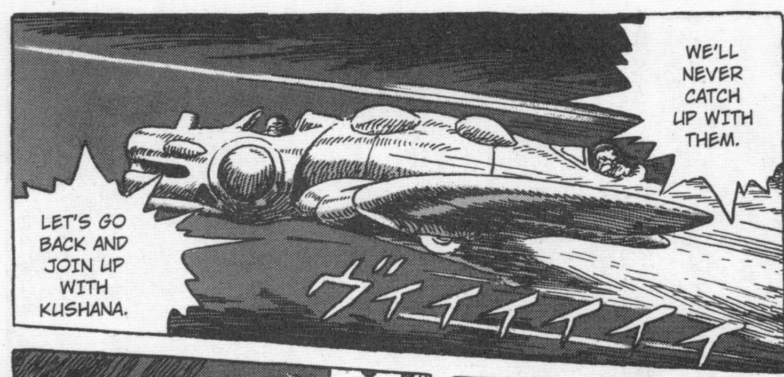
WE'LL NEVER CATCH UP WITH THEM.
LET'S GO BACK AND JOIN UP WITH KUSHANA.
ヴィイイイイイ

DAMN IT, OLD MAN, I SAID, GIVE IT UP!!

DID YOU HEAR ME!? THE ENGINE IS GOING TO EXPLODE!

PRINCESS ...

DON'T GIVE UP THE GHOST... YET, NAUSICAÄ. WE'RE COMING!

YOU JUST KEEP ON BABY-SITTING THAT MONSTER 'TIL WE GET THERE.

ENGINE CRITICAL! SHUTTING DOWN!!

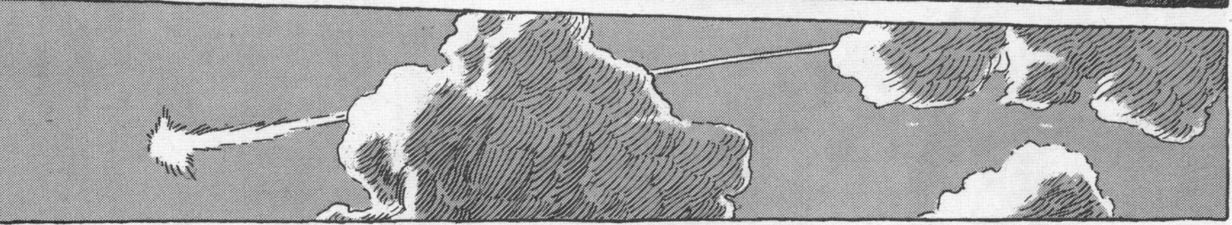

WE MUST BE MOVING AT A FANTASTIC SPEED, YET THE AIR IS STILL.

ドックーン
ドックー
HIS HEART-BEAT ...
IT'S SO SLOW.

HE'S HOLDING ON TO ME SO GENTLY.
HE REALLY THINKS I'M HIS MOTHER.

IT'S GETTING STRONGER ...!?

THERE'S SOME-THING WRONG WITH THIS LIGHT. MY HEART IS POUNDING.

LET ME OUT!! I WANT TO SEE OUTSIDE.

ヒュー
THE AIR OUTSIDE THE LIGHT IS SO COLD AND THIN.

ズル

ジジジ……

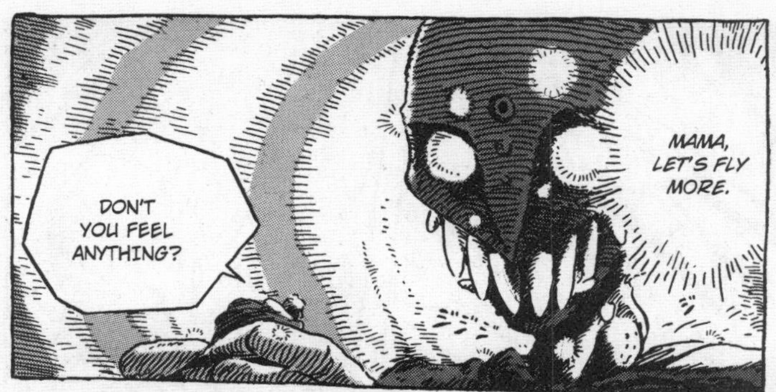
DON'T YOU FEEL ANYTHING?
MAMA, LET'S FLY MORE.

ハァハァ
SOME-THING IS HAPPENING TO HIM.
YOU'RE NOT WELL...

I'LL LAND.

LET'S LAND AND REST FOR A WHILE.
THERE'S DEFINITELY SOMETHING WRONG.

WE'RE SO HIGH UP. I WONDER IF THESE ARE THE GOSS MOUNTAINS.

I NEED AIR.

キラッ
I FEEL DIZZY.

WHO COULD IT BE AT A TIME LIKE THIS?

SHIPS. A FLEET. EVERYTHING IS GETTING DARK.

フワッ
ジュー
ジュルルルル
ジュルルルル
ジュー
ジジジ
ハア
MAMA.
MAMA.
LET ME...
CATCH MY
BREATH...
ハアハア
MY
BODY...
WON'T
MOVE...
EH!?
グラ
ドウ
UNH!
ダン

MAMA, WHERE ARE YOU?
MAMA ...

UNH ...

IT'S--

I'M AFRAID... MAMA...

MAMA... MAMA... MY BODY... WON'T MOVE...

IT'S ALL RIGHT. I'M RIGHT HERE.

SEE? I'M RIGHT HERE. DON'T WORRY. I WON'T LEAVE YOU.

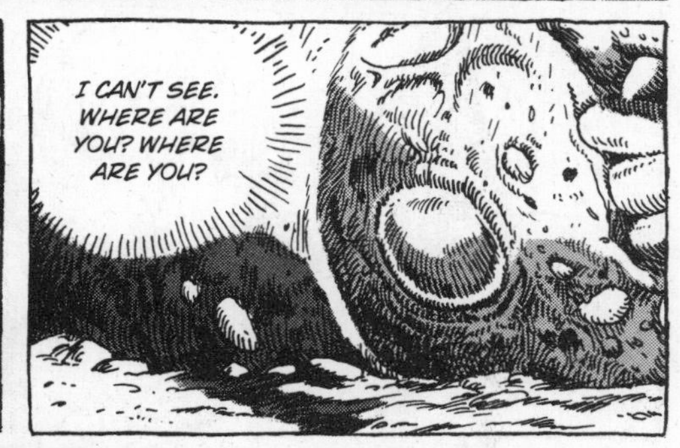
I CAN'T SEE. WHERE ARE YOU? WHERE ARE YOU?

YOU JUST REST A WHILE. THEN YOU'LL FEEL BETTER.

YOU POOR THING. YOU MUST BE EXHAUSTED. YOU'VE BEEN WORKING MUCH TOO HARD FOR A NEWBORN BABY.

AND YET I GO ON PRETENDING TO BE HIS MOTHER, SMILING AND ENCOURAGING HIM.

I'M HOPING FOR THIS CHILD'S DEATH.
ガチ
ガチ

HOW HURT HE WOULD BE IF HE COULD LOOK INSIDE MY HEART...

SNOW.

...IF HE KNEW THAT HE SHOULD NEVER HAVE BEEN BORN.

ANCIENT WRITING... IT'S A TRADEMARK!

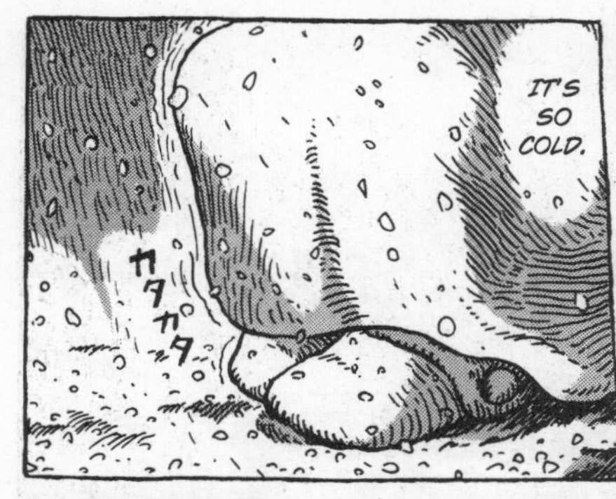
IT'S SO COLD.
カタカタ

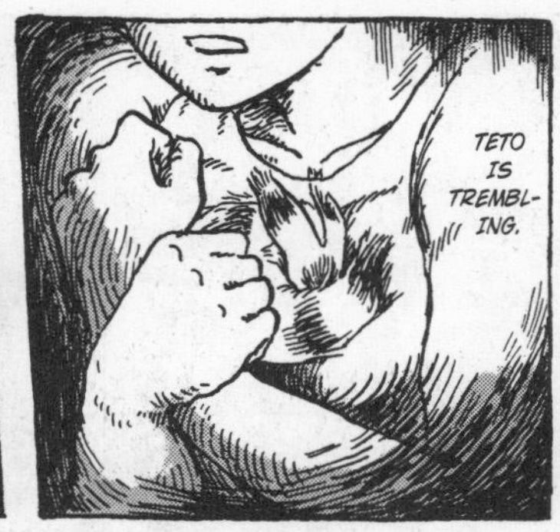
TETO IS TREMBLING.

I CAN'T DIE HERE. I HAVE TO SEAL THE DOORS OF THE CRYPTS OF SHUWA... TO ENSURE THAT NOTHING LIKE THIS CAN EVER BE MADE TO HAPPEN AGAIN.

ググ…

THIS LIGHT !?

IT'S WARM.
HE'S SUCH A KIND CHILD.

BRING MORE OXYGEN BOTTLES!
AND CLOSE THAT DAMNED DOOR!!

I TOLD YOU WE SHOULD HAVE CROSSED THE SEA OF CORRUPTION.

WHILE WE SIT HERE, OUR FATHER IS NO DOUBT OFF TO CAPTURE THE SECRETS OF THE CRYPTS OF SHUWA FOR HIMSELF.

CURSE THIS INSUFFERABLE COLD. OF ALL THE PLACES TO BE GROUNDED.
DON'T TALK. I HAVE A SPLITTING HEADACHE.

THEY SHOULD NEVER HAVE SENT UP A SHIP IN THIS WEATHER!

THE SCOUT SHIP WE SENT OUT TO SURVEY A COURSE HAS FINALLY COME BACK.
HAH! WE'D BE DISCOVERED FOR SURE IF WE TRIED THAT!

SEND UP A FLARE!! THEY CAN'T SEE A THING FROM UP THERE!!

グヮーー
HMPH! ANOTHER CRASH. AS IF WE HAVE SHIPS TO SPARE.

NOT THAT WAY!! YOU'RE HEADED STRAIGHT FOR THE CLIFF!!
ガァァァァ

ワ
ワ

THE ONE THE DOROKS STOLE FROM PEJITEI?
A GOD WARRIOR!? YOU MEAN THAT COMET WE SAW WAS A GOD WARRIOR?

HMMM. A GOOD OMEN... OR POSSIBLY A BAD OMEN.
COULD THIS BE A GIFT OF GOOD FORTUNE?

IT SEEMS TO HAVE LANDED IN A VALLEY IN THE NEXT GROUP OF MOUNTAINS OVER.
I'M AFRAID I DON'T HAVE ANY DETAILS. THAT'S ALL OUR SCOUT WAS ABLE TO TELL ME BEFORE HE DIED.

シュ
シュー

.....
.....
スー

ジュー
シュー
ジュー
ジュジュ

ハア ハア
THAT MUST BE IT THERE!

IT'S HUGE. IS IT DEAD?
CONTACT OUR MAIN FORCE. LET'S GO, MEN!

DAMN! THE ICE IS THIN.

WHAT'S THAT SMELL !?

THIS ISN'T ORDINARY STEAM!
IS IT ROTTING !?

ググ
IT'S MOVING! IT'S ALIVE!!

LOOK!! ITS FINGERS--!!
GOOD GODS, WHAT A STENCH!

YOU'RE NOT KUSHANA'S TROOPS, ARE YOU?

YOU MUSTN'T STAY HERE. PLEASE LEAVE RIGHT AWAY.

IF YOU STAY HERE, YOU'LL BE--!?

WHO THE HELL ARE YOU!? SOME KIND OF MONSTER!?

STAY BACK! THIS CHILD GIVES OFF A POISONOUS LIGHT.

PULL BACK!! THAT THING'S DANGEROUS!
シュ
シュ
シュ
シュ
シュー
カァ
WAH!
OH, NO!
ドン
ガー!
チュン!
チ...

ジュ

DON'T SHOOT !!

HA ...

チュン
チュン
HAHA ...
HAHAHA ...

ワー
ダダダ

HE'S ENJOYING HIMSELF !?

...!!

STOP !!
DON'T SHOOT !!

シュー
シュー
シュー

タッ

HE SENSED THAT I WAS UPSET.

THIS IS MY FAULT.
ズズズ

THIS MAN'S STILL ALIVE.
アア…

THERE'S NOTHING I CAN DO.
AH-H ... HELP ME ...
IT'S SO HOT ... IT ...
ガシッ

HANG ON! I'LL PUT OUT THE FIRE!
AH ... AH-H ...

MAMA IS ANGRY. MAMA IS ANGRY!

HIS LEGS !!

ブチッ
ググ

ガクッ

ヨロ…

WE'VE GOT TO MOVE ON.

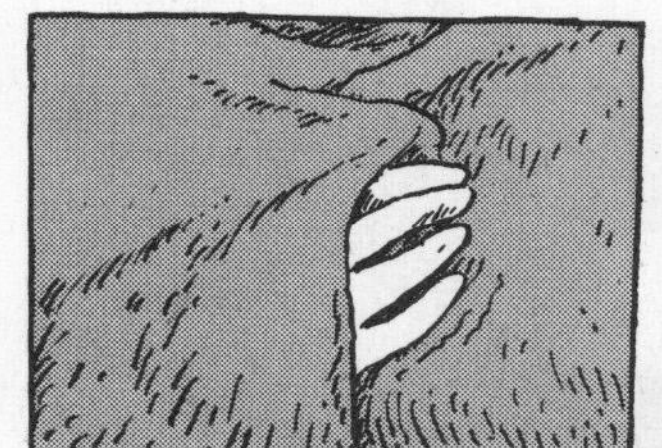

TETO IS GROWING WEAK.

SO AM I.
ハァ ハァ
IT'S THE POISONOUS LIGHT.

I HAVEN'T GOT MUCH LONGER.
AND I DON'T THINK HE DOES, EITHER.

THIS LIGHT ...

...HE'LL END UP LIKE THE MOLD.

IF I ABANDON THIS CHILD NOW...
YOU CAN MOVE, CAN'T YOU? RAISE YOUR HEAD.

I'M NOT ANGRY ANYMORE.
I'M SORRY. I KNOW YOU WERE JUST TRYING TO PROTECT ME.

ARE YOU ANGRY, MAMA?

HIS TOOTH !?

ズン

I LIKE TO FIGHT FOR MAMA.

I'M RESTED NOW. I CAN FLY. LET'S GO TO THE WESTERN LANDS.

ドーン

STAY CALM. DON'T GET UPSET.

MAMA ISN'T ANGRY! MAMA ISN'T ANGRY!

CHIKUKU ...!?

BEFORE WE FLY, I WANT YOU TO LISTEN VERY CAREFULLY TO WHAT I HAVE TO SAY.

YOU HAVE TO LEARN HOW TERRIBLE YOUR POWERS CAN BE.
BUT IT TAKES MORE THAN POWER TO BECOME A FINE PERSON.
WHY DID I SUDDENLY THINK OF CHIKUKU?

YOU'RE A VERY KIND CHILD WITH VERY STRONG POWERS.
LIKE CHI-KUKU.

IF YOU DIVIDE THE WHOLE WORLD INTO JUST ENEMIES AND FRIENDS, YOU'LL END UP DESTROYING EVERYTHING.
YOU TOO, CHIKUKU.

NOW, ARE YOU GOING TO DO AS I SAY AND BECOME A FINE PERSON?
SELM. PLEASE GUIDE ME.

THEN I WILL GIVE YOU A NAME.
I'M GOING TO USE THIS CHILD'S POWER TO SEAL THE CRYPTS OF SHUWA.

YES !!
I'LL BECOME A FINE PERSON!!

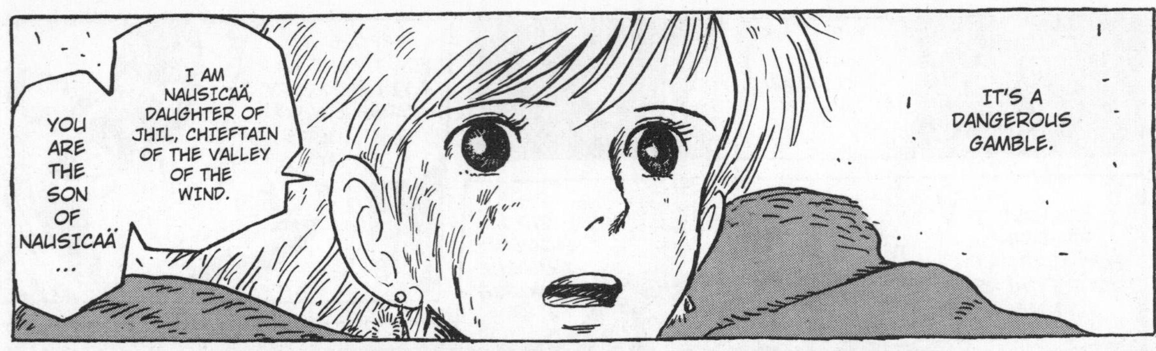
YOU ARE THE SON OF NAUSICAÄ ...
I AM NAUSICAÄ, DAUGHTER OF JHIL, CHIEFTAIN OF THE VALLEY OF THE WIND.
IT'S A DANGEROUS GAMBLE.

OHMA.
MY NAME IS OHMA.

...AND YOUR NAME IS OHMA.

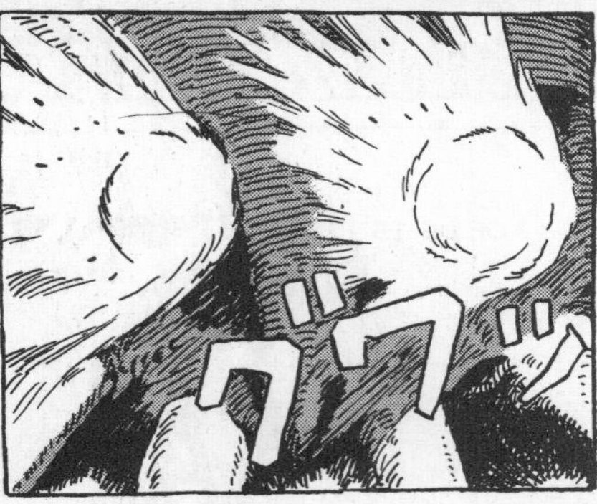

I GO WITH MY SMALL MOTHER TO THE WESTERN LANDS.

OHMA, SON OF NAUSICAÄ OF THE VALLEY OF THE WIND!!
GIRD IN RINGS OF LIGHT, OHMA IS BOTH ARBITRATOR AND WARRIOR.

HIS LEVEL OF INTELLIGENCE HAS SUDDENLY RISEN!! "ARBITRATOR"?!

OHMA,
WAIT.

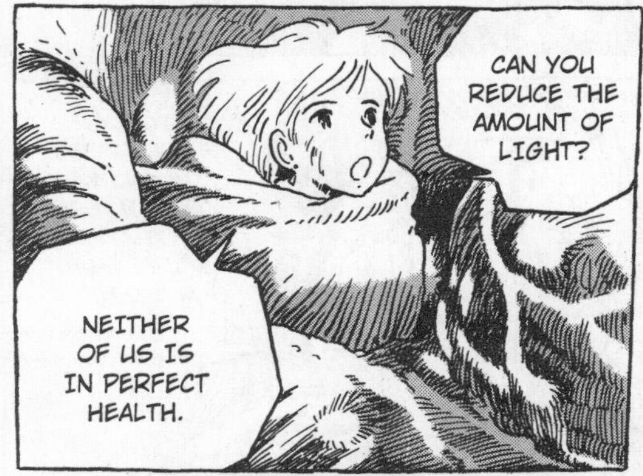
CAN YOU
REDUCE THE
AMOUNT OF
LIGHT?
NEITHER
OF US IS
IN PERFECT
HEALTH.

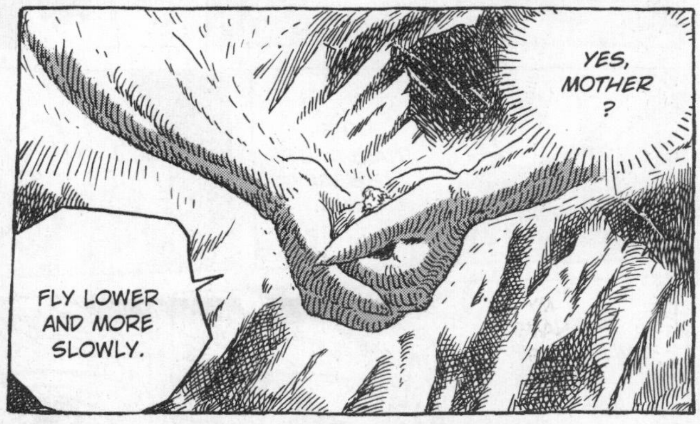
YES,
MOTHER
?
FLY LOWER
AND MORE
SLOWLY.

I WILL
DO WHAT
I CAN.

ALL WE KNOW
IS THE LEGEND
THAT TELLS THEY
DESTROYED THE
WORLD IN THE
SEVEN DAYS
OF FIRE.
IF THEY WERE MEANT
TO BE MERE WEAPONS,
INTELLIGENCE WOULD BE
NOTHING BUT A HINDRANCE.
YET THIS CHILD IS
BEGINNING TO DEVELOP
A PERSONALITY.

WE KNOW
NOTHING
ABOUT
OHMA'S
PEOPLE.

IT SEEMS THE PEOPLE OF OLD DIDN'T CREATE OHMA AND HIS KIND TO BE GODS OF DEATH.

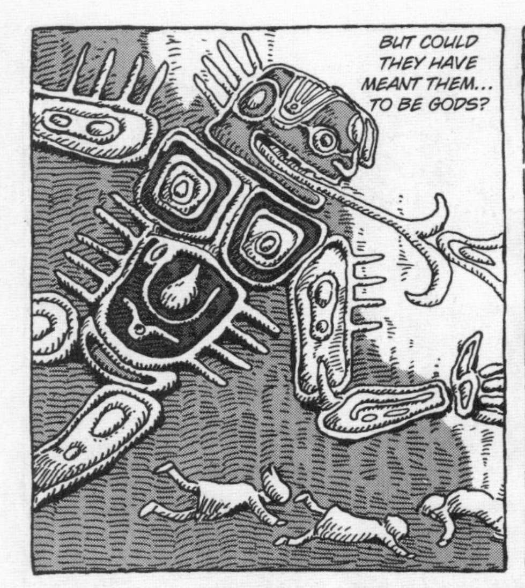
BUT COULD THEY HAVE MEANT THEM... TO BE GODS?

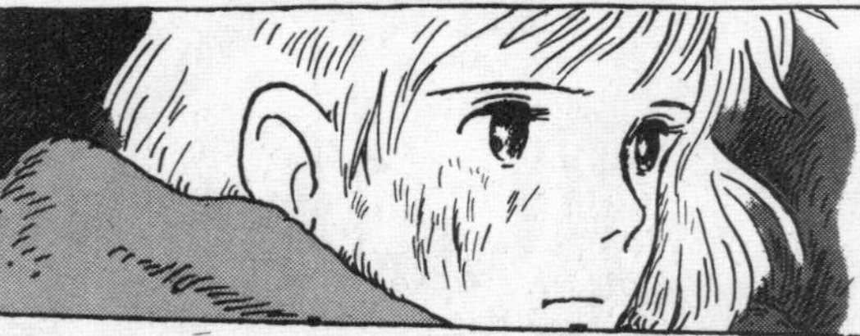
I WONDER IF THE CRYPTS OF SHUWA CONTAIN THE KEY THAT CAN SOLVE THAT MYSTERY.

THE NAUSEA IS UNBEAR-ABLE.

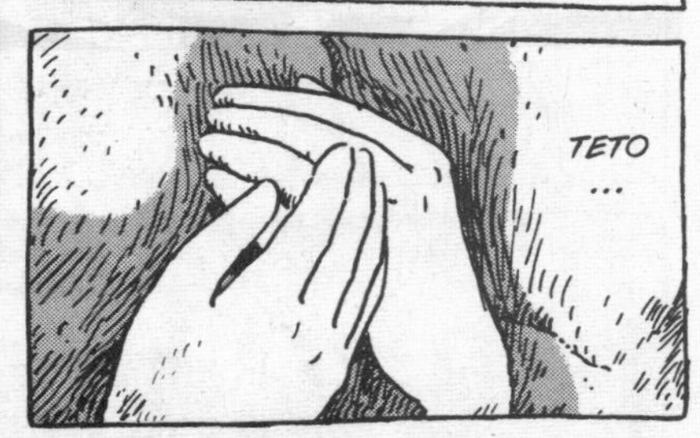
TETO ...

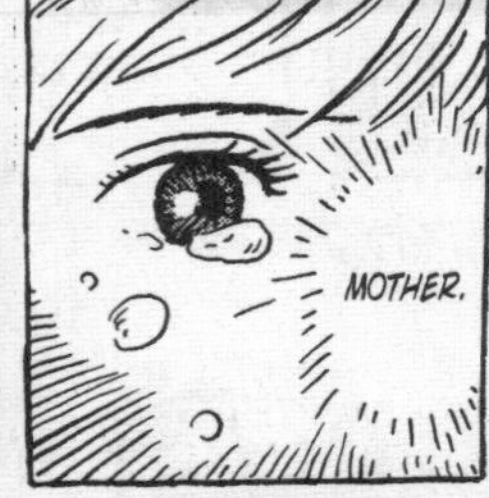
MOTHER.

THERE ARE ARMED MEN NEARBY.

THERE, BEYOND THE MOUNTAIN TO THE LEFT.
ウオオー
ALERT !!
THE GOD WARRIOR IS FLYING PARALLEL TO US ON OUR STAR-BOARD SIDE!!

TELL ALL THE SHIPS TO HOLD THEIR FIRE!!
IT'S MOVING TOWARD US!!

IDIOTS!! WE TOLD YOU TO SIDLE UP TO THEM WITHOUT BEING SPOTTED!
ゴオオー

IT'S *GRABBED* US BY OUR BOW!!
WE CAN'T STEER THE SHIP!!

IT DOESN'T SEEM TO INTEND TO ATTACK US.
DON'T RESIST!! DO EXACTLY AS IT SAYS.

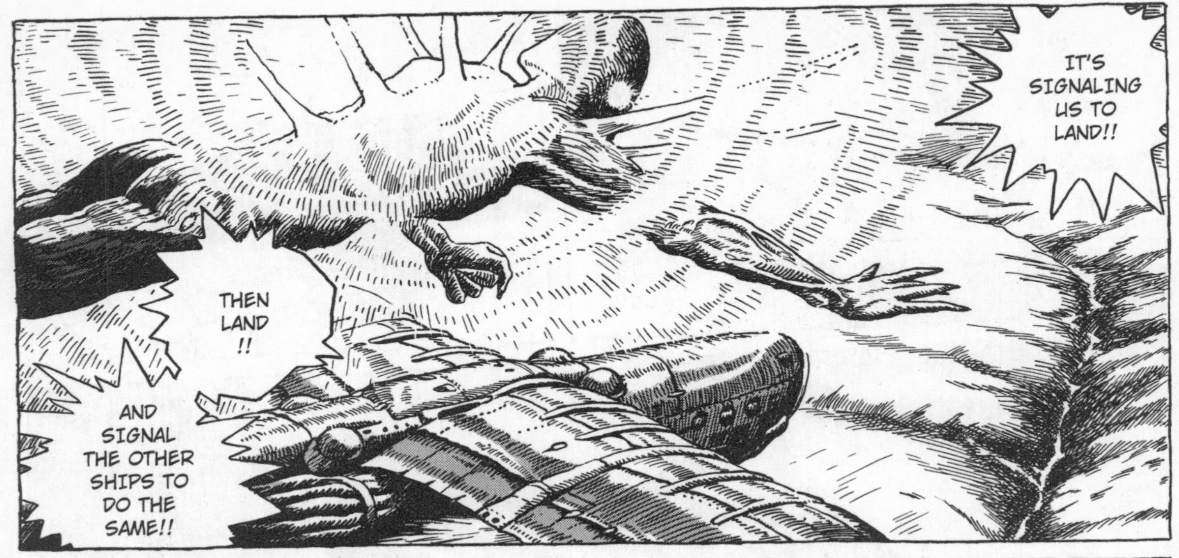
IT'S SIGNALING US TO LAND!!
THEN LAND!!
AND SIGNAL THE OTHER SHIPS TO DO THE SAME!!

WE WILL GREET THIS CREATURE AS IF IT WERE ROYALTY! IS THAT CLEAR?
HURRY WITH THE CARPET!!

ジュ

HONOR GUARD!! FALL IN!!

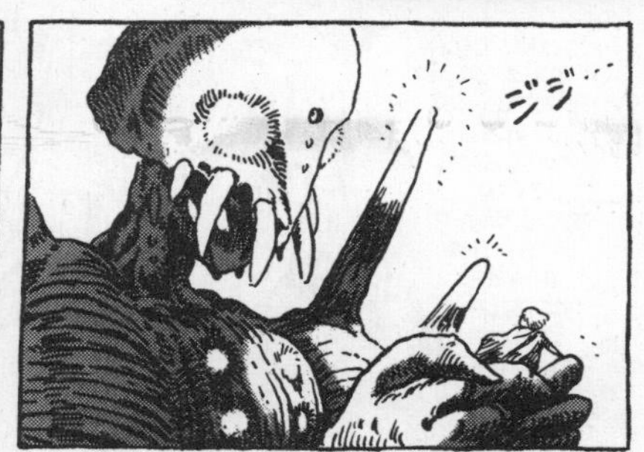
ジジ…

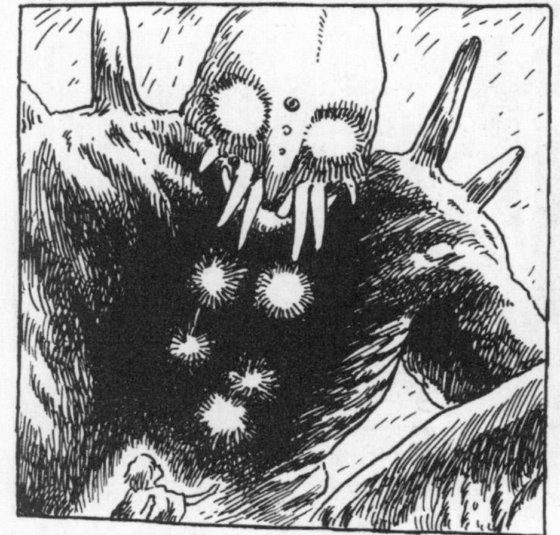

WH-WHAT IS THIS STENCH?
SHE'S TALKING WITH THE GOD WARRIOR. IS SHE A GOD OR A DEVIL?

SHE'S NOT ONE TO BE FRIGHTENED OFF BY BLUFF OR BLUSTER.
SHE STEPS ON THE ROYAL CARPET WITHOUT THE SLIGHTEST HESITATION.

THE HOLY EMPEROR IS DEAD ...
...AND THE GREATER PORTION OF THE DOROK LANDS HAVE BEEN SWALLOWED UP BY THE SEA OF CORRUP-TION.

YOU'RE THE NEW UNIT FROM TORUMEKIA, AREN'T YOU?
YES ...

THE WAR IS OVER. PLEASE RETURN TO YOUR HOMELAND.

ARE YOU A DIVINE MESSENGER? MIGHT WE AT LEAST ASK YOUR NAME?

I WILL NOT ASK YOURS...

...SO I WILL NOT OFFER MY OWN. I WILL GIVE YOU ONE WORD OF WARNING, THOUGH. STAY AWAY FROM THIS CHILD. HE GIVES OFF A POISONOUS LIGHT.

I HAVE PAINFUL NEWS FOR YOU. YOUR SCOUTING PARTY WAS WIPED OUT BY THIS CHILD'S LIGHT.

"CHILD"? THIS GOD WARRIOR IS YOUR CHILD?
A-A POISONOUS LIGHT!?

I KNOW ...
...YOU ARE AFTER THE SECRETS OF THE CRYPTS OF SHUWA.

WE ARE ON OUR WAY TO SEAL THE CRYPTS OF SHUWA FOR ETERNITY.

YOU MUST NOT GO THERE.

LOOK. THE GIRL'S AS PALE AS A GHOST.

VERY LITTLE LAND REMAINS ON THIS PLANET FOR HUMAN USE.
YOU TORUMEKIANS HAVE THE GOOD FORTUNE OF INHABITING A LARGE PORTION OF THAT LAND!! WHAT MORE CAN YOU ASK FOR?

SHE CAN BARELY STAND. IT IS SHE WHO HAS BEEN POISONED BY THE MONSTER'S LIGHT!

WE ARE BUT REINFORCEMENTS. THE KING IS ALREADY ON HIS WAY TO SHUWA.

BUT OUR ORDERS TO ATTACK SHUWA COME DIRECTLY FROM OUR FATHER, THE KING. TO DEFY THOSE ORDERS WOULD BE TREASON.
IT IS AS YOU SAY. NOW THAT THE HOLY EMPEROR IS DEAD, THERE IS NOTHING TO BE GAINED BY CONTINUING THIS WAR.

WE HAVE ALREADY LOST OUR BROTHERS AND SISTER TO THIS WAR.
OUR SOLDIERS AND OUR PEOPLE ARE EXHAUSTED FROM THIS WAR. WE WERE OPPOSED TO THIS CAMPAIGN.

HE MAY BE REACHING TO UNBOLT THE DOORS TO THE CRYPT AS WE SPEAK.

SO MUCH HAS BEEN LOST IN THIS WAR, BUT THE GODS HAVE NOT TAKEN EVERY-THING FROM US.
OUR SISTER IS ALIVE.
INDEED.

KUSHANA IS ALIVE. IT WAS SHE WHO GAVE ME THIS CAPE.
IS THAT TRUE!?

PLEASE, STOP A WHILE AND TELL US MORE.
MEN! THIS GUEST IS TO RECEIVE FIRST-CLASS TREATMENT.

IT MUST HAVE BEEN THE GODS THEMSELVES WHO BROUGHT YOU TO US.

I CAN SEE THAT YOU ARE TIRED. ALLOW US TO GIVE YOU SOMETHING HOT TO DRINK.

MOTHER
...

I'M ALL RIGHT. JUST A BIT DIZZY...

OHMA
...
ハア ハア
BEWARE THESE MEN...

MOTHER
!!

バタン

ワ

STAY CALM!! YOU HAVEN'T GOT A CHANCE AGAINST THAT THING. DON'T ATTACK.
PROTECT THEIR HIGH-NESSES !!

TH-THE POISONOUS LIGHT...

IT DOESN'T WANT TO JEOPARDIZE ITS MASTER. THIS IS OUR CHANCE.
IT'S NOT ATTACKING.

ゴッ

THOUGH I'M SURE YOU MEAN NO HARM, THAT LIGHT IS A POISON!!
THE LIGHT YOU GIVE OFF IS EATING AWAY AT HER.

IF YOU CARE FOR THIS PERSON, YOU MUST STAY AWAY FROM HER.
GOD WARRIOR!! PLEASE HEAR WHAT WE HAVE TO SAY!!

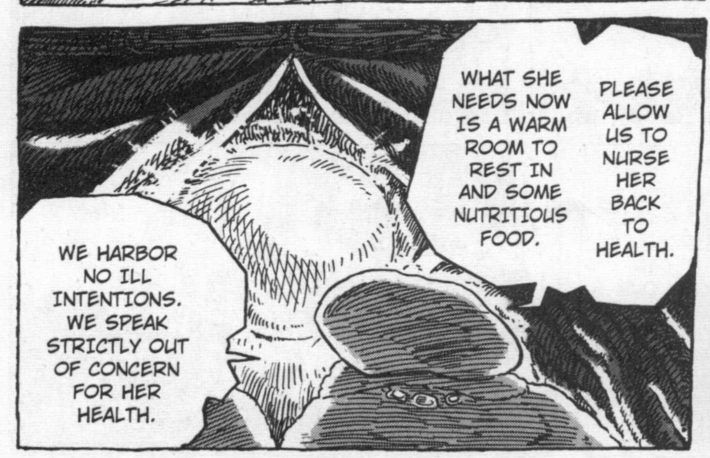
WE HARBOR NO ILL INTENTIONS. WE SPEAK STRICTLY OUT OF CONCERN FOR HER HEALTH.
WHAT SHE NEEDS NOW IS A WARM ROOM TO REST IN AND SOME NUTRITIOUS FOOD.
PLEASE ALLOW US TO NURSE HER BACK TO HEALTH.

IT WOULD BE BEST IF YOU COULD WATCH OVER HER FROM A SAFE DISTANCE.
OTHER-WISE, SHE IS SURE TO DIE!!

IF YOU ARE GOING TO SHUWA, WE WILL BE HAPPY TO TAKE HER THERE IN OUR SHIP.

THE GOD WARRIOR IS TURNING BACK!!
IT HEEDED THE WORDS OF THEIR HIGHNESSES.

THAT MONSTER. I COULD SWEAR IT SMIRKED AT US. IT SAW THROUGH OUR WORDS.
ABSURD. IT'S NOTHING BUT A MAN-MADE WEAPON.

HIGH-NESSES!! ARE YOU ALL RIGHT !?

TREAT HER WITH THE GREATEST CARE!!
IT HAS ITS EYE ON US.

WHAT'S TAKING THE PHYSICIAN SO LONG?!
HURRY UP AND BRING OUR GUEST INSIDE.
STRIKE THE TENTS!!

GOD WARRIOR! WE ARE READY TO DEPART FOR SHUWA!!

WE ASK THAT YOU TAKE TO THE SKY AHEAD OF US AND WATCH OVER OUR FLEET.

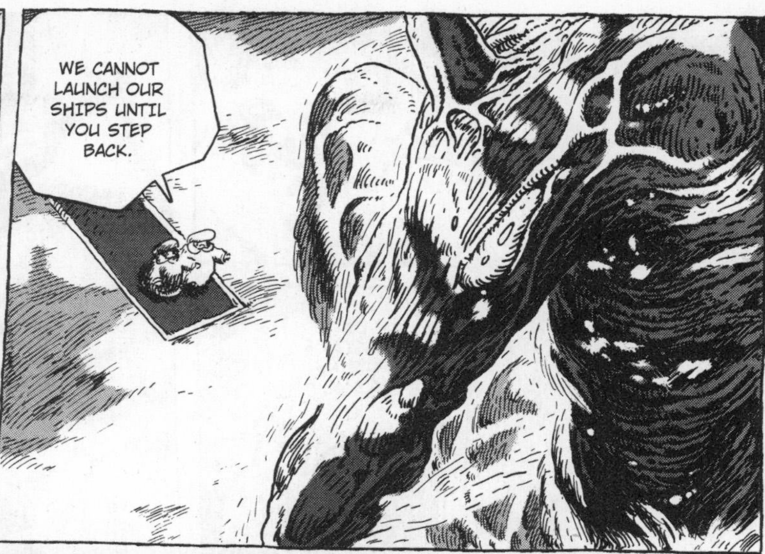
WE CANNOT LAUNCH OUR SHIPS UNTIL YOU STEP BACK.

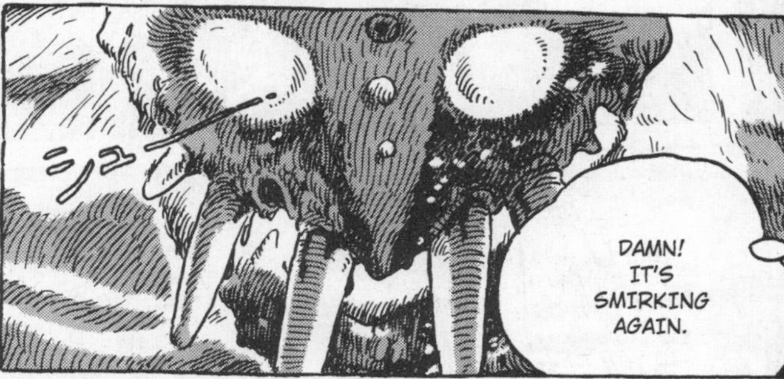
シュ
DAMN! IT'S SMIRKING AGAIN.

I-IS IT MY IMAGINATION OR IS THE LIGHT INCREASING !?

ジジ…
THE POISONOUS LIGHT!!
I-IT'S FLOATING UP.

FLY, GOD WARRIOR !!
BUT THE GIRL'S LIFE IS IN OUR HANDS.
DO AS WE COMMAND, OR YOUR MASTER WILL--

カアッ

WE DID IT!!
IT FOLLOWED OUR ORDERS!!

WH-WHAT IS THIS !?
ボタボタ

THE MONSTER'S ROTTING FLESH.

AH !!
THE STENCH !!

THE GOD WARRIOR IS CIRCLING ABOVE OUR HEADS!!
LAUNCH AT ONCE.
AND HEAT THE BATH!

ゴゴゴゴ

ウオオオー

FORGIVE ME, YOUR HIGHNESS ...

...BUT I CANNOT TREAT THAT GIRL. SHE IS A WITCH!

THERE'S A MAD SQUIRREL FOX ON HER CHEST THAT WON'T LET US NEAR HER.
AND WHAT'S MORE ...

...A-A VOICE INSIDE OUR EARS...
HMPH! THEN LEAVE HER BE.

DO NOT TOUCH MY MOTHER. STAND BACK.

AS LONG AS WE HAVE THE GIRL, IT CAN'T LAY A FINGER ON US.
WE'LL JUST CONTINUE OUR TRIP TO SHUWA.
AND IF OUR FATHER SHOULD ATTACK US, I THINK WE CAN COUNT ON THE GOD WARRIOR TO DEFEND US.

DO YOU THINK IT COULD BE THAT THING'S VOICE?
THE GIRL'S A WITCH!! NOTHING ABOUT HER WOULD SURPRISE ME.

HMPH! BEHAVING AS IF IT IS SOME SORT OF GOD.

AT ANY RATE, THE GOD WARRIOR IS FLYING QUIETLY OVER OUR FORMATION.

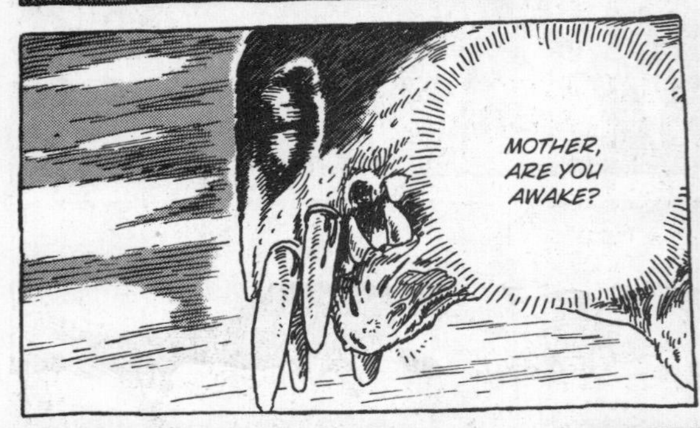
MOTHER, ARE YOU AWAKE?

MOTHER.

THOSE TWO THINK THAT BY TAKING YOU HOSTAGE ...
...THEY CAN USE MY POWERS FOR THEIR BENEFIT.

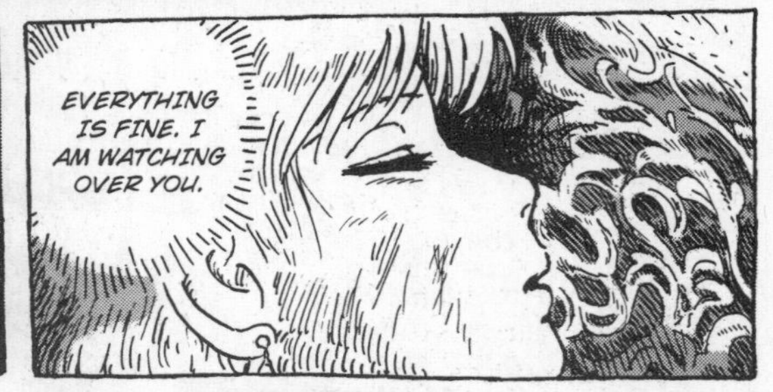
EVERYTHING IS FINE. I AM WATCHING OVER YOU.

I'LL ALLOW THEM TO CONTINUE TO THINK SO FOR THE TIME BEING.
THIS WOULD SEEM TO BE THE BEST SITUATION FOR YOUR BODY RIGHT NOW.

IN THE MEANTIME, I WILL OBSERVE AND CONSIDER WHETHER THESE TWO DESERVE TO LIVE OR NOT.

OHMA... JUST WHO ARE YOU ...?

IT IS DIFFICULT TO BELIEVE THAT THEY ARE OF THE SAME RACE AS YOU, MOTHER.

I AM OHMA, ARBITRATOR AND WARRIOR ...
... AND JUDGE.

"JUSTICE"!?

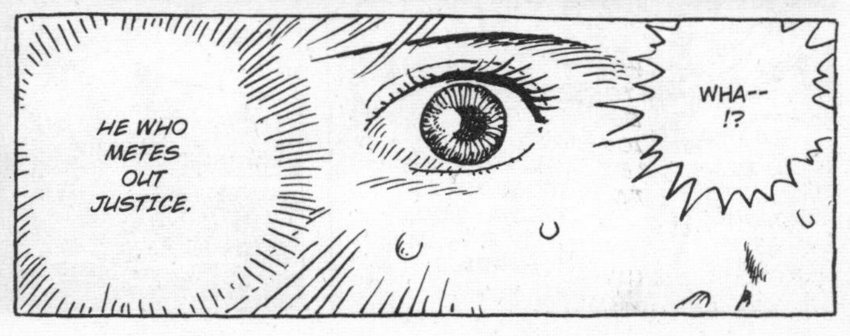
HE WHO METES OUT JUSTICE.
WHA-- !?

ヴオOOOO

OH-H, THAT WAS ASBEL PILOTING.

ガガガ

THE PRINCESS IS HEADED FOR SHUWA, ALONE, WITH THE GOD WARRIOR.
AH-H, I THOUGHT AS MUCH.

WE'LL BE LEAVING AT ONCE, SIR.
I THOUGHT THAT WAS TOO CLEAN A LANDING FOR MITO.

LOOK YONDER.
YOU THOUGHT AS MUCH !?

YES, JUST LAST NIGHT.
THE WORM-HANDLERS. SO THEY'VE COME BACK.

ゾロ

ワラワラ
ダッ
WAH! HERE THEY COME NOW.

HOW DID THEY KNOW? DO THEY HAVE SUCH POWERS, TOO?

THEY CAME WEEPING, SAYING THE PRINCESS HAD GONE SOMEPLACE THEY COULD NOT REACH ON FOOT.

THERE'S A LIMIT TO HOW MUCH OUR SHIP CAN CARRY. YOU MEN HAVE TOO MUCH BAGGAGE.
WE CAN'T POSSIBLY CARRY ALL OF YOU.

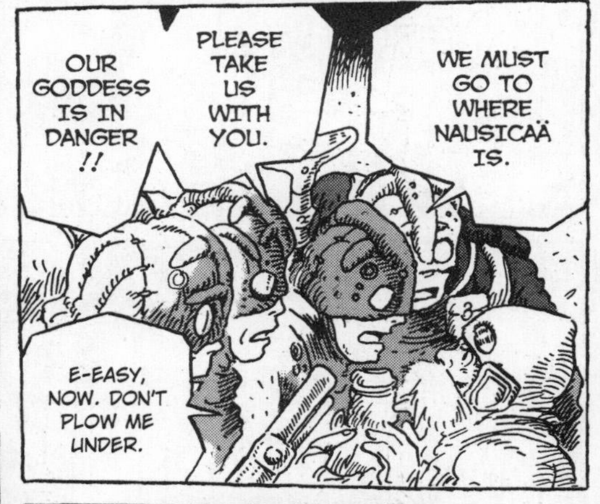

WE MUST GO TO WHERE NAUSICAÄ IS.
PLEASE TAKE US WITH YOU.
OUR GODDESS IS IN DANGER !!
E-EASY, NOW. DON'T PLOW ME UNDER.

B-BUT ...
LET'S TAKE THEM WITH US. THEY MAY BE ABLE TO HELP US.

THEY'RE AS QUIET AS THE DEAD.

IT'S A PITY, BUT PERHAPS NOW THEY'LL GIVE UP.

WORMHANDLERS CARRY ALL THEIR EARTHLY POSSESSIONS WHEREVER THEY GO.
THEIR POSSESSIONS ARE MORE IMPORTANT TO THEM THAN THEIR LIVES. THEY WOULD NEVER THROW AWAY ANY OF THEIR BAGGAGE.

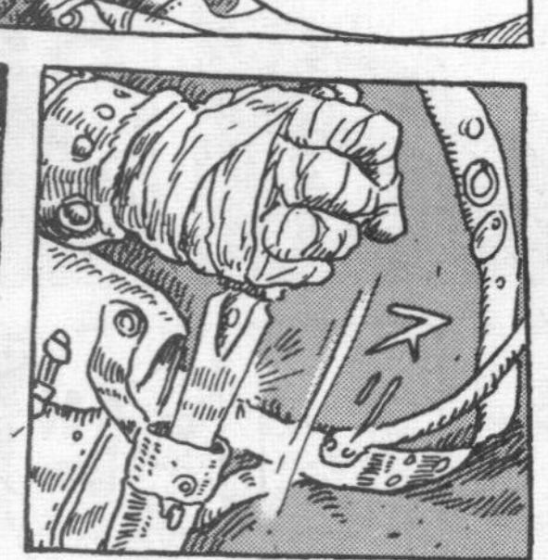

WHAT IN BLAZES ARE YOU DOING!?

WAH-H-H !!

WORM-HANDLERS KILLING THEIR OWN WORMS...!?

ガサ
ガシャ

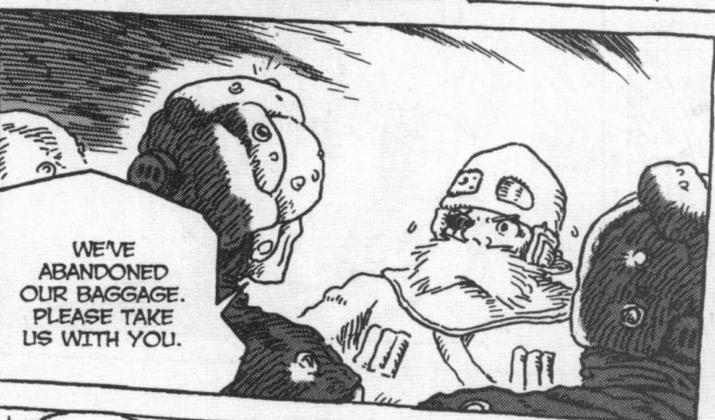
WE'VE ABANDONED OUR BAGGAGE. PLEASE TAKE US WITH YOU.

ドサ

THAT WOULD HAVE BEEN EVEN MORE CRUEL.
IT IS COLD HERE. THERE IS NOTHING FOR THEM TO EAT. IF WE HAD SET THEM FREE, THEY WOULD HAVE DIED A SLOW DEATH.

BUT SURELY YOU DIDN'T HAVE *TO KILL* THEM!?

PLEASE!! TAKE US WITH YOU!!
WE'VE ABANDONED OUR POSSESSIONS IN ORDER TO PROTECT NAUSICAÄ!!
WE WORM-HANDLERS HAVE ABANDONED OUR WORMS!!

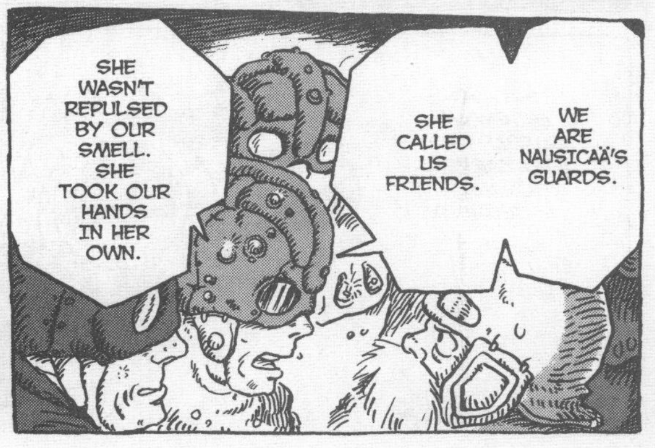
SHE WASN'T REPULSED BY OUR SMELL. SHE TOOK OUR HANDS IN HER OWN.
SHE CALLED US FRIENDS.
WE ARE NAUSICAÄ'S GUARDS.

THANK YOU. I HOPE YOU'LL COME WITH US TO WHEREVER OUR PRINCESS LEADS US. TO THE ENDS OF THE EARTH, IF NEED BE.
YOU AND WE ARE THE SAME.
オー
オー
オー

I...

I DON'T KNOW WHAT TO SAY.

LET US GO!! TO THE ENDS OF THE EARTH IF NEED BE!!

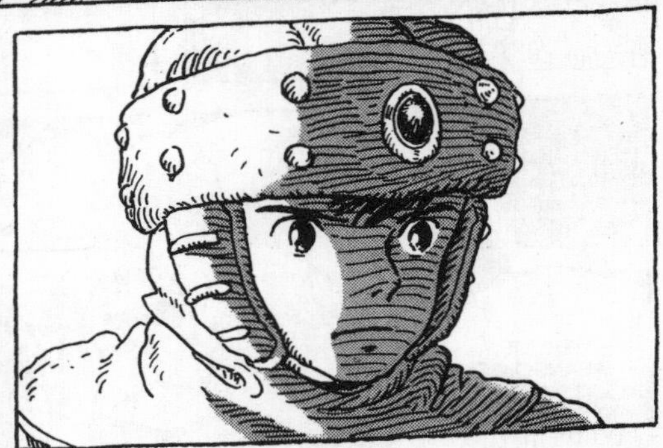

...IS THE THREAD THAT JOINS US ALL TOGETHER.

NAUSICAÄ...

US. THE DOROKS. EVEN KUSHANA AND THE WORM-HANDLERS.

SUCH AN ENORMOUS BURDEN THAT GIRL CARRIES ON HER SHOULDERS.

WITHOUT NAUSICAÄ, WE WOULD ONLY QUARREL AND SPLINTER.
グ"
グ"

"RASTEL'S ELDER BROTHER..."
"I'VE NEVER FORGOTTEN THE PERSON WHO MADE THIS BANDAGE FOR ME."

I'LL BE DAMNED IF I LET HER DIE.

LET US HURRY!! TO THE LAND OF SHUWA, WHERE NAUSICAÄ SAID SHE WAS GOING!!
ヴォロロロロ

ALL ABOARD !!

STERN COCKPIT READY!!

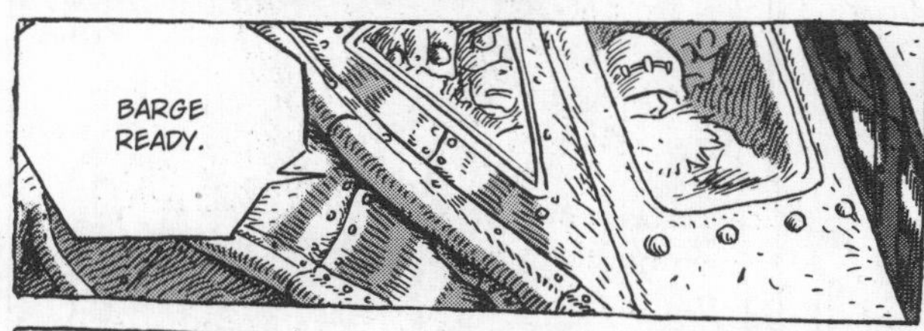
BARGE READY.

ガガガ

WAIT FOR ME, MY BELOVED WINDRIDER.
ウオオオー

AS A RESULT OF THE DAIKAISHO*, TWO-THIRDS OF THE DOROK LANDS HAVE BEEN ENGULFED BY THE SEA OF CORRUPTION, AND THE AREAS BORDERING THIS FUNGI FOREST LIE ABANDONED.

ONCE MIGHTY CITY WALLS ARE DEVOURED BY THE SEA OF CORRUPTION, AS WELL AS EVERY VILLAGE AND TOWN.

THE FOREST CONTINUES TO GROW. SCATTERED ISLANDS OF THE FOREST REACH OUT TO EACH OTHER, SPREADING ACROSS THE GAPS THAT SEPARATE THEM.

FIRST, THE SMALLER INSECTS COME.

THE LARGER INSECTS THAT FOLLOW CARRY WITH THEM VARIOUS SPORES, THUS THE YOUNG FOREST RAPIDLY GROWS INTO A COMPLEX ECOSYSTEM.

THE LOWEST LAYER OF THE ATMOSPHERE IS PERVADED BY A DENSE MIASMA, UNTIL THE MOUNTAIN PEAKS THAT RISE ABOVE THE REACH OF THE FOREST FLOAT LIKE ISLANDS IN THE SEA OF CORRUPTION.

*DAIKAISHO: THE GREAT STAMPEDE OF FOREST INSECTS TRIGGERED BY THE DOROK COUNCIL OF PRIESTS' ILL-FATED ATTEMPT TO USE A GENETICALLY ENGINEERED STRAIN OF FOREST MOLD AS A BIOLOGICAL WEAPON AGAINST TORUMEKIA.

ON ONE SUCH MOUNTAIN HUDDLES A MASS OF HUMAN SURVIVORS.

YOUR HIGHNESS, I'VE FOUND YOU A CLOAK. IN THIS STRONG WIND, YOU'LL --

I'M FINE AS I AM. I ALREADY HAVE A CLOAK.
HM!?

NAUSICAÄ IS WEARING IT.

THE IMMORTAL EMPEROR... ***IS DEAD!!***

NAUSICAÄ HAS LIFTED THE YOKE OF A CENTURY!!

THIS IS HOW THEY CELEBRATE? BY CHANTING SCRIPTURES?

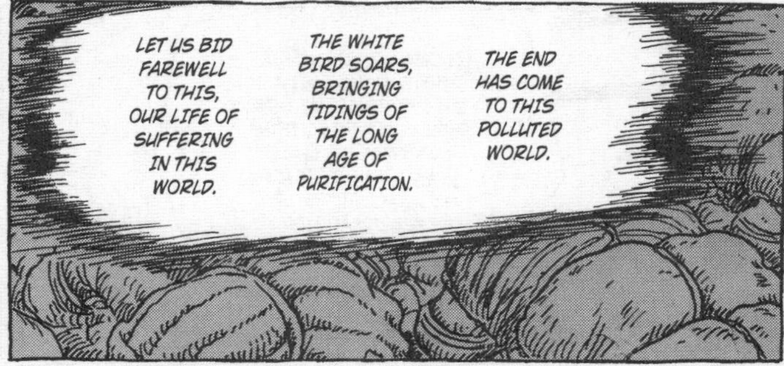

LET US BID FAREWELL TO THIS, OUR LIFE OF SUFFERING IN THIS WORLD.
THE WHITE BIRD SOARS, BRINGING TIDINGS OF THE LONG AGE OF PURIFICATION.
THE END HAS COME TO THIS POLLUTED WORLD.

IT WAS FORBIDDEN BY THE COUNCIL OF PRIESTS, BUT MUST HAVE BEEN SECRETLY PASSED ON FROM GENERATION TO GENERATION.
THIS IS AN OLD NATIVE SUTRA.

THEY BELIEVE NAUSICAÄ IS THE WHITE-WINGED APOSTLE... THE ONE WHO SHALL LEAD THEM TO PARADISE.
WH-WHAT DID YOU SAY!?

O, GREAT WHITE BIRD! O, BLUE-CLAD ONE! LEAD US TO THE PURE LAND!

YOU MEAN THE BLUE-CLAD ONE IS NOT A SAVIOR BUT A **GOD OF DEATH!?**

THE SAME PROPHECY AT TIMES REPRESENTS A HOPE FOR A BETTER LIFE IN THIS WORLD, AND AT OTHERS A YEARNING FOR PEACE IN THE AFTERLIFE.
THEY HAVE LOST EVERYTHING TO THE DAIKAISHO. IT WILL TAKE SOME TIME FOR THEM TO RECOVER.

BESIDES, SINCE ANCIENT TIMES THE SHADOW OF DEATH HAS HUNG HEAVILY OVER THE DOROK LANDS.

THE HOLY EMPEROR WAS NOT THE ONLY ONE. THE DOROK KING BEFORE HIM, AND THE DYNASTY BEFORE THAT... ALL STRUGGLED WITH THAT SHADOW, ONLY TO BE SWALLOWED UP IN THE END BY NOTHINGNESS.
THE CRYPT OF SHUWA... AND ITS MASTER.

I HAVE HEARD THERE IS A DEEP, BLACK, AND ENORMOUS CRYPT IN THE LAND OF SHUWA.
THROUGHOUT HISTORY, DOROK RULERS HAVE INVARIABLY BUILT THEIR CAPITALS AROUND THAT CRYPT.
I WON'T REST 'TIL I'VE SEEN FOR MYSELF WHAT IS TO BE SEEN IN THAT LAND THAT LIES IN SHADOW...

...'TIL I'VE SEEN THE MASTER OF THE CRYPT.

<WOMAN OF TORUMEKIA, THE WAR HAS ENDED. IT IS FITTING THAT THEE SHOULD RETURN TO THINE OWN LAND. WE SHALL REMAIN IN THIS PLACE AND AWAIT THE RETURN OF THE GREAT BIRD.>
<WE SHALL NOT GO TO SHUWA. THE GREAT BIRD TOLD US NOT TO FOLLOW HER.>

WE'LL DISCUSS THIS. PLEASE WAIT.

THEY THINK WE MEAN TO ATTACK SHUWA AND ARE USING NAUSICAÄ'S NAME TO FOOL THEM.

WHAT HAVE THEY STARTED BICKERING ABOUT?
YUPA TOLD THEM WE WOULD LIKE TO BORROW A SHIP TO FLY TO SHUWA.

THE THIRD ARMY WAS ONCE MADE UP OF 6,000 YOUNG MEN. FEWER THAN 200 REMAIN.
AND THE DOROK PEOPLE HAVE SUFFERED FAR GREATER LOSSES.

I CAN'T BLAME THEM. THERE MAY HAVE BEEN A DAIKAISHO, BUT THERE HAS YET TO BE A TRUCE.
BESIDES, THEY'RE LITTLE MORE THAN A DISORDERLY MOB.

WE'LL WAIT.
AH... YES... OF COURSE, YOUR MAJESTY.
HMPH. EVEN KUSHANA'S BEGINNING TO SOUND LIKE NAUSICAÄ.

KUROTOWA, LOOK BEHIND YOU.

GIVE ME A HUNDRED TROOPS, YOUR HIGHNESS, AND I CAN TAKE THAT FLOATING FORTRESS.

HERE, PRAYING FOR THE COUNTLESS DEAD AND FOR THE HOLY EMPEROR.

ギ
WHERE'S CHARUKA ?

WE CAN TALK HERE.
WE HAVE SOMETHING IMPORTANT TO SPEAK TO YOU ABOUT.

I'LL BE HAPPY TO STEP OUTSIDE IF YOU'LL RELEASE THESE OTHERS AS WELL.

WE *CAN'T* TALK HERE. NOW PLEASE DON'T GIVE US ANY TROUBLE.

I DO NOT DESERVE SPECIAL TREATMENT.
REGARDLESS OF WHETHER WE SERVED THE HOLY EMPEROR OR THE HOLY EMPEROR'S BROTHER, WE ALL SERVED ON THE COUNCIL OF PRIESTS AND SHARE THE SAME BURDEN OF SIN.

YOU'RE NOT LIKE THESE OTHERS! NAUSICAÄ HERSELF TRUSTS YOU!
AND WE KNOW YOU'VE DONE EVERYTHING YOU CAN TO HELP US.

SHE IS ACCOMPANIED BY A MAN WHO IS SAID TO BE NAUSICAÄ'S MENTOR. THEY ARE ASKING TO BORROW A SHIP TO FLY TO SHUWA, AND ARE REFUSING TO BUDGE UNTIL THEY GET ONE.

THE TORUMEKIAN PRINCESS, WHO BROUGHT THE EMPEROR'S COFFIN, HAS PROPOSED A TRUCE.

IF SOMETHING DOESN'T HAPPEN SOON, WE ARE GOING TO END UP BATTLING THE TORUMEKIAN TROOPS AGAIN.
THIS IS NOT THE TIME TO DISCUSS THIS.

IF WE DO BATTLE NOW, FAR MORE ARE CERTAIN TO DIE. WE ARE ASKING YOU TO SHARE YOUR WISDOM WITH US, CHARUKA.
WE SAPATANS HAVE ALREADY LOST MOST OF OUR WARRIORS-- AS HAVE THE OTHER CLANS.

THE WARRIORS OF THE MANI TRIBE ARE IN A RAGE, AND SPEAK OF AVENGING THEIR FALLEN BRETHREN BY SLAUGHTERING THE TORUMEKIANS.

NO! WE'RE SIMPLY SAYING WE DON'T WANT TO DIE AS PRISONERS!!
AND WHEN THE BATTLE IS DONE YOU'LL MAKE SLAVES OF US AGAIN!!

THE TORUMEKIAN TROOPS ARE AS MUCH OUR ENEMIES AS THEY ARE YOURS!!
IF THAT IS THE CASE, RELEASE US AND GIVE US ARMS!

WHERE IS CHIKUKU? IS CHIKUKU AWAKE YET?
H-HE'S STILL ASLEEP.

SILENCE!! THERE IS NO POINT IN FURTHER BLOODSHED!!

WAKEN CHIKUKU! DUMP A BUCKET OF WATER ON HIM IF THAT'S WHAT IT TAKES!!
WHEN HE AWAKES, I'LL GO WITH YOU.

IF I STEP IN NOW, IT WILL SIMPLY ADD FUEL TO THE FIRE. THERE ARE MANY WHO RESENT THE ACTIONS I TOOK AS MILITARY COMMANDER.
THIS IS NOT GOOD.

HOW LONG DO THEY INTEND TO DISCUSS THE MATTER!? IT'S ALREADY PITCH BLACK OUT.

THEY SAY THE CHILDREN ARE STARVING. THEY WOULD LIKE TO OPEN THE SHIP'S PANTRY, IF THEY MAY.

HM? WOMEN ...?

I'LL SHOW THEM THE WAY.

OF COURSE. IT WAS YOUR FOOD TO BEGIN WITH.

KETCHA.

THIS IS IT. THERE SHOULD BE MORE IN THE BACK.

I TRIED TO STOP THEM, BUT THEY WOULDN'T LISTEN. THEY ARE FILLED WITH HATRED OF THE TORU-MEKIANS.

THESE WOMEN ARE ALL CARRYING EXPLOSIVES.
THE TRIBES-MEN ARE PLANNING AN ATTACK.

THEY MAY NOT BE ABLE TO BECOME LIKE NAUSICAÄ, BUT THEY CAN FOLLOW HER PATH.
WE HAVE TO STOP THEM.

IT'S HOPELESS. THEY CAN'T POSSIBLY BECOME LIKE NAUSICAÄ.

♪

IT SEEMS THEY'VE MADE UP THEIR MINDS.
THIS DOESN'T LOOK GOOD.

IN THE END, WE TREAD THE BLOOD-DRENCHED PATH...

IT'S GROWING COLD, YOUR MAJESTY. PLEASE COME INSIDE.

MEN!

HER MAJESTY HAS GIVEN THE ORDER TO FALL OUT.
GO BACK INSIDE AND EAT.

ザワ
ザワ
THOSE ON WATCH, STAY BEHIND.
BEHAVE NATURALLY, BOYS. DON'T RUSH.

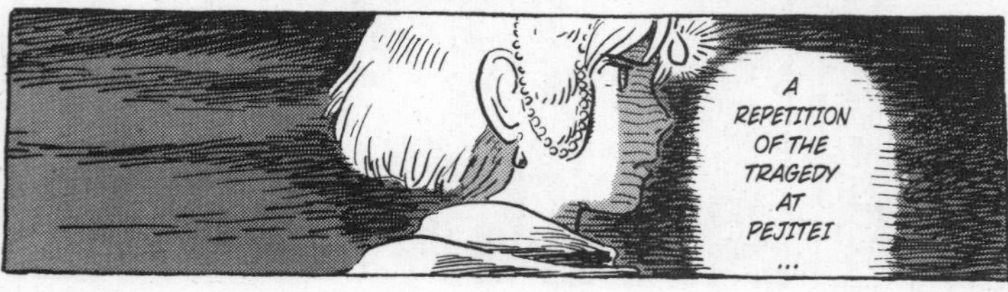
A REPETITION OF THE TRAGEDY AT PEJITEI ...

HAVE THEY HAD NO TRAINING AT ALL? I CAN SEE THEIR EVERY MOVE.

KEEP IT QUIET! SEAL THE HATCHES! DON'T LET A SINGLE SOLDIER IN!
CAPTURE THE WOMEN IN THE PANTRY. THEY MAY BE A SPECIAL ATTACK UNIT.

DOROK WARRIORS ARE NOT WHAT THEY USED TO BE.

IF THEY CANNOT PUT ASIDE THEIR HATRED OF US, THEN LET THEM ATTACK.

MY OWN HATRED, AS WELL.

NEITHER SIDE WILL WIN. WE'LL SIMPLY TURN THIS SPOT INTO AN OCEAN OF BLOOD AND BRING THIS ENDLESS CYCLE OF HATRED TO ITS VIOLENT CONCLUSION.
EVEN IF THEY SUCCEED IN KILLING ME, MY MEN ARE CERTAIN TO FIGHT TO THE LAST.

WHAT'S SHE DOING? THIS WASN'T PART OF OUR PLAN.

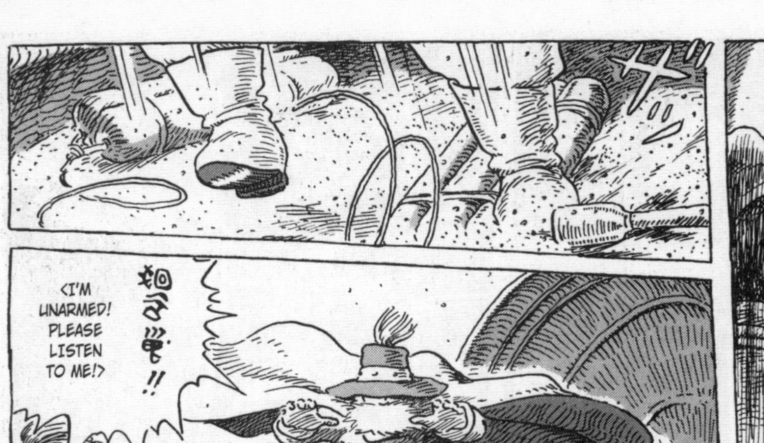
<I'M UNARMED! PLEASE LISTEN TO ME!>

<REMEMBER! REMEMBER THE WAY OF THE HOLY ONE!>

<THE WAR IS OVER. WE MUST NOT ALLOW ANY MORE BLOODSHED.>

<WOULD HE HAVE TOLD YOU TO PLANT BOMBS IN GRAIN AND SEEK VENGEANCE AT THE COST OF YOUR OWN LIVES?>

WAIT! MASTER YUPA IS TRYING TO REASON WITH THEM!!

<NO OUTSIDER CAN UNDERSTAND THE SUFFERING AND HUMILIATION WE'VE ENDURED!!>
<THAT WOMAN WAS EVEN WILLING TO BECOME THE BRIDE OF THE EMPEROR!>

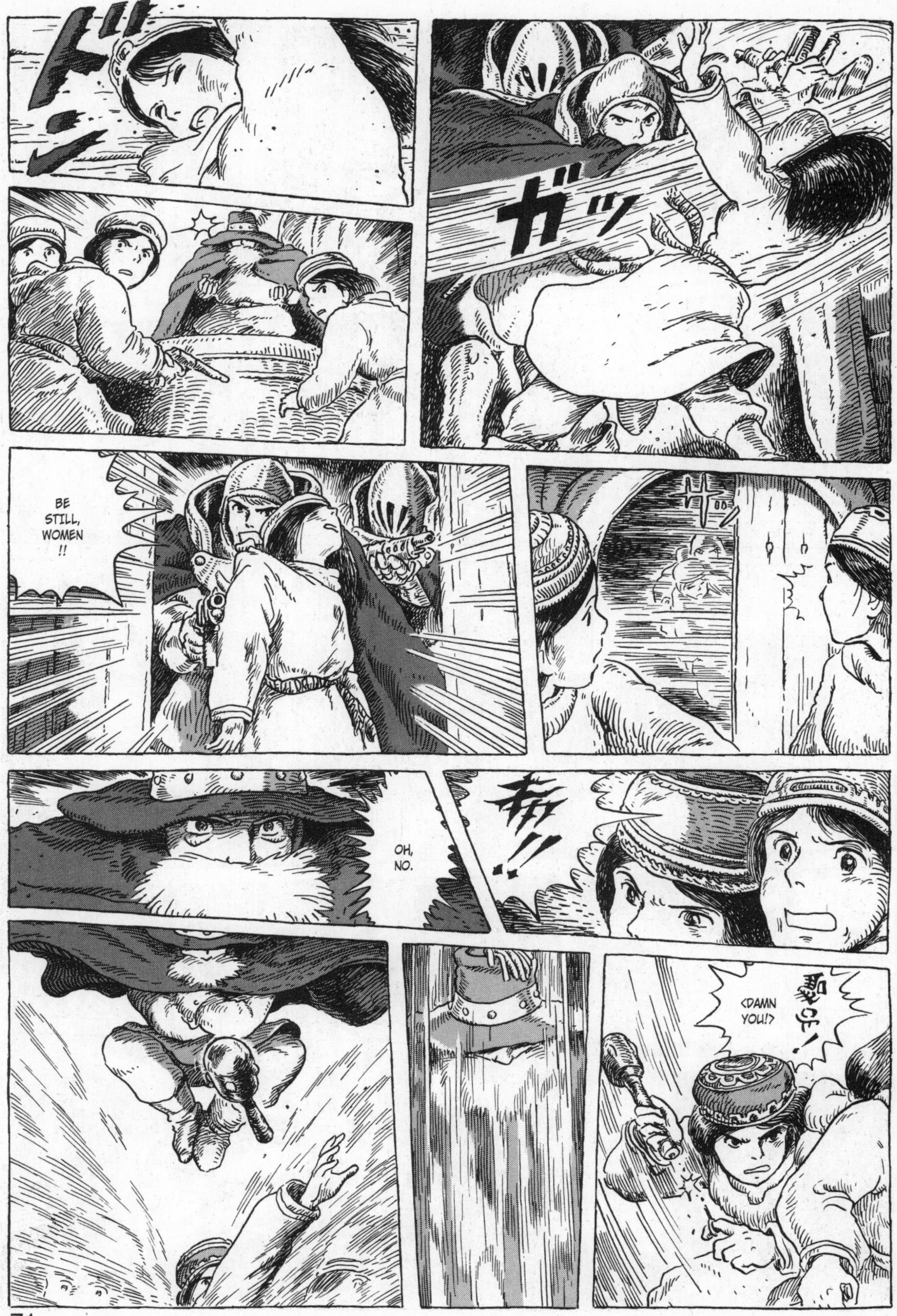

BE STILL, WOMEN !!
OH, NO.
<DAMN YOU!>

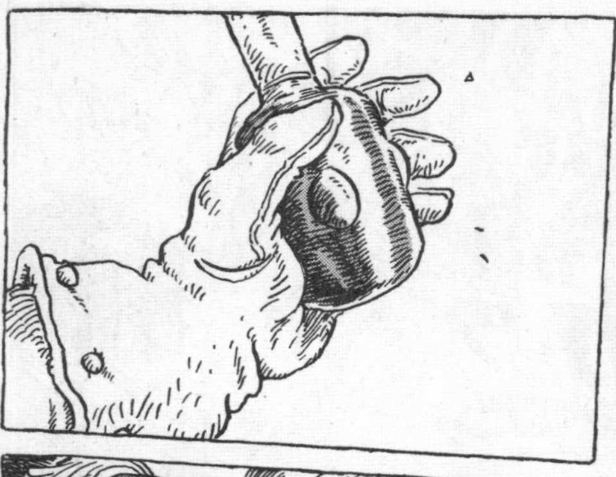

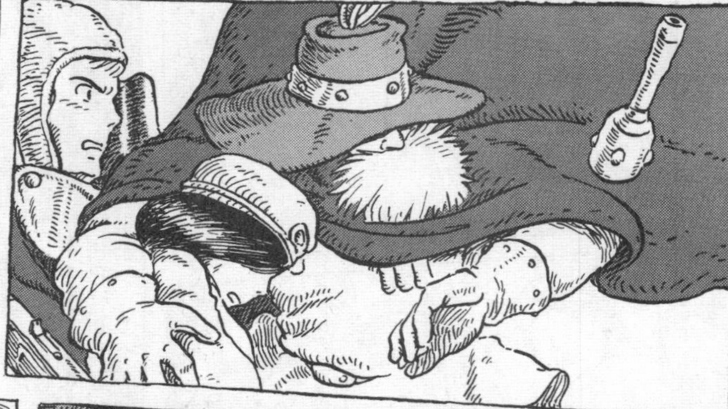

<GET DOWN!!>

MASTER YUPA!!

ヴォムム

THE WOMEN HAVE GONE INTO ACTION!

DAMN! I STILL HAVEN'T GOTTEN KUSHANA INSIDE.

MY EYES ARE CRYING OF THEIR OWN FREE WILL.

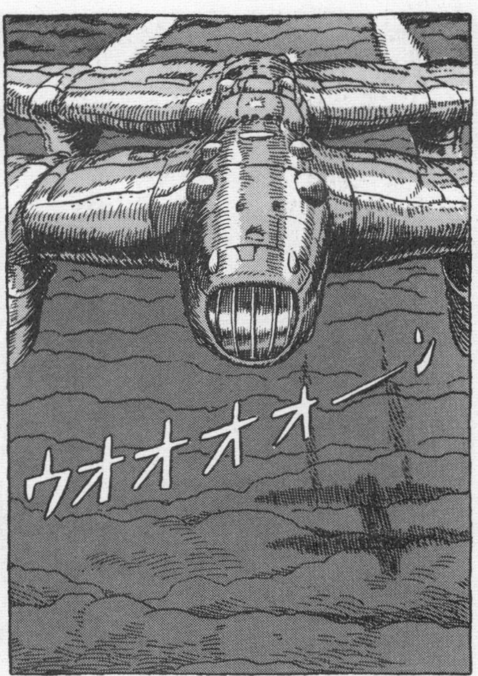
ウオオオオーン

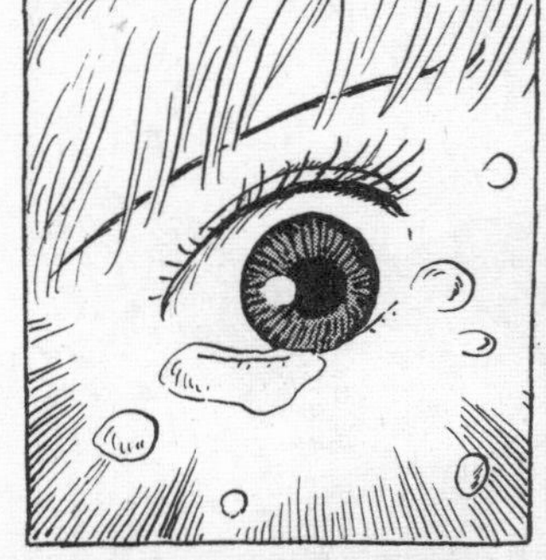

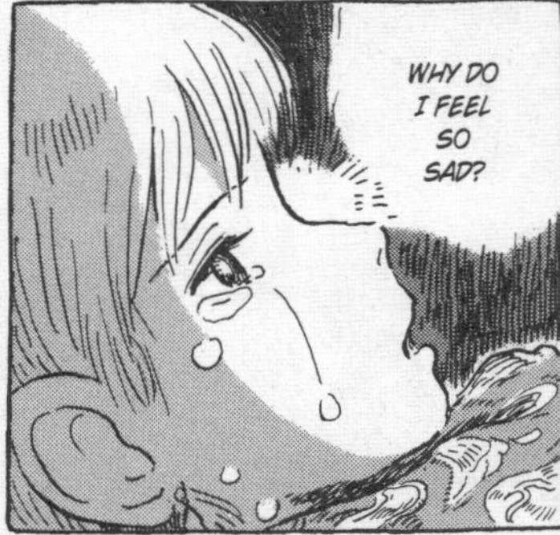
WHY DO I FEEL SO SAD?

AH-H-H !!

TETO... YOU'VE DIED.

...!?
MY ARM !?

オオオオオ

WHO ...?

I OFFER THIS ARM AS PROOF OF MY SINCERITY. PLEASE UNDER-STAND.

SEE TO KETCHA. SHE'S UNCONSCIOUS.

WHY DON'T THEY COME?
SURELY THAT EXPLOSION WAS SUPPOSED TO BE THE SIGNAL.

ゴオオオ

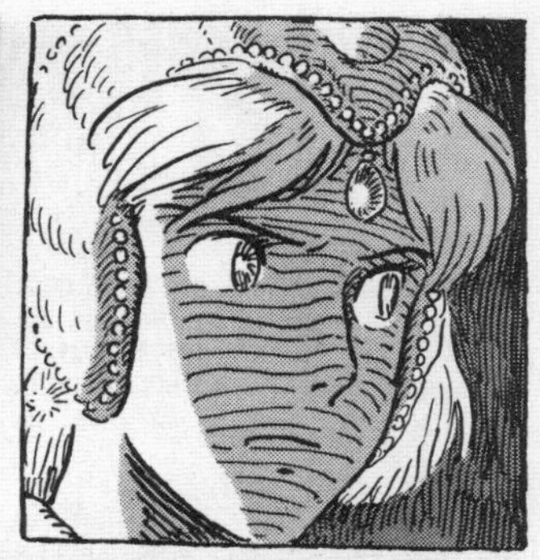

!?

WELL, SHALL WE GET STARTED?

M-MISS ...?

YOU MEN WILL PROTECT HER MAJESTY WITH YOUR ARMOR AND SHIELDS.

HER MAJESTY IS HUNGRY.
YOU'RE LATE! HOW LONG CAN IT TAKE TO MAKE A MEAL?
THE MOMENT I STEP UP TO HER MAJESTY'S SIDE, WE ATTACK.

DAMN, IT'S A LONG WALK.

YOU SNIPERS TAKE OUT THEIR FIRST LINE IN ONE GO. SHOW NO MERCY TOWARD WOMEN OR CHILDREN.

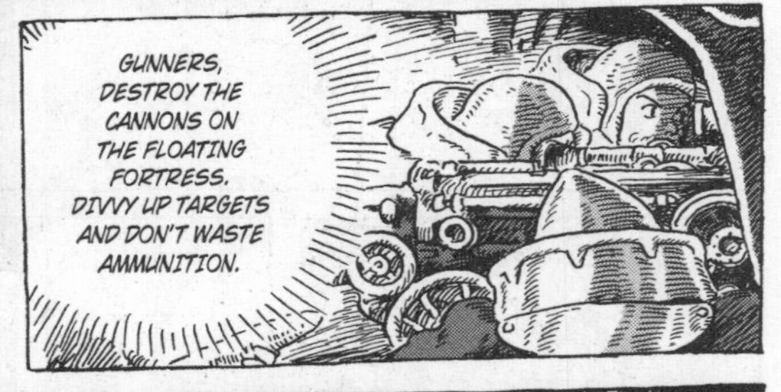
GUNNERS, DESTROY THE CANNONS ON THE FLOATING FORTRESS. DIVVY UP TARGETS AND DON'T WASTE AMMUNITION.

M-MASTER YUPA... Y-YOUR ARM...
THE DANGER ABOARD THE SHIP HAS PASSED. YOU MUSTN'T MAKE THE FIRST MOVE.
ADJUST YOUR EYES TO THE DARKNESS AND TAKE A LOOK AT THOSE PEOPLE.

HALT !!

THEY'RE FORMING A HUMAN WALL IN FRONT OF THE TROOPS.
THERE MUST HAVE BEEN A SPLIT BETWEEN THEM.

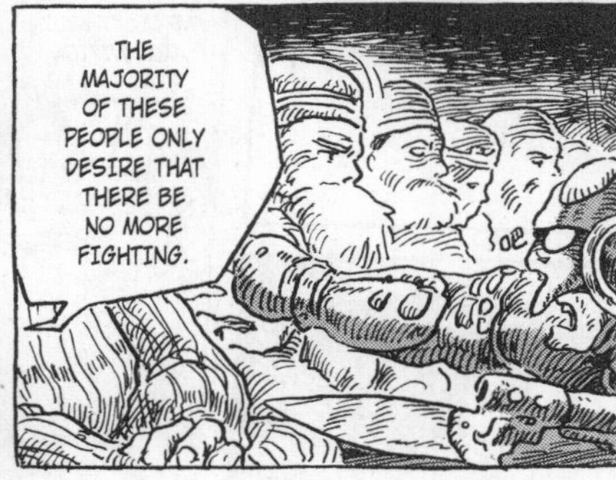

THE MAJORITY OF THESE PEOPLE ONLY DESIRE THAT THERE BE NO MORE FIGHTING.

THAT IS WHY THEY ARE RISKING THEIR OWN LIVES IN ORDER TO CALM THE ANGER OF THE WARRIORS.

THOUGH THERE MAY BE THOSE AMONG THEM WHO ARE BLINDED BY HATRED, THESE ARE THE MOST HUMAN OF HUMANS, LOST IN THE DEPTHS OF DESPAIR.

AN ARMY THAT WOULD GO UP AGAINST CIVILIANS... IS HEADED DOWN THE PATH OF ASURA*, WITH NO HOPE OF EVER RETURNING.

YOU SPEAK THE TRUTH, MASTER YUPA.
IF THERE WAS ANY WAY TO AVOID THIS, I GLADLY WOULD.
BUT MY PATH IS ALREADY AWASH WITH AN OCEAN OF BLOOD. THERE IS NO HOPE OF REDEMPTION FOR ME.

*ASURA: A SUBHUMAN DEMON THAT REVELS IN WAR AND HATRED.

!!
IT'S NOT THE SAPATANS ALONE. OUR OWN MONKS ARE AMONG THEM.

WHAT SHOULD WE DO? WE'VE LOST THE OPPORTUNITY FOR A SURPRISE ATTACK.
DAMN THESE SAPATAN COWARDS!

TO HELL WITH THE COWARDS!! I'LL GO ALONE!!

THAT VILLAIN, CHARUKA. HE'S FINALLY FOUND HIS OPPORTUNITY, HAS HE?

TORU-MEKIAN SWINE!!

ザッ
ドカ
ドカ

AH!!
F-FORGIVE US, HOLY ONE!!

THE HOLY ONE HAS RETURNED!!
IT'S THE HOLY ONE!!
BE STILL AND WATCH!!
D-DON'T MAKE A MOVE!!
AH!
EVER FOR-WARD, MY DARLING WIND.
MASTER YUPA... IS PASSING AWAY.

MASTER YUPA !!

オオオオ

WAH-H-H
KETCHA, DON'T GRIEVE FOR ME.

MASTER YUPA !!

THE DEBT IS MORE THAN PAID!
B-BLESS-INGS ON YOU ...

PEOPLE OF THE MANI TRIBE, I NOW RETURN THE LIFE THAT WAS GRANTED ME BY YOUR HOLY ONE.

BLOOD... BLOOD HAS NOT SULLIED BUT CLEANSED YOU.

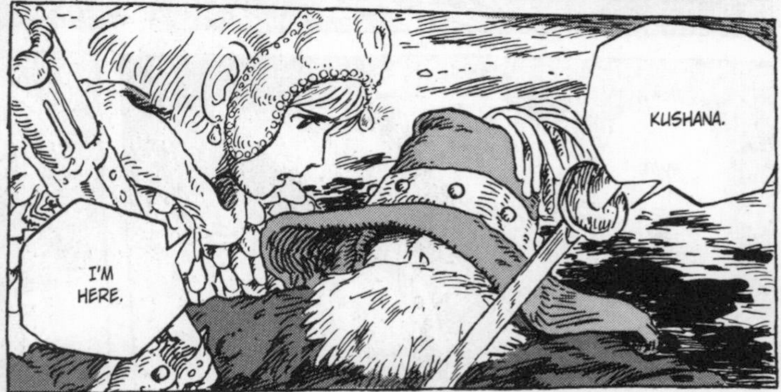
KUSHANA.
I'M HERE.

IT IS THE PATH OF RIGHTEOUS RULE THAT BEFITS YOU, NOT THE PATH OF ASURA.

PUT ME DOWN. I CAN WALK.
I JUST HELPED A LITTLE.

CHIKUKU, WAS THAT YOUR DOING AGAIN?
NO.

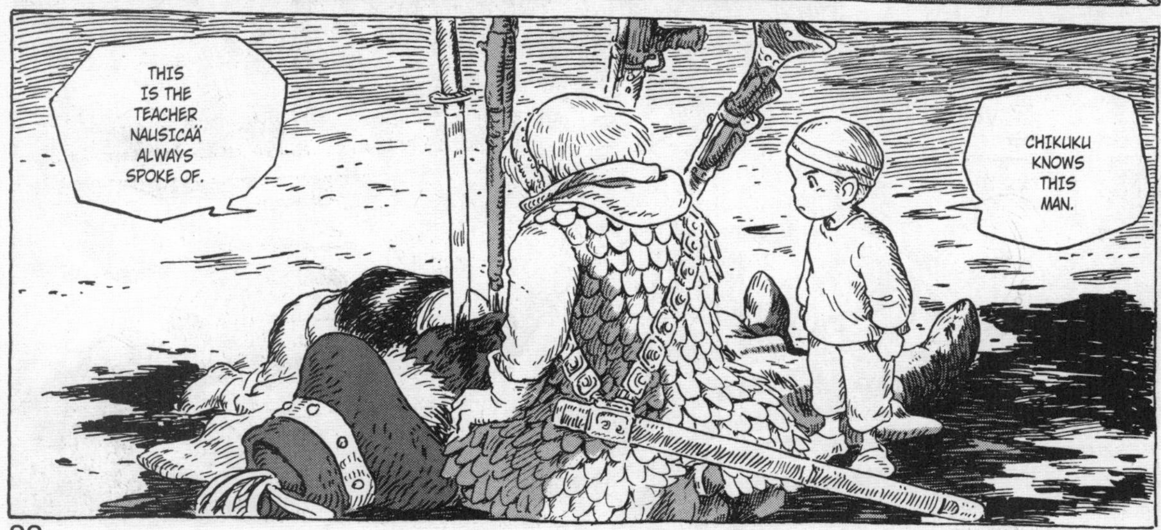
THIS IS THE TEACHER NAUSICAÄ ALWAYS SPOKE OF.
CHIKUKU KNOWS THIS MAN.

WE CAN BURY THIS MAN HERE.
THAT IS WHAT NAUSICAÄ WANTS US TO DO.

NAUSICAÄ TOLD ME ABOUT YOU, TOO, KUSHANA.

SHE SAID YOU ARE A DEEPLY WOUNDED BIRD.

SHE SAID YOU ARE ACTUALLY A GENTLE BIRD WITH BROAD WINGS AND A BIG HEART.

CHIKUKU AND KUSHANA SHOULD BE FRIENDS.

OHMA, COME TO ME.

YES, MOTHER ?
TAKE ME OUT OF HERE. I WANT TO BURY TETO.

ウオオオ

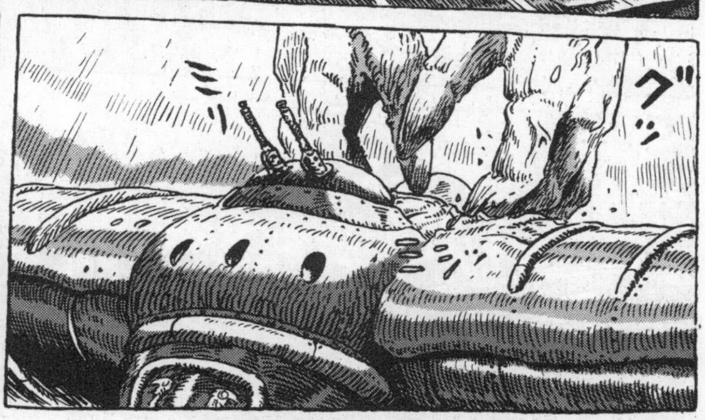
グッ

EMERGENCY!! THE GOD WARRIOR IS CLOSING IN! IT'S DIGGING ITS TALONS INTO THE PORT WING!!

THE WING'S GOING TO BREAK!!
THE GIRL'S IN THE GUN SUPPORT! SHE MUST HAVE CALLED HIM!!
BATTLE STATIONS!! WAKE THEIR MAJESTIES, IMMEDIATELY!!

FOOLS! WHY DID YOU LET HER OUT OF HER ROOM!?
OUT OF THE WAY! WE'LL DRESS LATER!

グラ
AIEE !!

バタバタ
CURSES!! SHE'S ESCAPED!!

バタバタ

PLEASE COME BACK!! YOU'RE IN NO CONDITION TO GO ANY-WHERE!!
バタバタ

オオオ
AT LEAST PUT SOME WARMER CLOTHES ON!!
IF YOU MUST GO, ALLOW US TO ACCOMPANY YOU!!

TH-THE GOD WARRIOR SPOKE!!

SO, YOU'D LIKE TO COME WITH US?

コク

WELL? YOU WANT TO COME, DON'T YOU?

EEEE!!
PUT US DOWN!

N-NO!!
グイ

HEAR ME, TORUMEKIAN TROOPS!! WE HAVE REACHED AN AGREEMENT.

DO YOU REALLY WANT ME TO LET GO OF YOU?
LET GO OF US!!

AH!!
W-WE'LL GO WITH YOU!!

THE TWO PRINCES WILL GO WITH ME TO SHUWA. ACCORDINGLY, THERE IS NO NEED FOR YOU TO PROCEED FURTHER. REVERSE DIRECTION AND RETURN TO YOUR HOMES.

チカ チカ
RETURN TO YOUR HOMES AND LIVE IN PEACE!!
ANY RESPONSE FROM THE FLAGSHIP !?

THE FLAGSHIP IS NOT RESPONDING !!
WH-WHAT SHOULD WE DO? REVERSE DIRECTION?
WE CAN'T JUST LEAVE THEIR MAJESTIES TO DIE!!

ワワッ

パウ

WAH !!

THE NEXT WILL ENGULF YOU IN FLAMES. BEGONE AND DO NOT COME BACK.

ゴゴゴ
R-RETREAT !!
ウオオー
ワワ

W-WAIT ...

WHY THE FUSS? THIS IS WHAT YOU WANTED, IS IT NOT?

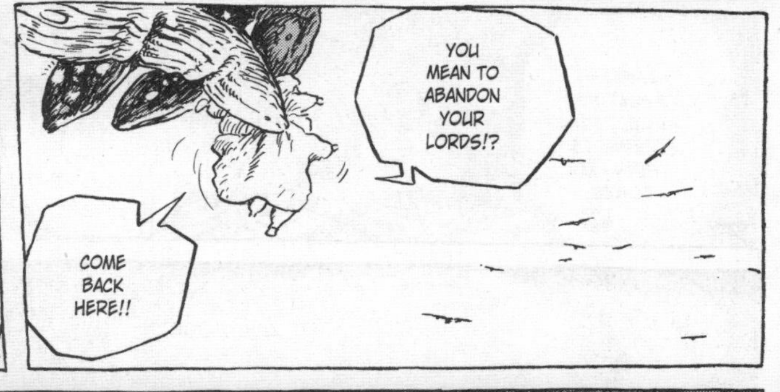
YOU MEAN TO ABANDON YOUR LORDS!?
COME BACK HERE!!

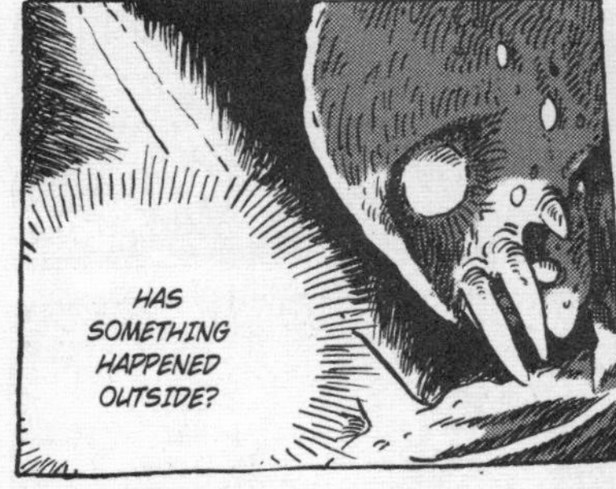
HAS SOMETHING HAPPENED OUTSIDE?

OHMA.
OPEN YOUR HAND.

OHMA, THESE MEN...?

THEIR TROOPS HAVE RETURNED TO THEIR HOMES...
...BUT THESE TWO INSISTED ON ACCOMPANYING YOU.

THE TROOPS WENT HOME? OHMA, WHAT DID YOU DO?

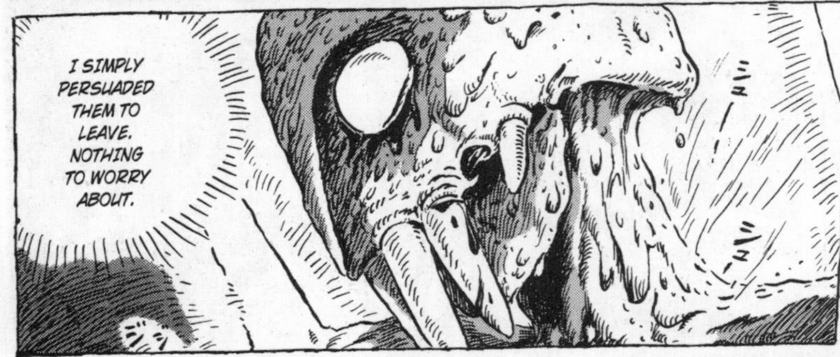
I SIMPLY PERSUADED THEM TO LEAVE. NOTHING TO WORRY ABOUT.

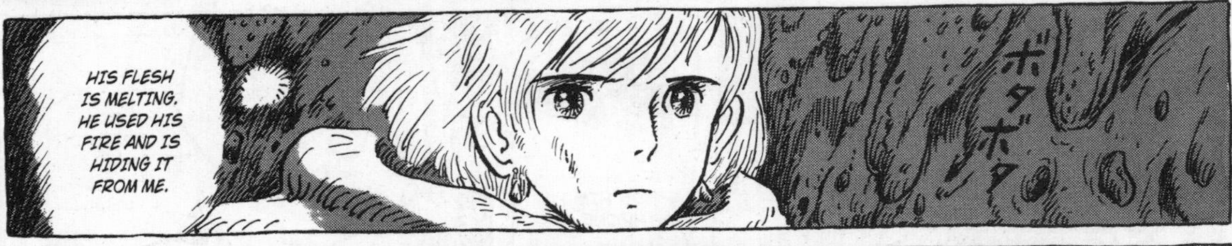
ボタボタ
HIS FLESH IS MELTING. HE USED HIS FIRE AND IS HIDING IT FROM ME.

IS IT BECAUSE HE DOESN'T WANT ME TO WORRY?
OR IS HE SPEAKING...
...AS AN ARBITRATOR?
DAWN IS BREAKING.

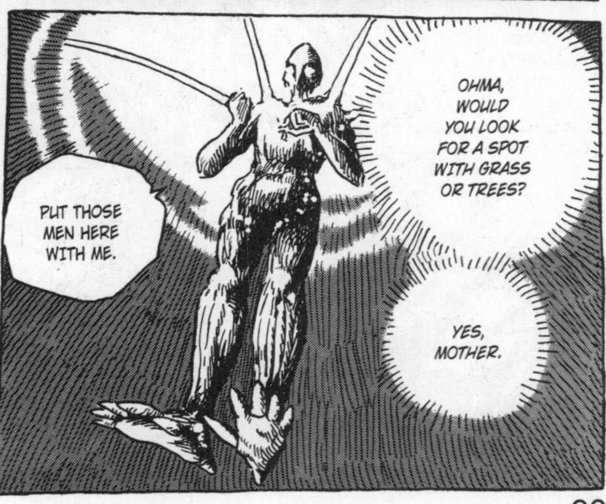
OHMA, WOULD YOU LOOK FOR A SPOT WITH GRASS OR TREES?
PUT THOSE MEN HERE WITH ME.
YES, MOTHER.

TRY TO LAND AS SOON AS POSSIBLE.
S-SPARE US!

I'M NOT SURE. PERHAPS.
E-EXPOSURE TO THIS LIGHT RESULTS IN CERTAIN DEATH!?

...BEFORE THEY ARE OVERLY EXPOSED TO HIS LIGHT.

OUR FATHER INTENDS TO BECOME IMMORTAL LIKE THE HOLY EMPEROR.

WE'VE LONG BEEN PREPARED TO DIE. PLEASE TAKE US WITH YOU TO SHUWA.

PERHAPS!? WE'RE MORE CERTAIN TO DIE IF THEY DROP US OFF IN THE MIDDLE OF NOWHERE.

OUR FATHER SEES HIS OWN CHILDREN AS NOTHING BUT USURPERS WHO WOULD ROB HIM OF HIS THRONE.

IF WE HAD NOT PLAYED THE PART OF COWARDLY FOOLS ALL OUR LIVES, WE WOULD LONG SINCE HAVE BEEN MURDERED.

IF THAT TYRANT SUCCEEDS IN BECOMING IMMORTAL, HEAVEN HELP US ALL.

HOW TRAGIC ...
AH! SO YOU SYMPATHIZE WITH OUR PLIGHT!?

THIS MOST RECENT WAR, TOO, IS HIS WAY OF TESTING US.
IF WE HAD ACTUALLY INVADED SHUWA, WE WOULD SURELY HAVE BEEN ASSASSINATED IMMEDIATELY.

... TO THINK OF ALL WHO DIED FOR SUCH A WAR.

MOTHER, I'VE SPOTTED A TREE.

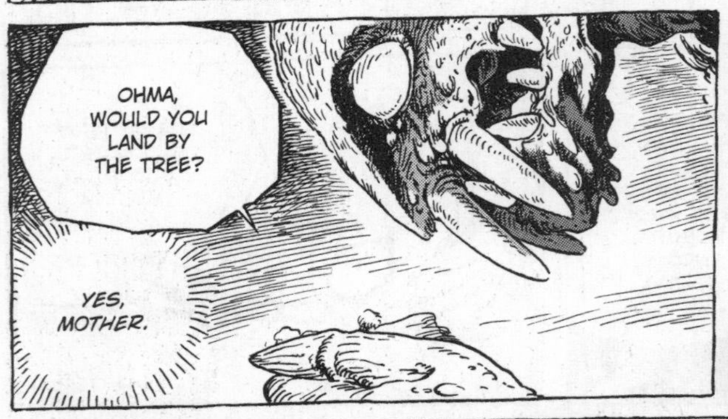
OHMA, WOULD YOU LAND BY THE TREE?
YES, MOTHER.

THE RUINS OF A TOWN.

W-WAIT! WE'LL GO WI--

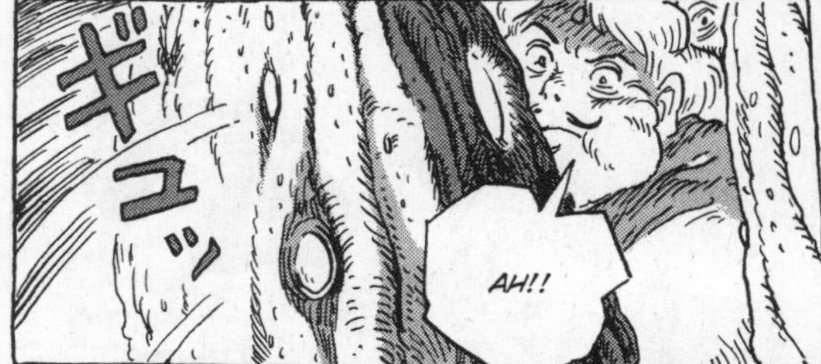
ギュッ
AH!!

WHAT A MAGNIFICENT TREE. IT MUST BE MORE THAN A THOUSAND YEARS OLD.

YOU MUSTN'T INTERFERE WITH MOTHER. STAY WHERE YOU ARE.

...AND FEEL THE BREEZE IN THE LEAVES AND THE BIRDS THAT NEST IN THE BRANCHES.

I'M SURE TETO WON'T BE LONELY HERE. EVENTUALLY HE'LL BECOME PART OF THE TREE.

FORGIVE ME FOR LEAVING YOU HERE THIS WAY.
GOODBYE.

ブスブス

I JUST ASSUMED THE TOWN WAS ABANDONED. I HOPE OHMA'S LIGHT DOESN'T POISON THE SOIL.

GOAT DROPPINGS. IS THERE SOMEBODY HERE?

AH!

<HAVE YOU NOT COME FROM THAT WORLD WHERE COUNTLESS CORPSES LIE SCATTERED WITH NARY A BURIAL NOR PRAYER?>

BROTHER, THERE'S SOMETHING WRONG WITH THE GOD WARRIOR!

YOU NEEDN'T WORRY ABOUT THAT. MY BEASTS ARE QUITE CLEVER. WHERE IS IT YOU ARE GOING IN SUCH A HURRY?
TO SHUWA... TO SEAL THE DOORS OF THE CRYPT.
?

IN ANY EVENT, YOU WON'T BE ABLE TO LEAVE ANYTIME SOON WITH YOUR GIANT ESCORT IN *THAT* CONDITION.

THE DOORS OF THE CRYPT...

グラリ
EEE !

MOTHER... I'M AFRAID I...

OHMA !!

ARE YOU IN PAIN?

ゲホ

ハア
ゼイゼイ
ゼイ

SHE "CALLED" ITS NAME WHEN SHE SAW IT FALL.

AN EVEN CURIOUSER SIGHT. SHE SPEAKS WITH THE GOD OF DEATH.
ゼイ
ゼイ

ヒイイイ
UNH... MY HEAD...

"OHMA."
IN THE ANCIENT EFTAL TONGUE, THAT MEANS "INNOCENCE."
IS SHE THE ONE WHO GAVE IT THAT NAME?

KEST.
IT'S BECAUSE YOU RAN, AND YOU DO NOT HAVE BODIES THAT ARE FIT TO RUN. THE AIR IS THIN HERE.
ウウウ
ウッ

H-HELP US! THE GOD WARRIOR'S POISONOUS LIGHT...
ゼイ
ゼイ
I... I CAN'T BREATHE.

CARRY THESE TWO INSIDE.
トコトコ

EE!
HOLD ON TO HIS HORNS.
ヒョイ

トコ

STAY BACK. YOU MUSTN'T COME NEAR THIS CHILD.
シュー
シュ

OHMA, I WILL TAKE CARE OF YOUR MOTHER FOR A WHILE.
WE'LL LET HER REST BEYOND THE REACH OF YOUR LIGHT.

HE'LL BE FINE ONCE HE'S RESTED A-!?

YOU KNOW OHMA'S NAME!?
REST EASY. I SHALL NOT REVEAL THIS CREATURE'S NAME TO ANYONE.

YOU THINK YOU'RE IN ANY CONDITION TO LEAVE? YOU CAN BARELY STAND.
ヒョイ
AH ...

THAT'S RIGHT. YOU'RE BOTH GOOD CHILDREN.

MOTHER... GO... OHMA... WILL BE... FINE...

...AS MY MOTHER.

THIS MAN HAS THE SAME SMELL...

AH-H !!

FROM THE SKY IT LOOKED LIKE NOTHING BUT RUINS.

AN OLD-FASHIONED WINDMILL.

ギィイイイ

IT SEEMS THEY'VE TAKEN TO YOU.

NOW, NOW. CLEAR THE WAY.

KEST, YOU SAW TO THE OTHER TWO?

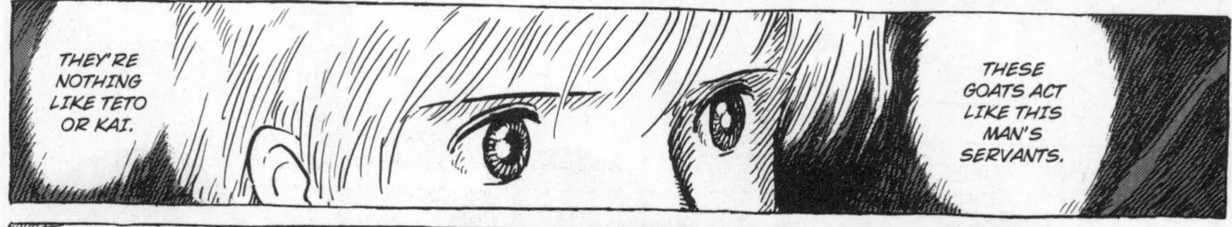
THEY'RE NOTHING LIKE TETO OR KAI.
THESE GOATS ACT LIKE THIS MAN'S SERVANTS.

DON'T BOTHER OUR GUEST, CHILDREN.

I'LL HAVE THEM PREPARE A MEDICINAL BATH IMMEDIATELY. REST NOW.

WHERE AM I? HEAVEN?

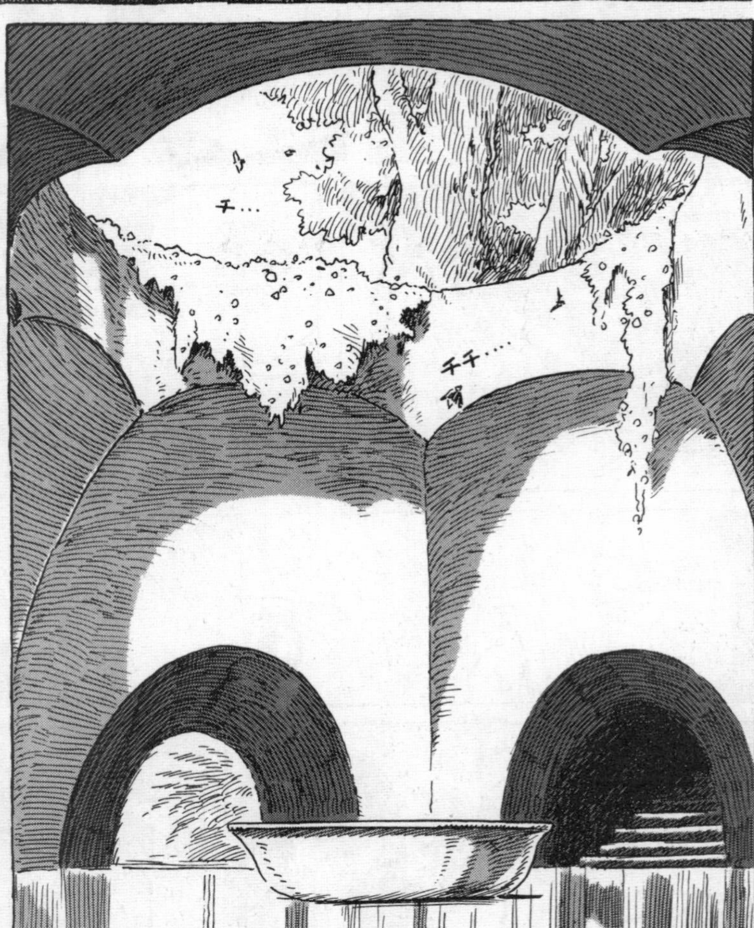
チ…
チチ…

コト

A BATH!? BUT WHEN ...?

AH !!

I MUST HAVE FALLEN ASLEEP AS SOON AS I LAY DOWN.

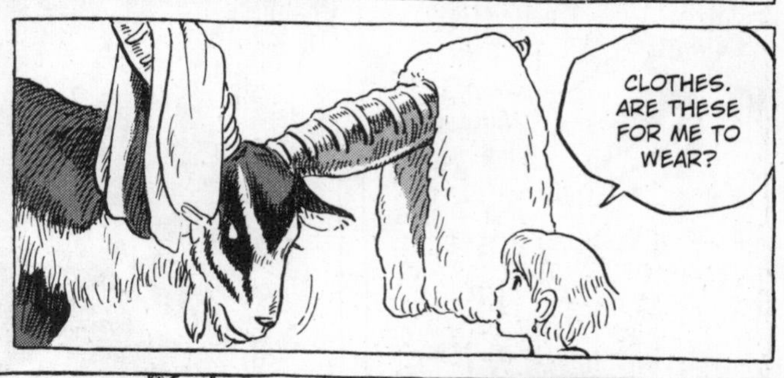
CLOTHES. ARE THESE FOR ME TO WEAR?

SUCH BEAUTIFUL FABRIC.

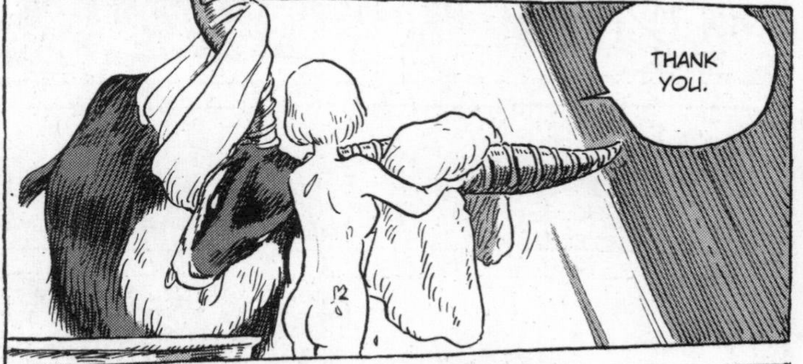
THANK YOU.

MY BODY FEELS SO LIGHT.
THIS BATH HAS THE MOST UNUSUAL SCENT.

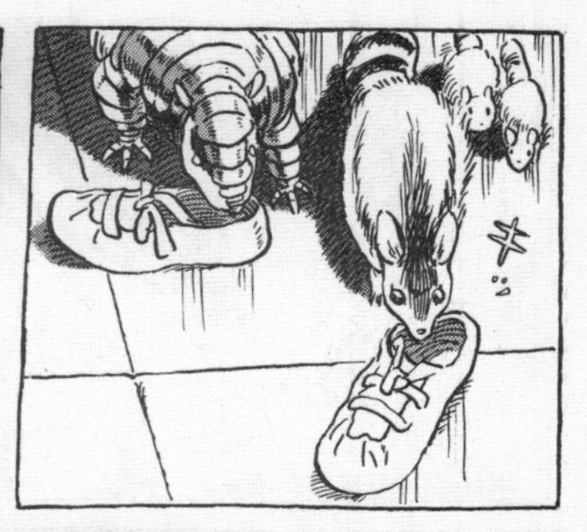

EVEN SHOES !

HEE HEE. THEY FIT PERFECTLY.

OH, MY!

IS THIS FOR ME? OH, WONDERFUL. I'M STARVING.

THANK YOU, KEST.

...THESE CHILDREN ...
THIS FRUIT ...
... THE TREES AND PLANTS ...
...THESE ARE ALL SPECIES THAT BECAME EXTINCT AGES AGO.

WHAT A PEACEFUL PLACE.
I FEEL WONDERFUL.

HMM. THERE'S SOMETHING I'M SUPPOSED TO REMEMBER. WHAT WAS IT...?

MUSIC ...
I WONDER IF IT'S HIM.

WHAT AN ENORMOUS MANOR.

IT'S COMING FROM QUITE A DISTANCE.

IT'S COMING FROM IN HERE.

WHO ...?

IT'S SIMPLY MARVEL-OUS.
ALL THE MUSIC MANKIND EVER PRODUCED ESCAPED THE SEVEN DAYS OF FIRE AND HAS BEEN PRESERVED HERE!
IT'S INCREDIBLE. THIS SHELF HERE CONTAINS THE WORKS OF THE GREAT MASTERS OF THE AGE OF THE SEVEN-NOTE SCALE.

I COULD HAVE SWORN HE WAS SOMEONE I KNOW.
Y-YES.

THIS ROOM IS A TREASURE TROVE OF MUSIC AND LITERATURE THAT WAS SUPPOSED TO HAVE BEEN LOST LONG AGO!

AH, PLEASE, PLEASE, COME IN. DO YOU LIKE THIS PIECE?

SUCH PURITY AND SIMPLICITY OF STRUCTURE. JUST LOOK AT THIS CHORD...

WAIT A MINUTE. IF WE REARRANGE IT A BIT, I BELIEVE WE CAN PLAY THIS ON THIS INSTRUMENT.
JUST LOOK AT THIS. THE GENIUSES WEREN'T LEGENDS-- THEY ACTUALLY LIVED!

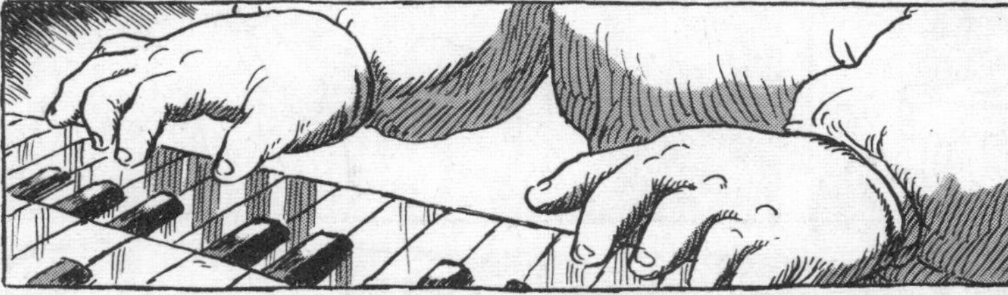

I'LL PLAY THE STRING AND WOODWIND PARTS. THIS INSTRUMENT TRULY IS MARVELOUS.
YOU PLAY THE KEYBOARD PARTS.

TETO
...
ザワ
ザワ
"TETO"!?
...!?
OHMA
!?
TETO...
OHMA.

OH, WELL. I KNEW IT WAS BOUND TO HAPPEN.

KEST.

OUR LATEST PLAYERS ARE QUITE SKILLED.

I'LL BE RIGHT THERE.

NO.
WHA -!?

OHMA !!
I HAVE TO GO !!

DON'T GO.
NO.
WHAT IS THIS PLACE !?
WOULD YOU PLEASE KEEP IT DOWN? WE'RE TRYING TO CONCENTRATE.
DIDMXV

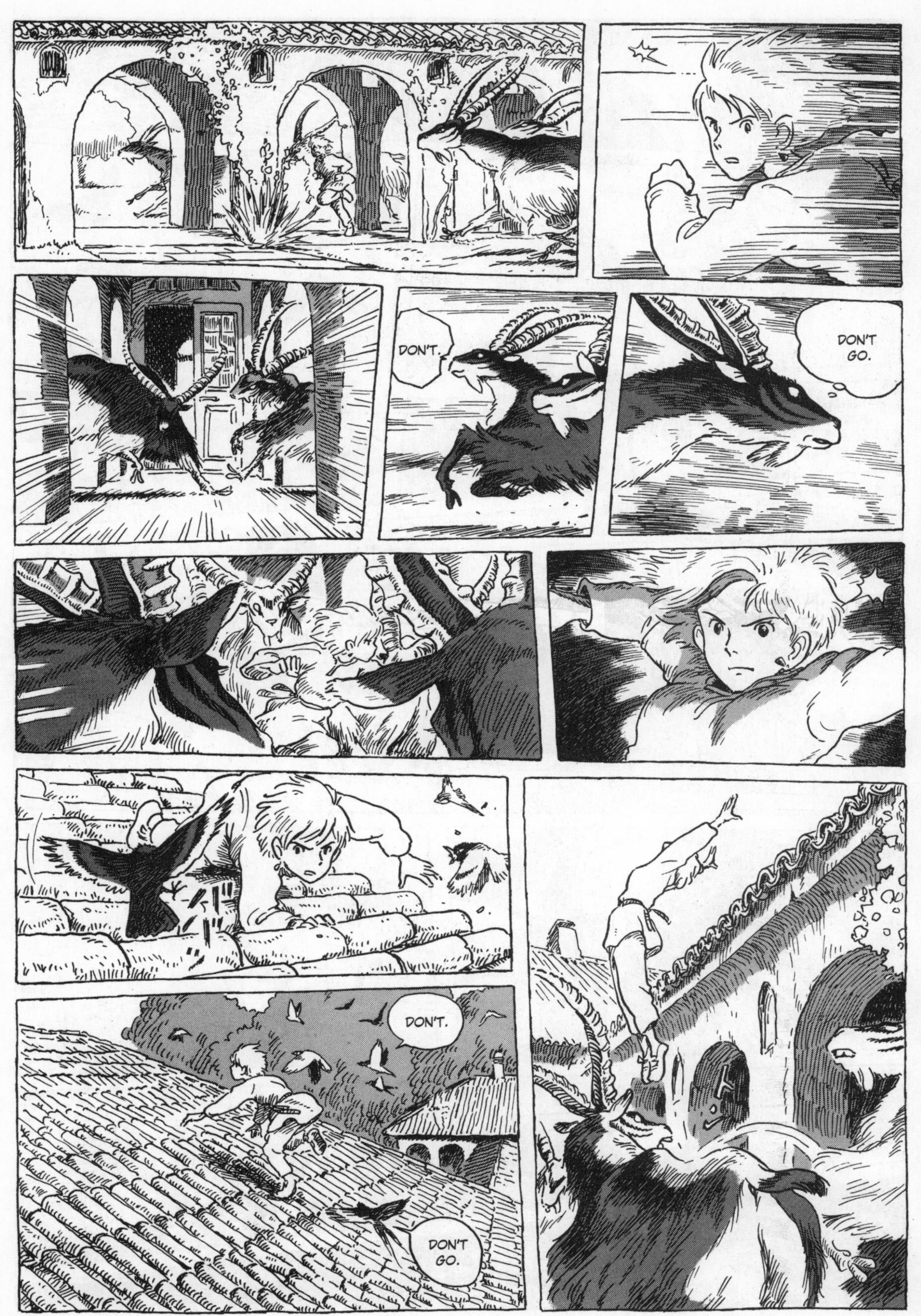
DON'T.
DON'T GO.
DON'T.
DON'T GO.

THOSE FARMERS ARE HEEDRA!!
YOU MUSTN'T GO.
DON'T GO.
WHY WOULD HEEDRA ...!?
DON'T.
STAY.
STAY HERE.
COULD THIS BE... THE CRYPT !?

TH-
THERE'S
NO
SOUND!!

IT'S
MITO
!!

THEY'RE
DIS-
APPEARING
INTO EMPTY
SKY.

THAT'S WHY
IT LOOKED
LIKE NOTHING
BUT RUINS
WHEN I SAW
IT FROM
ABOVE.
THIS
GARDEN
IS MADE
TO BE
INVISIBLE
FROM THE
OUTSIDE
!!

BARGE!! WHAT'S
GOING ON BACK
THERE? YOU'RE
ROCKING US!!

THEY'VE
DIS-
APPEARED
!!
I'VE GOT
TO GET
OUT OF HERE.
I'VE GOT TO
GET BACK
TO OHMA.

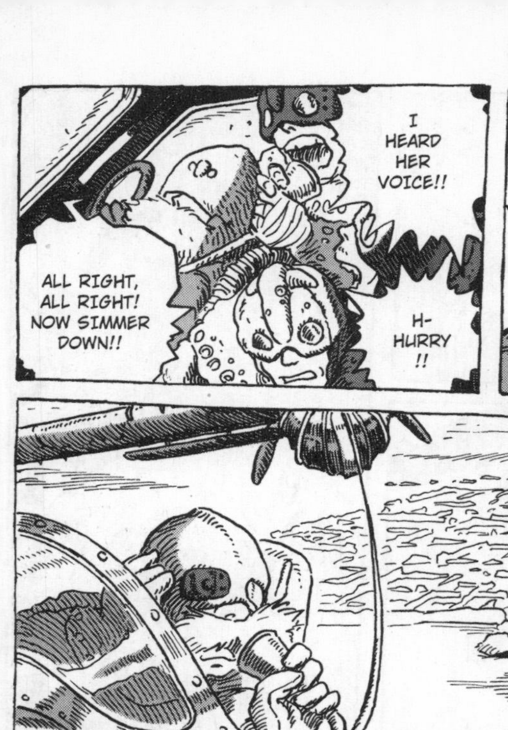
I HEARD HER VOICE!!
H-HURRY!!
ALL RIGHT, ALL RIGHT! NOW SIMMER DOWN!!

WHAT'S GOING ON!?
MITO!! HOLD ON! THE WORMHANDLERS ARE--!
スーー

WHAT!? THE PRINCESS!?

NAUSICAÄ CALLED OUT TO US!!
I HEARD IT, TOO! SHE'S SOMEWHERE NEARBY!

MITO!!
YOU'RE ALL TALKING AT ONCE!! HOW DO YOU EXPECT ME--

THE VOICE HAS DISAPPEARED!!
BRING US DOWN!!
AH! IT'S GONE! I CAN'T HEAR HER ANYMORE!!
I HEARD IT, TOO!! WE'VE GOT TO LAND!!
グラグラ

!?
THEY'RE HUGE! THOSE ARE THE GOD WARRIOR'S PRINTS.
WHY IS HE WALKING RATHER THAN FLYING?

FOOT-PRINTS ON THE PORT SIDE!!

KUI'S MAKING A RUCKUS, TOO!
THESE LADS REALLY MAY HAVE HEARD THE PRINCESS'S VOICE!

LET'S GO! THE FOOTPRINTS SHOULD LEAD US TO THE PRINCESS.
THE FOOTPRINTS LEAD TO SHUWA. NAUSICAÄ WILL BE WHEREVER THE GOD WARRIOR IS.
MITO! WE'LL SEARCH THIS AREA!

THE BARGE IS FREE. INCREASING SPEED!
バウウ

タン

ALL RIGHT !!
JUST DON'T WANDER TOO FAR FROM THE BARGE. WE'LL COME BACK TO PICK YOU UP LATER.

ザッ

THIS IS REAL MOSS.

THERE'S NO SIGN THERE EVER WAS A GATE HERE AT ALL.

THE GATE IS GONE!?

BUT THIS IS WHERE WE CAME IN!!
ザッ

バッ

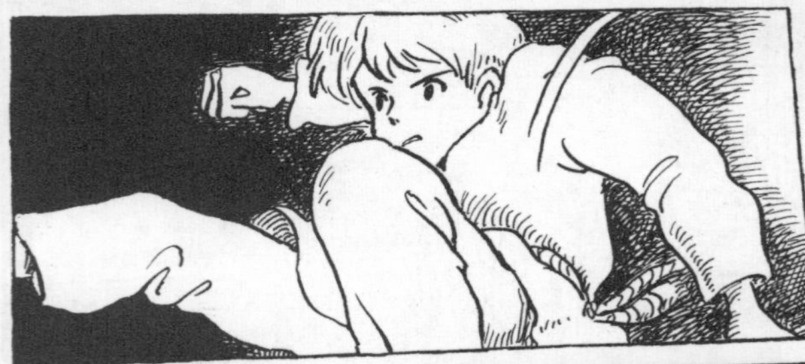

パッ

YOU CERTAINLY ARE A HANDFUL, AREN'T YOU?

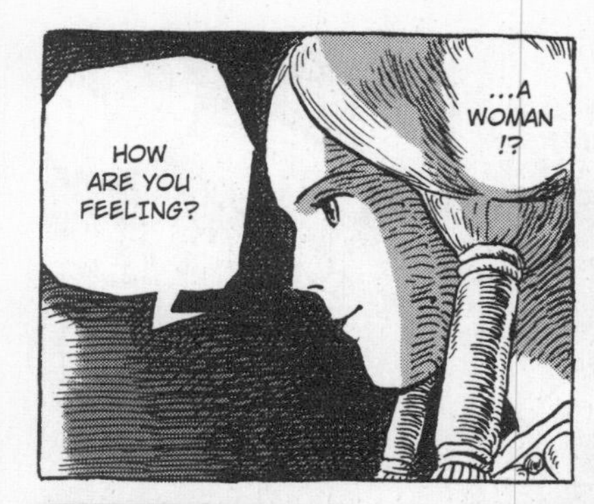
HOW ARE YOU FEELING?
...A WOMAN !?

Y- YOU'RE --!

IF I HADN'T STEPPED IN, YOU WOULD HAVE MELTED RIGHT INTO THE WALL.

COME ON, NOW. LET ME SEE YOUR TONGUE.
OPEN YOUR MOUTH.

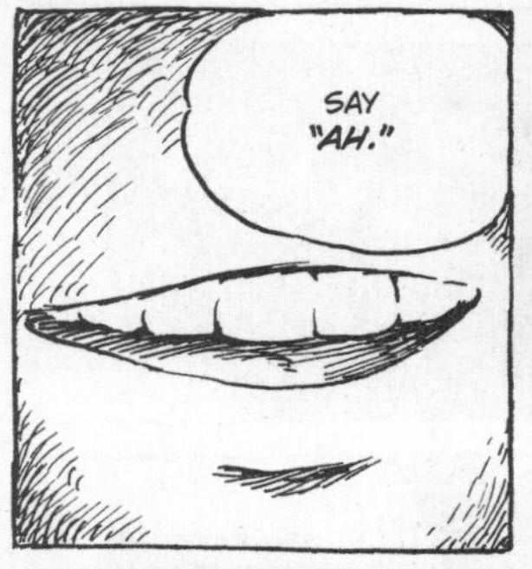
SAY "AH."

THERE'S A GOOD GIRL.

ビクッ

AH-H-H-H

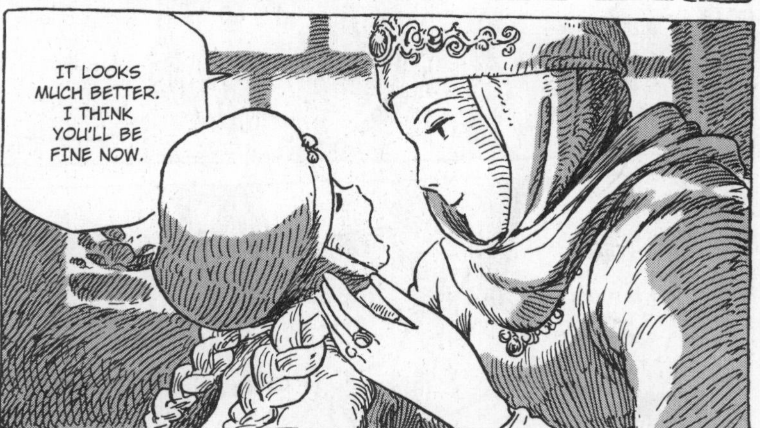
IT LOOKS MUCH BETTER. I THINK YOU'LL BE FINE NOW.

BUT YOU MUSTN'T GO OUT- SIDE.

THIS IS THE ONLY PLACE YOU'LL FIND THE PEACE YOU'VE BEEN LOOKING FOR.

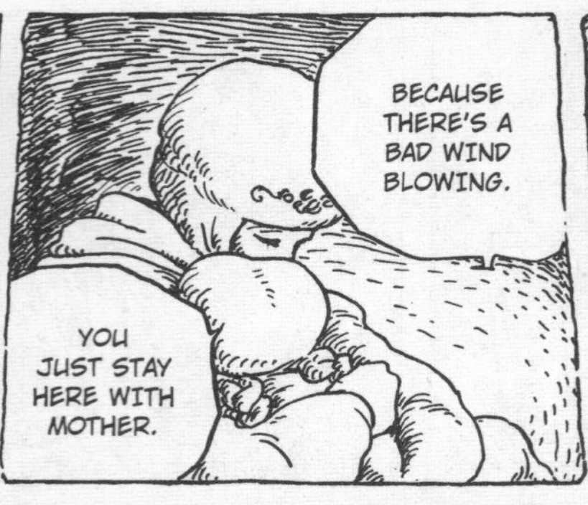
BECAUSE THERE'S A BAD WIND BLOWING.
YOU JUST STAY HERE WITH MOTHER.

WHY ?
WHY CAN'T I GO OUTSIDE?

THAT'S RIGHT. GO TO SLEEP NOW.

STAY HERE... FOREVER?

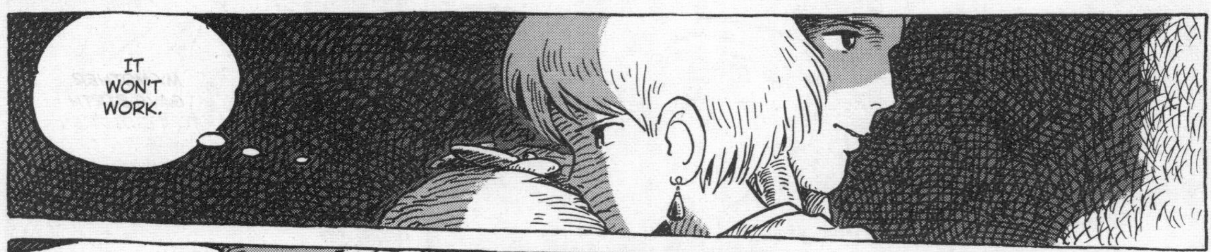
IT WON'T WORK.

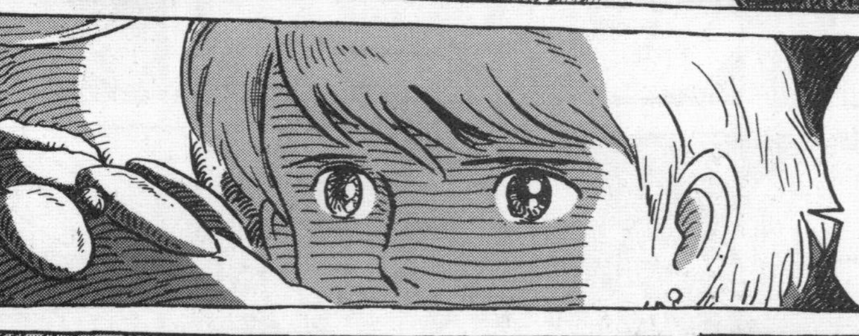
YOU HAVE THE POWER TO READ A PERSON'S HEART INSTANTLY. YOU EVEN CHANGE YOUR OWN FORM TO SUIT EACH GUEST!

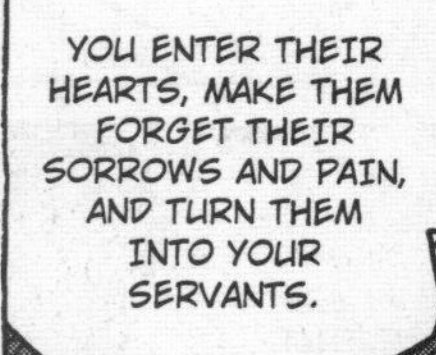
YOU ENTER THEIR HEARTS, MAKE THEM FORGET THEIR SORROWS AND PAIN, AND TURN THEM INTO YOUR SERVANTS.

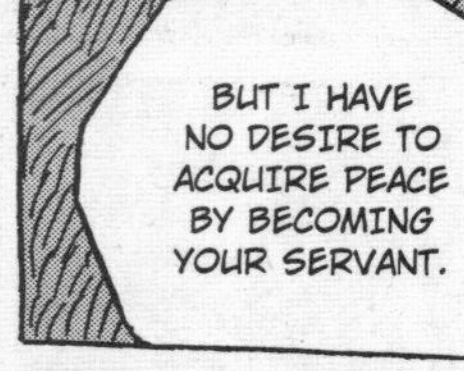
YOU SAVED MY LIFE.
BUT I HAVE NO DESIRE TO ACQUIRE PEACE BY BECOMING YOUR SERVANT.

BOTH YOUR BODY AND SPIRIT WERE IN NEED OF HEALING.
DO YOU DENY THAT YOU WERE LONGING FOR YOUR MOTHER WHEN I HELD YOU?

BUT I CLOSED MY HEART THE MOMENT I GAVE OHMA HIS NAME. I'M BEYOND YOUR REACH.

AT SUCH TIMES, HER FACE WAS THE FACE OF A STRANGER.

I REMEMBERED MY MOTHER BECAUSE YOU HAVE THE SAME SCENT OF DEATH ABOUT YOU AS SHE DID!

I WAS AFRAID THAT IF I SPOKE TO HER, SHE MIGHT NOT REMEMBER ME.
SO I WOULD STAND THERE SILENTLY UNTIL SHE FINALLY NOTICED ME.

MY MOTHER WAS KIND, BUT SHE OFTEN USED TO SIT BY THE WINDOW AND STARE OUTSIDE.

MY SISTERS AND BROTHERS ABSORBED THE POISON THAT HAD GATHERED IN MY MOTHER'S BODY AND DIED IN HER PLACE.
MY MOTHER GAVE BIRTH TO 11 CHILDREN. I WAS THE ONLY ONE WHO LIVED TO MATURITY.

THE IMAGE OF MY MOTHER THAT YOU SHOWED ME WAS A TRAP. MY OWN DESIRE WAS THE LURE.
MY MOTHER TAUGHT ME THAT THERE ARE SOME WOUNDS THAT CAN NEVER BE HEALED. BUT SHE DIDN'T LOVE ME.

BUT YOU INSIST ON GOING TO THE CRYPT!
ONCE IN A GREAT WHILE I HAVE A VISITOR SUCH AS YOU.

I WON'T ASK WHO YOU ARE.
AND I WON'T ASK WHAT THE PURPOSE OF THIS TRAP IS, BUT...

COME WITH ME.
スー

SOME 200 YEARS AGO A BOY VERY MUCH LIKE YOU VISITED US HERE.

HE GOT ALONG VERY WELL WITH KEST AND THE OTHER BEASTS, AS WELL AS THE HEEDRA.
HE WAS A TALENTED SCRIBE AND MUSICIAN, AND LOOKED UPON ME AS HIS MENTOR.

TAKE CARE UNTIL YOU'VE ADJUSTED. THE AIR HERE IS SWEET BUT STRONG.

TOMB-STONES.
IT'S THE SAME AS THE AIR IN THE DAYS BEFORE HUMANKIND BEGAN TO USE THE "FIRE."

ONE DAY, THE BOY LEFT THIS GARDEN.
HE LEFT ME A NOTE.

THE NOTE READ, "I WANT TO SAVE HUMANITY."
HE TOOK FOUR HEEDRA WITH HIM.

SO THEN IT *IS* POSSIBLE TO LEAVE THIS GARDEN.
HA, HA. YES, EVEN WE SLIP UP SOMETIMES.

HE WENT ON TO BECOME THE FIRST HOLY EMPEROR.
HEEDRA!? YOU MEAN TO SAY THAT BOY WAS--!?

WHEN HE WAS YOUNG, HE WAS A GENUINELY COMPASSIONATE PHILOSOPHER-KING. THERE WAS NOTHING HE WANTED MORE THAN FOR THE PEASANTS TO BE AT PEACE.
THAT LASTED ABOUT 20 YEARS. WHEN THE PEASANTS PROVED TO BE INCORRIGIBLY STUPID, HE GREW TO HATE THEM.

I BELIEVE YOU MET HIS CHILDREN, THE CHILDREN WHO SUCCEEDED HIM.

YOU, WHO THINK YOURSELF A MESSIAH, HAVE UNLEASHED THAT MONSTER ON THE WORLD.
TAKE THE GOD WARRIOR AND THE HEEDRA AS WELL.
CRAWL AROUND WITH THE WHOLE BLOODY LOT ON YOUR SHOULDERS, AND THEN SEE IF YOU CAN SAVE THE WORLD!!

I AM OHMA, SON OF NAUSICAÄ.
HE WHO METES OUT JUSTICE.

LUWA CHIKUKU KULABALUKA WILL FOLLOW NAUSICAÄ!
THE SAME PATH THAT HAS BEEN TROD OVER AND OVER AGAIN...

YOU HUMANS TREAD THE SAME PATHS OVER AND OVER AGAIN.

EVERYONE BELIEVES THEY ALONE WILL NOT ERR.
YET NONE CAN ESCAPE FROM THE CYCLE WHEREIN KARMA GIVES BIRTH TO KARMA, SORROW GIVES BIRTH TO SORROW.

YOU DO NOT LOVE HIM, YET YOU GAVE THAT GOD OF PLAGUES A NAME. WHY?
WAS THAT YOUR REVENGE AGAINST THE MOTHER WHO DID NOT LOVE YOU?
WHA-- ? NO, I--

THIS GARDEN IS THE PLACE WHERE ALL CHAINS CAN BE SEVERED.
YOU SAW THE TWO TORU-MEKIAN PRINCES?
FOR THE FIRST TIME IN THEIR LIVES, THEY ARE EXPERIENCING PEACE AND JOY.

.....

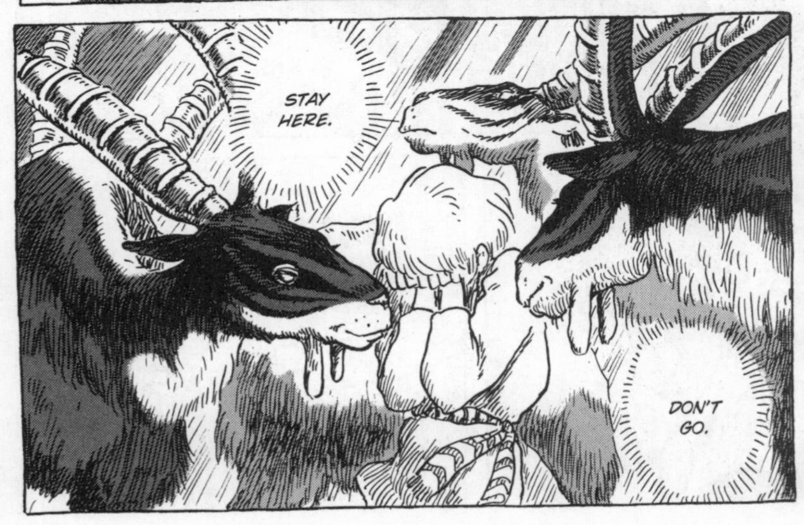
STAY HERE.
DON'T GO.

ヴィイイイイム
BLACK SMOKE UP AHEAD !!
IS IT THE GOD WARRIOR !?

WE'VE REACHED THE END OF THE PLAINS. IT'S SHUWA !!

MITO! LOOK STAR-BOARD!!

THE TORU-MEKIAN ARMY IS ATTACKING !!
IT'S THE VAI EMPEROR !!

ITS BODY IS A MESS! JUST WHAT DOES IT MEAN TO DO!?

IS THE PRINCESS WITH THAT THING!?
I CAN'T TELL. I'LL MOVE IN CLOSER.

THE AIR OUTSIDE IS VERY BAD.
DON'T GO.
STAY HERE.
DON'T GO.
DON'T!
DON'T CRY.
I'M LOSING MY CONVICTION.
WHAT YOU ARE TRYING TO DO...
...HAS BEEN ATTEMPTED BY OTHER HUMANS MANY TIMES BEFORE.
WE ALL LIKE YOU.
PLEASE DON'T GO. PLEASE.
SELM ...
GIVE ME THE STRENGTH TO GO ON.
HELP ME, SELM.

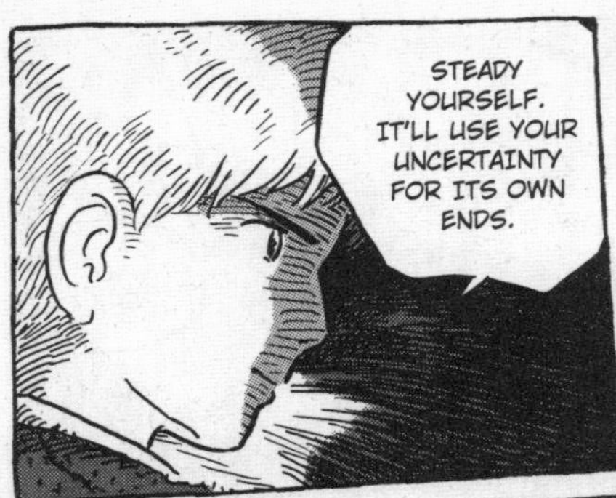
STEADY YOURSELF. IT'LL USE YOUR UNCERTAINTY FOR ITS OWN ENDS.

SELM !?

IT HAS NOTICED MY PRESENCE ALREADY.
IT, TOO, HAS THE ABILITY TO LEAVE ITS BODY. A VERY WELL-MADE HEEDRA INDEED.

HEEDRA !? THIS PERSON-- !?

AN IMMORTAL WATCHDOG CREATED BY THE PEOPLE OF THE ANCIENT WORLD.

IMMORTAL !?
IT'S PROBABLY BEEN ALIVE FOR AT LEAST A THOUSAND YEARS.

AN AMAZING GIRL! I WOULDN'T HAVE THOUGHT YOU COULD BREAK THROUGH MY BARRIER AND BRING IN AN UNINVITED GUEST.
ARE YOU ONE OF THOSE WHO ABANDONED FIRE?

SEVERAL OF YOUR PEOPLE HAVE VISITED OUR GARDEN BEFORE. THEY ALL TURNED OUT TO BE WONDERFUL GUESTS.
HERE THEY FOUND A PEACE THAT CANNOT BE ATTAINED SIMPLY BY ABANDONING FIRE AS YOUR PEOPLE HAVE. THEY BECAME GOOD GARDENERS.

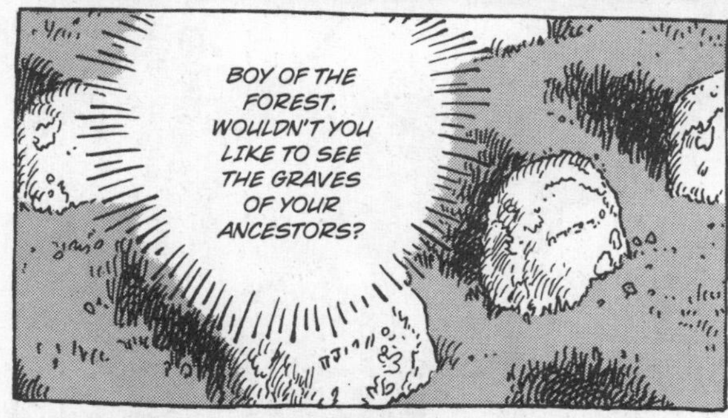
BOY OF THE FOREST. WOULDN'T YOU LIKE TO SEE THE GRAVES OF YOUR ANCESTORS?

WHAT HE SAYS IS NO DOUBT TRUE. TIME AND AGAIN OUR PEOPLE HAVE SENT REPRESENTATIVES TO SHUWA.
BUT WE BECOME POWERLESS WHEN WE LEAVE THE FOREST.

YOUR HEART IS GRIPPED BY UNCERTAINTY AND DOUBT.
WHY DO YOU HIDE THOSE FEELINGS FROM THE GIRL?

HA, HA, HA. A COUNTERATTACK? YOU FEEL SAFE BECAUSE YOUR BODY IS FAR AWAY? ARROGANT BOY.

MASTER OF THE GARDEN.
YOUR FRIENDS PASS AWAY ONE AFTER THE OTHER, AND YET YOU GO ON LIVING. JUST WHAT IS IT YOU ARE GUARDING?

WE WILL ALL DIE!?

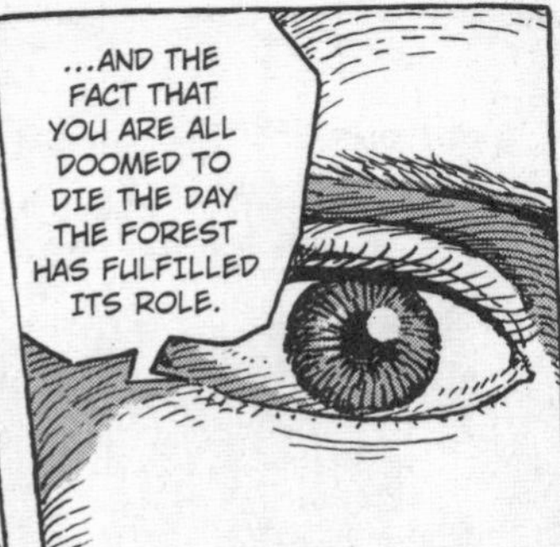
...AND THE FACT THAT YOU ARE ALL DOOMED TO DIE THE DAY THE FOREST HAS FULFILLED ITS ROLE.

SURELY YOU AND YOUR PEOPLE HAVE DISCOVERED THE MEANING OF THE SEA OF CORRUPTION...
...WHY IT IS THAT HUMANS CANNOT LIVE IN THE PLACE WHERE THE FOREST ENDS...

AH!!

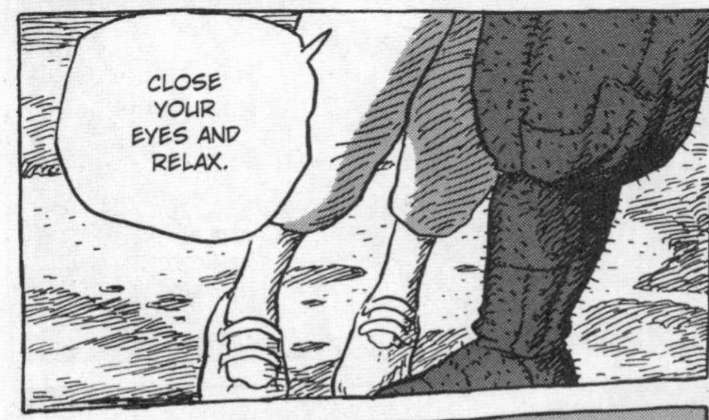
CLOSE YOUR EYES AND RELAX.

SELM.
TRUST ME, NAUSICAÄ. TURN YOUR BODY OVER TO ME FOR THE MOMENT.

MASTER OF THE GARDEN, IF YOU THINK YOU CAN SHAKE ME WITH YOUR INTERROGATION, YOU ARE MISTAKEN.

CHILD OF THE FOREST, LONG AGO YOUR PEOPLE SENT SCOUTS TO THE PLACE WHERE THE FOREST ENDS...SEVERAL TIMES. BUT NOT ONE OF THEM EVER CAME BACK. EVERY ONE OF THEM VOMITED BLOOD AND DIED.
NOW IT IS CONSIDERED TO BE A HOLY AND FORBIDDEN PLACE. WHY DO YOUR PEOPLE GO ON DECEIVING THEMSELVES THAT A PLACE THAT CAN ONLY BE VISITED IN SPIRIT SOMEHOW REPRESENTS HOPE?

AND NOT JUST HUMANS. THE PLANTS AND ANIMALS WERE CHANGED, TOO.

YOU KNOW THAT THE HUMAN BODY IS DIFFERENT FROM WHAT IT ONCE WAS.
THAT IT HAS CHANGED TO SUIT A POLLUTED WORLD.

THE CREATURES THAT LIVED WHEN THE EARTH AND SKY WERE PURE COULD NEVER LIVE IN THE SHADOW OF THE SEA OF CORRUPTION.

HAVE YOU NEVER THOUGHT IT ODD THAT HUMANS CAN SURVIVE EXPOSURE TO THE MIASMA WITH ONLY FLIMSY MASKS TO PROTECT THEM?

THE UNPOLLUTED AIR OF THIS GARDEN IS SWEET AND STRONG.
IF I HAD DONE NOTHING TO THIS GIRL'S BODY, HER LUNGS WOULD BE SPEWING BLOOD.

SO YOU'RE SAYING WE CANNOT LIVE WITHOUT THE POISON?

STAY CALM!
IT'S A TRICK !!

IT'S ALL RIGHT, SELM.
THANK YOU FOR COMING, SELM. NOW I CAN SEE THINGS MORE CLEARLY.

...THAT WE BLIND OURSELVES BY LOOKING AT THE WORLD SIMPLY IN TERMS OF "PURITY" AND "CORRUPTION".
I'VE ALWAYS FELT...

PLEASE, TELL ME MORE!!

IN MY VALLEY, WE LET THAT WATER SIT IN THE RESERVOIR FOR A WHILE BEFORE USING IT TO WATER THE CROPS, AND WE BOIL IT BEFORE DRINKING IT.
PLANTS FROM THE SEA OF CORRUPTION RAISED ON THAT WATER GAVE OFF NO MIASMA AND REMAINED SMALL. BUT THE AQUATIC PLANTS OF THE VALLEY WOULDN'T GROW IN THAT WATER.
WHEN I RAISED PLANTS FROM THE SEA OF CORRUPTION USING PURE, UNDER-GROUND WATER, I DISCOVERED THAT THE CAUSE OF THE MIASMA IS IN THE SOIL.

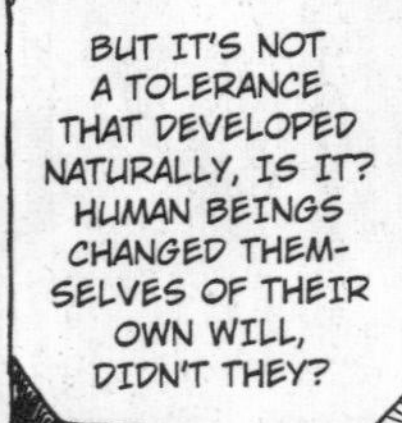
THE WATER SURELY BECOMES CONTAMINATED WHILE SITTING IN THE RESERVOIR, YET THE PLANTS GROW BETTER THAT WAY!

BUT IT'S NOT A TOLERANCE THAT DEVELOPED NATURALLY, IS IT? HUMAN BEINGS CHANGED THEM-SELVES OF THEIR OWN WILL, DIDN'T THEY?

YOU SAID THAT ALTHOUGH WE MAY LONG FOR A PURIFIED WORLD, WE COULD NEVER SURVIVE THERE-- THAT THE HUMAN BODY IS DIFFERENT FROM WHAT IT ONCE WAS.

HE HAS DISAPPEARED. HE HAS CEASED HIS ATTACK.

HMM. I'VE BEEN TAKEN OFF GUARD BY A CLEVER VISITOR.

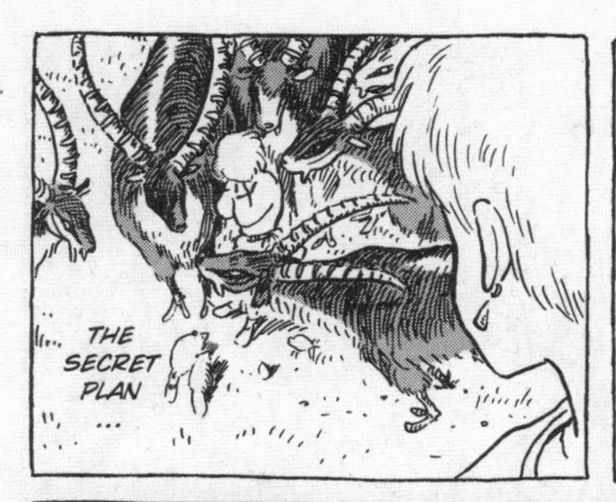
THE SECRET PLAN ...

NOW I SEE EVERY-THING CLEARLY.
I FEEL STRANGELY, ALMOST FRIGHT-ENINGLY SERENE.

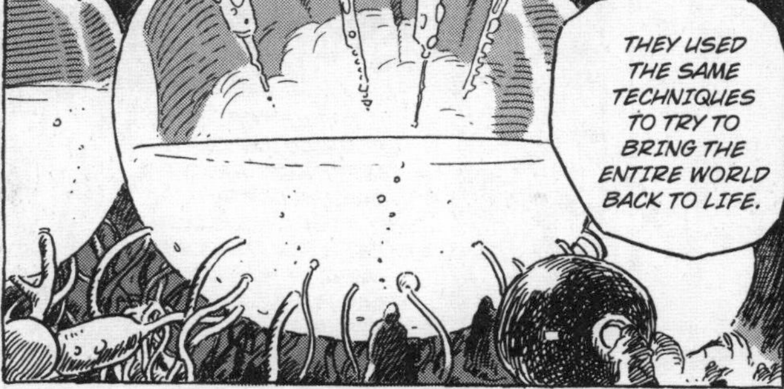
THEY USED THE SAME TECHNIQUES TO TRY TO BRING THE ENTIRE WORLD BACK TO LIFE.

TECHNIQUES TO CRYSTALLIZE CONTAMINATED MATTER AND RENDER IT HARMLESS.

AROUND THE TIME OF THE SEVEN DAYS OF FIRE, WHEN THE WORLD HAD BECOME POLLUTED IRREVOCABLY, A GROUP OF PEOPLE REMADE HUMAN BEINGS AND OTHER LIFE FORMS.

THAT WAS THE SOURCE OF THE SUDDEN APPEARANCE 1,000 YEARS AGO OF THIS INCREDIBLE NEW ECOSYSTEM!

ARE YOU SAYING THE FOREST WAS CREATED BY THE HANDS OF HUMAN BEINGS!?
THAT'S RIGHT.
IF WE TAKE THAT TO BE TRUE, EVERY-THING BECOMES CRYSTAL CLEAR.

AN ECOSYSTEM WITH A GOAL. ITS VERY EXISTENCE RUNS CONTRARY TO THE LAWS OF NATURE!

THE SEA OF CORRUPTION IS ATTEMPTING TO REVIVE A BARREN EARTH IN JUST A FEW THOUSAND YEARS. WHEN ITS ROLE IS OVER, IT WILL DIE. IT WAS PLANNED FROM THE BEGINNING.

OUR LIVES ARE LIKE THE WIND ... OR LIKE SOUNDS.
WE COME INTO BEING, RESONATE WITH EACH OTHER...

... THEN FADE AWAY.

ONE THOUSAND YEARS AGO, HUMANITY MUST HAVE BEEN IN THE DEPTHS OF DESPAIR. THE PEOPLE SOUGHT DESPERATELY FOR SOME GLIMMER OF HOPE. THE TECHNOLOGY USED TO CREATE AN ECOSYSTEM AND REMAKE LIVING CREATURES LIVES ON IN THE UPKEEP OF THIS GARDEN.

YOUR IDEAS WILL SHAKE THE VERY FOUNDATIONS OF MY PEOPLE.
WE HAVE ALWAYS FELT THAT THE FOREST IS A SACRED LIFE FORM.

ACCORDING TO THE PLAN, WE SHOULD BE WELL ALONG THE PATH TO REBIRTH, BUT IN REALITY, FOOLISHNESS HAS CONTINUED, AND NIHILISM AND DESPAIR HAVE ONLY SPREAD.

I DON'T UNDERSTAND. HOW COULD FOOLISH HUMANS CREATE SUCH A LIFE FORM AS AN OHMU?

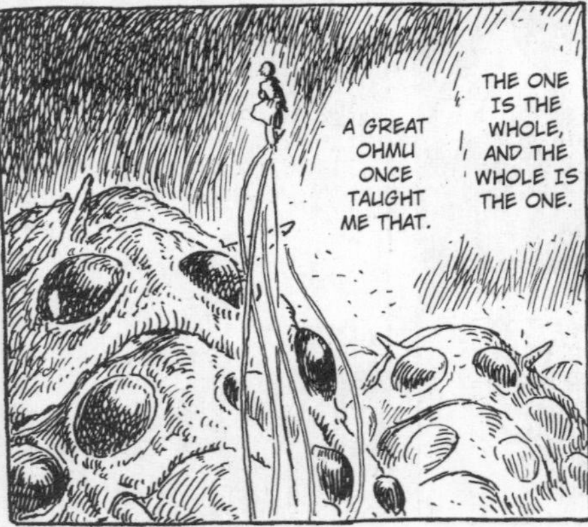
THE ONE IS THE WHOLE, AND THE WHOLE IS THE ONE.
A GREAT OHMU ONCE TAUGHT ME THAT.

I STILL FEEL THAT WAY.

EVERY LIFE FORM, NO MATTER HOW SMALL, CONTAINS THE OUTSIDE UNIVERSE WITHIN ITS INTERNAL UNIVERSE.

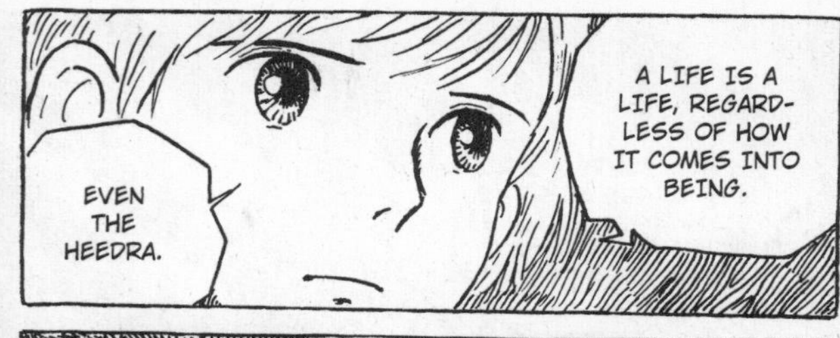
A LIFE IS A LIFE, REGARDLESS OF HOW IT COMES INTO BEING.
EVEN THE HEEDRA.

AND YOU'RE SAYING THE SECRETS BUILT INTO THIS WORLD CAN BE FOUND IN THE CRYPT OF SHUWA.

...
THE GREATNESS OF A MIND IS DETERMINED BY THE DEPTH OF ITS SUFFERING.
EVEN THE MUTANT MOLD HAD A MIND OF SORTS.

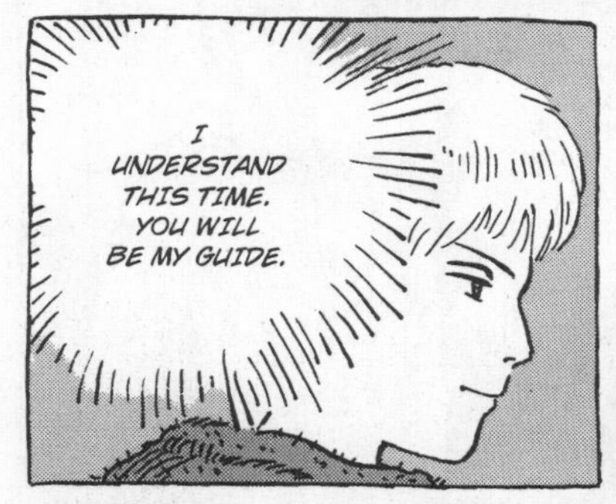
I UNDERSTAND THIS TIME. YOU WILL BE MY GUIDE.

I WILL GO THERE, SELM. NOT TO CLOSE THE DOORS BUT TO PRY THEM OPEN, IF NEED BE...AND DISCOVER THE TRUTH.

THIS GARDEN IS THE STOREHOUSE OF THE CRYPT. IT IS NOT ITS CENTER.

THOUGH OUR BODIES ARE FAR APART, I WILL GO WITH YOU. EVEN IF ALL THAT AWAITS US IS CRUSHING DESPAIR.

YOU'RE A STRONG CHILD. SO YOU WON'T CHANGE YOUR MIND ABOUT GOING?

HIDDEN SEEDS. SEEDS FOR REPLENISHING THE WORLD AFTER IT HAS BEEN PURIFIED.
I WONDER IF THERE ARE OTHER GARDENS LIKE THIS ONE?

I DON'T BELIEVE YOU ARE CAPABLE OF TAKING A LIFE. THAT IS WHY YOU CANNOT STOP ME.
YOU ARE CRUEL, YET KIND.

I HAD THOUGHT THE CRYPT MUST BE A PLACE WHERE MANUFACTURING TECHNIQUES AND KNOWLEDGE ARE PRESERVED.

PUREBRED SPECIMENS OF UNCON-TAMINATED PLANTS AND ANIMALS THAT WERE THOUGHT TO BE LONG SINCE EXTINCT...
...AGRICULTURAL PRODUCTS...
...MUSIC AND POETRY...
...AND THE VISITORS AND HEEDRA WHO KEEP THEM ALL ALIVE AND PASS THEM ON.

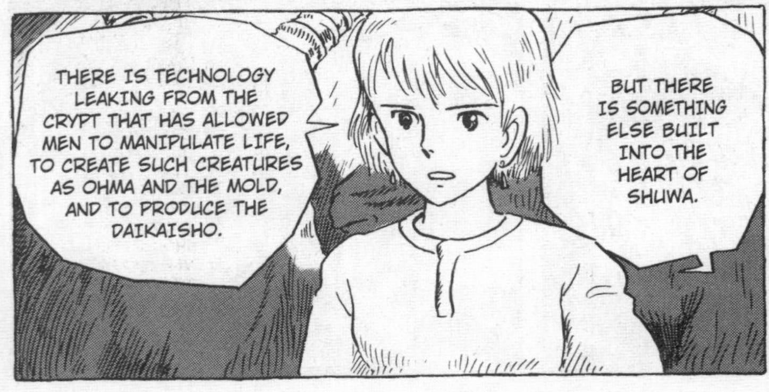
THERE IS TECHNOLOGY LEAKING FROM THE CRYPT THAT HAS ALLOWED MEN TO MANIPULATE LIFE, TO CREATE SUCH CREATURES AS OHMA AND THE MOLD, AND TO PRODUCE THE DAIKAISHO.
BUT THERE IS SOMETHING ELSE BUILT INTO THE HEART OF SHUWA.

THIS GARDEN CONTAINS THE ONLY THINGS HUMAN BEINGS WERE ABLE TO CREATE THAT ARE WORTH PASSING ON TO THE NEXT WORLD.

WHY IS THERE TECHNOLOGY PRESERVED IN THE CRYPT THAT SHOULD NOT BE PRESERVED, TECHNOLOGY THAT SPEWS A SHADOW OF DEATH?

YOU MUSTN'T.
YOU MUSTN'T GO.

YOUR SILENCE IS ANSWER ENOUGH.
IT IS TIME FOR ME TO GO.

MOTHER OF OHMA.
YOU MUSTN'T LET HER GO.

THOUGH I SHATTERED IT MYSELF, I WILL NEVER FORGET THE MOMENT OF TRANQUILITY YOU GAVE ME.
FARE-WELL. MY NAME IS NAUSICAÄ.

NAUSICAÄ. THAT IS A GOOD NAME.

I WON'T STOP YOU. BUT I WILL LEAVE THE DOOR OF THE GARDEN OPEN FOR YOU, SHOULD YOU EVER CHOOSE TO RETURN.

WILL NAUSICAÄ COME BACK?
NO.

THINGS ARE GOING TO BE DULL AGAIN FOR A WHILE, AREN'T THEY, KEST?

BUT SHE GAVE US HER NAME, DIDN'T SHE?

THERE'S SOMETHING ODD ABOUT THE RUINS OF THIS TOWN.
THERE ARE GRASS AND TREES HERE, YET THERE IS NO SIGN OF THEM.

FOUND ANYTHING ?

INTENTIONALLY !?

ALL SIGNS OF LIFE HAVE BEEN INTENTIONALLY ERASED.

IS IT THE PRINCESS !?

WHOA!
ダッ

KUI.

AH!!

?

NAUSICAÄ WAS BORN FROM THIS STONE!
I SAW IT, TOO!!

YOU'RE HERE, TOO!
WELL, I'LL BE.

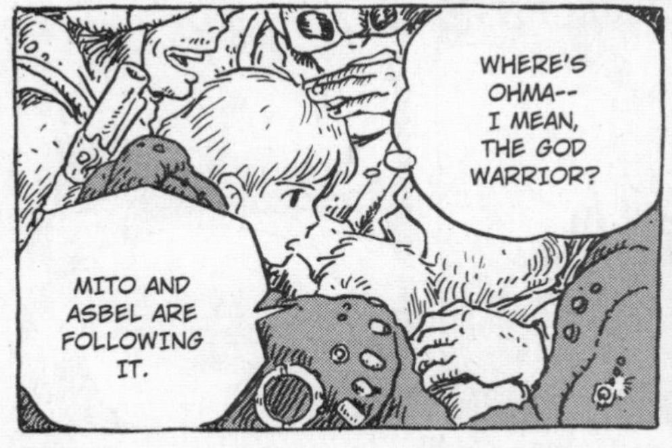
WHERE'S OHMA-- I MEAN, THE GOD WARRIOR?
MITO AND ASBEL ARE FOLLOWING IT.

THANK GOODNESS!
LOOK AT THE COLOR OF HER CHEEKS! SHE'S MUCH BETTER NOW.
THANK YOU. THANK YOU ALL.

OHMA ...
HA, HA!! JUST LOOK AT HOW FAST SHE CAN RUN!!

YOU SAY HE WAS WALKING !?

I CAN'T HEAR A THING.

OHMA, ANSWER ME.
OHMA.

BRING KUI! I MUST GO AFTER THE GOD WARRIOR.
WE WILL GO WITH YOU!!
ALLOW US TO GO WITH YOU!!

COULD HE HAVE LEFT BECAUSE HE THOUGHT I WOULD ONLY GET IN THE WAY?

MY CHEST ACHES.

YES, I'M SURE OF IT!!
I WILL GO TO SHUWA IN YOUR PLACE, MOTHER. YOU ARE IN NEED OF A REST.

THEY DID WHAT!?
YES, THEY INSISTED WE TAKE THEM WITH US IN THE BARGE.

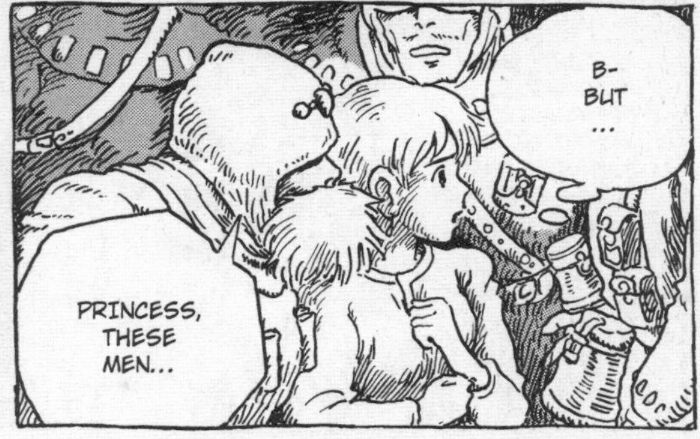
B-BUT ...
PRINCESS, THESE MEN...

HOW COULD WORM-HANDLERS KILL THEIR OWN WORMS?
THEY MEANT SO MUCH TO YOU.

BUT --!!

WE ARE NAUSICAA'S FRIENDS.
WE WANT TO DO WHAT WE CAN TO HELP YOU.
WE NEED NOTHING ELSE. WE HAVE ABANDONED EVERYTHING.

I'M SO SORRY!! YOU DID THIS ALL FOR ME...
YOU MUSTN'T CRY!!
DON'T CRY!!

THE BOY TOOK THE HEEDRA AND HEADED FOR SHUWA ...
...SAYING, "I WANT TO SAVE HUMANITY".

WE ARE NAUSICAA'S GUARDIANS.
LET US ACCOMPANY YOU!!

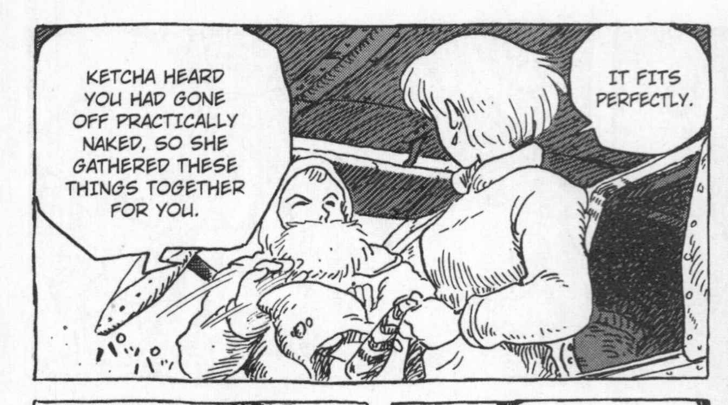

KETCHA HEARD YOU HAD GONE OFF PRACTICALLY NAKED, SO SHE GATHERED THESE THINGS TOGETHER FOR YOU.
IT FITS PERFECTLY.

NOW I TREAD THE SAME PATH WITH THE WORM-HANDLERS AND THE GOD WARRIOR.

WHY AM I DOING THIS...?

THANK YOU.
IT'S A BIT DIRTY, BUT I'D LIKE YOU TO WEAR MY CAP.

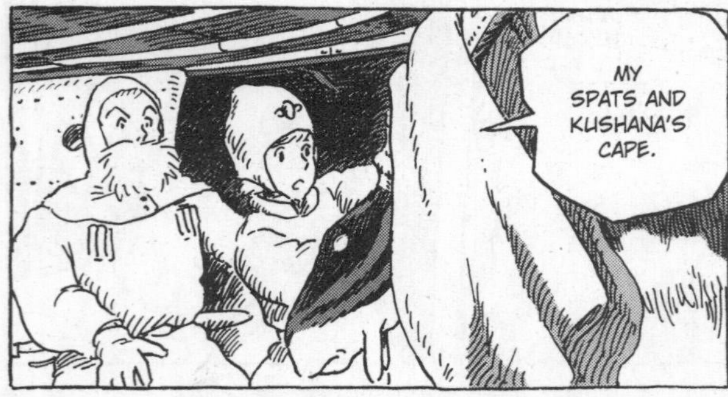

MY SPATS AND KUSHANA'S CAPE.

KEST !

FOR ALL I KNOW ...
THANK YOU, KEST.

ALL RIGHT, KUI.
BUT EVEN IF THAT'S THE CASE ...

I MAY BE GOING TO DESTROY HUMANITY.

PRINCESS. IT'S A BIT HEAVY, BUT...

WE'LL HAVE TO RUN TO SHUWA. SOMEONE TAKE THE LEAD AND SET THE PACE!

NO. I HAVE NO MORE NEED OF WEAPONS. I'LL SEE TO IT THAT MITO COMES BACK TO PICK YOU UP. UNTIL THEN, TAKE CARE OF THINGS HERE.

MAY THE BATTLE BE YOURS!!

THE AIR IS THIN HERE. DON'T BECOME OVEREAGER AND GO TOO FAST! IF ANYONE BECOMES TIRED, I'LL CHANGE PLACES WITH HIM!!
オオー

AND MAY WE SOON FIND OURSELVES HOME IN THE VALLEY OF THE WIND!

HUF
HUF

I'VE NEVER SEEN SUCH A PLACE.

HUF
HUF
HUF
HUF

THE SAND IS ALL RUST AND CRUSHED CERAMIC.

THESE ROCKY HILLS ARE A MELTED CITY!

SLOW THE PACE A BIT. THE OTHERS CAN'T KEEP UP.

HALT !!

ハァ
ハァ
ハァ
ハァ

TAKE A REST. DON'T COME NEAR THIS THING.

THIS IS TISSUE FROM OHMA.
ジジ…

シュー

NAUSICAÄ, WE HEAR CANNON FIRE.

THAT CHILD CAN BARELY WALK.

THEY'RE RIGHT. IT'S THE SOUND OF FIGHTING. BUT IT'S NOT OHMA.

I'VE GOT GOOD EARS. THE BEST!
SHH! BE QUIET.

THERE'S A BATTLE GOING ON FAR AWAY.

LET'S GO.
I MAY BE A WOMAN, BUT I'VE GOT STRONG LEGS. DON'T UNDERESTIMATE ME AND FALL BEHIND.

WH--!? BUT-
I'LL RUN, TOO. EVERYONE LOAD YOUR ARMS ON KUI.

OHMA! CAN YOU HEAR ME, OHMA?

I FEEL LIGHT AS A FEATHER.
WE WON'T FALL BEHIND!

AT THIS POINT, NAUSICAÄ AND THE WORMHANDLERS WERE SOME 20 LEAGUES* FROM SHUWA. BUT HERE WE MUST ROLL BACK THE CLOCK TO SET THE SCENE.

HUF
DON'T DO ANYTHING UNTIL I GET THERE! PLEASE!!
HUF
HUF

*GALLIC LEAGUES OF 1,500 PACES, OR ABOUT 1 1/8 MILES

YOUR MAJESTY, WE HAVE WON AN OVERWHELMING VICTORY. THE DOROKS ARE NO LONGER RESISTING IN ANY ORGANIZED FASHION.
SO WITHOUT ITS KING, THE COUNCIL OF PRIESTS IS NOTHING BUT A MOB, EH?

HAH. THEY EXPLOITED THEIR PEOPLE THIS MUCH. I PITY THEIR PEOPLE.
THESE ARE THE PRIESTS WHO HAVE COME TO SURRENDER. THEY BEG FOR THEIR LIVES IN EXCHANGE FOR THIS TREASURE.
DIVIDE THE BOOTY EQUALLY AMONG THE SOLDIERS. SEE THAT EVERY MAN GETS HIS SHARE. WHAT I SEEK LIES INSIDE THE CRYPT.

WHO ARE THE MEN HOLED UP IN THE CRYPT?
HMPH. A MESSENGER?

WHAT'S HE SAYING?

KILL THEM OFF ONE AT A TIME UNTIL THEY CONFESS.
SPARE US!! I BEG YOU!! WE TRULY DO NOT KNOW!!

WE DO NOT KNOW!! WE ARE BUT HUMBLE PRIESTS!!
THE CRYPT IS A SACRED PLACE. WE ARE NOT PERMITTED TO ENTER IT.

<YOU MUST NOT DISTURB THE CRYPT.>
<THE CRYPT'S STRENGTH IS AWESOME. YOU MUST PULL BACK YOUR TROOPS AND WAIT FOR A MESSENGER TO APPEAR.>

THERE'S NOT A SINGLE LOOPHOLE TO BE SEEN.

SO THAT'S THE CRYPT, IS IT? IT'S AS BLACK AS PITCH.
ズーン
ズズーン

THEY SEEM TO BE FIRING FROM THAT EYE ABOVE THE DOOR, PREVENTING OUR MEN FROM STORMING THE CRYPT.
ガーン

THE EMPTY MOAT THAT SURROUNDS THE CRYPT IS 300 METERS DEEP. THE ONLY WAY TO ENTER IS TO CROSS THAT BRIDGE.
ズーン
ズズーン
ガーン
ズズーン

キイイーン
キーン

BRING UP THE CANNON! AIM FOR THAT EYE!
ガウン

STORMING PARTY! WE'LL MOVE UNDER COVER OF THE SMOKE BOMBS!!

THAT'S NOT ORDINARY CERAMIC. THE SHOTS ARE SIMPLY BOUNCING OFF.
WE'LL HAVE THE ENGINEER CORPS GIVE IT A TRY.

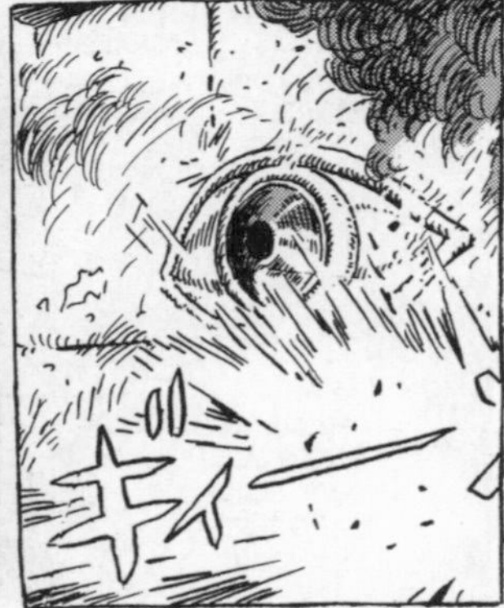
キイー

FIRE !!
GO!!
DAMN!! NEXT!!

タタ

ジュン

THE SMOKE ISN'T WORKING. I'LL GO!

CALL OFF THE ATTACK. THIS IS A WASTE OF TROOPS.

THAT BRIDGE IS MADE OF THE SAME STONE AS THE CRYPT. THERE ISN'T A SCRATCH ON IT.

ヴィ…

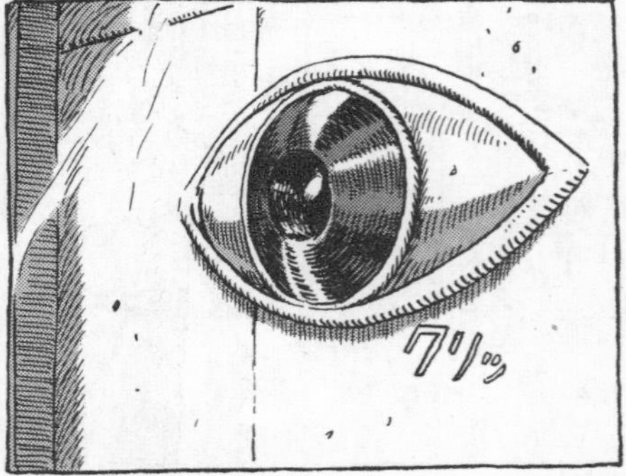
クリッ

RETREAT !!
HURRY, YOUR MAJESTY!
TIT FOR TAT, AND THEN SOME, EH?

ゴオオオオオ

COUNTER-ATTACK !!
THESE LIGHT CANNONS ARE USELESS AGAINST THAT THING!

YOUR MAJESTY, ALLOW US TO ATTACK FROM THE AIR WITH HEAVY BOMBS--
NO, THE CONTENTS OF THE CRYPT MUST NOT BE DAMAGED.
A MESSAGE !!

YOUR MAJESTY! A-A GOD WARRIOR IS APPROACHING FROM THE CLIFFS TO THE EAST!
A GOD WARRIOR ?

ワ
ワ

ワ
ワ

ズル

STOP THE BATTLE !!

I WANT TO SEE YOUR KING. WHERE IS YOUR KING?
I WILL NOT ALLOW THIS BATTLE TO CONTINUE!

NO DOUBT ABOUT IT, SIR! THAT THING'S ACTING ALONE.
ウォオオオー
IT MEANS TO INTERFERE WITH THE BATTLE!!

DAMN THESE OLD EYES OF MINE! I CAN'T SEE CLEARLY!

FIRE! FIRE!!

DESIST IMMEDIATELY! THIS IS YOUR FINAL WARNING!!

BRACE YOURSELF! HE'S GOING TO FIRE!!

A FLASH !?
ハァハァ
ゴオオオオ
ガ
WE'VE LOST THE ENGINE! MAKING AN EMERGENCY LANDING!!
DAMN! WE'RE GOING TO CRASH!!

HUF
HUF
HUF

THE GOD WARRIOR'S FIRE.
FIRE.

LET'S HURRY !!

OHMA. YOU'VE BEGUN?

I MUST GO THERE. I'M THE ONE WHO MADE THIS GAMBLE.

A REPETITION OF THE SEVEN DAYS OF FIRE.

ゴオオオ
ゴゴゴゴ
ゴゴゴゴゴ
ゴオオオ

SHOW YOURSELF, KING!!

YOU ARE LATE. SO YOU ARE THE KING?
YES, I AM THE SOVEREIGN OF THE TORUMEKIAN EMPIRE.
STAND BACK, ALL OF YOU. YOU'RE IN THE WAY.

YOUR MAJESTY!! IT'S TOO DANGEROUS!!

THERE'S NO POINT IN COWERING IN A HOLE NOW.
MY, MY. HE CERTAINLY MADE A MESS OF THE PLACE.

I AM THE ARBITRATOR WHO ENDS ALL WAR.
I COME TO THIS LAND AT THE BEHEST OF MY MOTHER. I WILL ALLOW NO MORE FIGHTING.

AND WHO ARE YOU WHO APPEARS TO ME IN A SEA OF FLAMES AND CALLS TO ME!? SPEAK YOUR NAME!!

THIS THING ISN'T A DOROK WEAPON!?

GATHER YOUR TROOPS AND RETURN TO YOUR COUNTRY AT ONCE.

AS LONG AS THE CRYPT REMAINS IN THIS ABOMINABLE LAND, SUMMONING TO ITSELF EVIL MEN, THIS LAND SHALL KNOW NO PEACE.

WE DID NOT COME TO THIS LAND WITHOUT GOOD REASON!!
WE DID NOT WISH FOR WAR.

COME WITH ME.
YOUR MAJESTY! NO!!

THE MONSTER SMIRKS. HEH, HEH. IT'S BEEN A LONG TIME SINCE I'VE ENJOYED A TASTE OF TRUE FEAR.

IF YOU ARE INDEED AN ARBITRATOR, THEN NO ONE WELCOMES YOU MORE THAN I. I WISH TO SPEAK WITH THOSE INSIDE THE CRYPT.
THEY REFUSE TO RESPOND TO MY APPEALS.

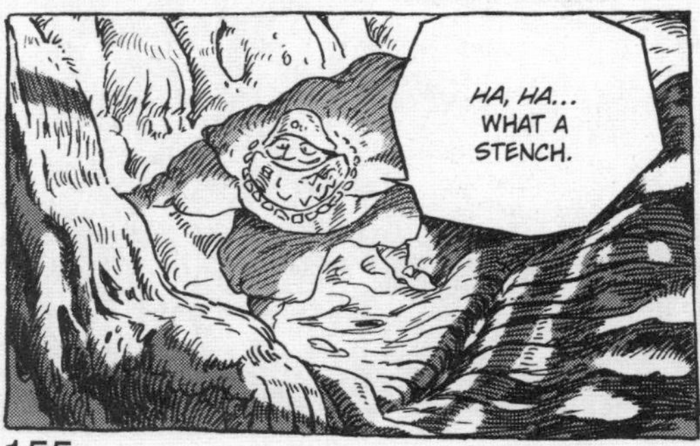
HA, HA... WHAT A STENCH.

SUMMON THEM WITH YOUR POWER.

WHY, THIS THING IS ROTTING.

THAT'S OUR EMPEROR FOR YOU. NOT EVEN A MONSTER CAN SHAKE HIM.
MAJESTY !!

ゴオオオ
ゴオオオオ

THERE IT IS. THAT IS THE STRUCTURE THAT IS THE NEST OF EVIL.
BE CAREFUL. THEY HAVE A TERRIBLE WEAPON.

I HAVE COME TO SEAL THE DOORS OF THE CRYPT FOR ETERNITY. YOU WILL EVACUATE IMMEDIATELY.

HEAR ME, OCCUPANTS OF THE CRYPT! MY LIGHT HAS THE POWER TO BURN AND MELT EVERYTHING IT FALLS ON.

WAIT! WHAT DO YOU MEAN, "SEAL THE DOORS"?! WE WANT TO NEGOTIATE WITH THEM.
ALL PEACE BEGINS WITH NEGOTIA-TION!!

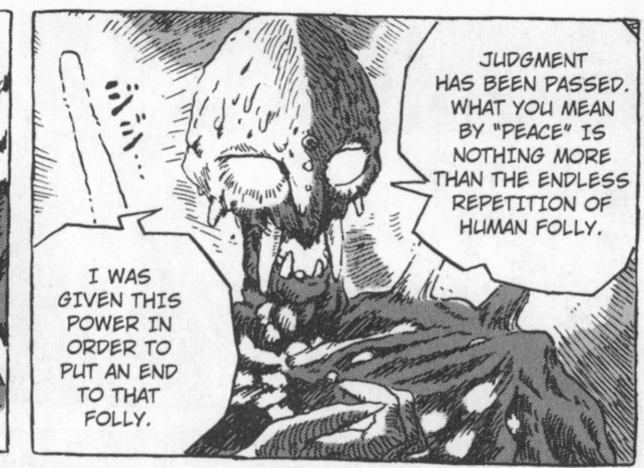
JUDGMENT HAS BEEN PASSED. WHAT YOU MEAN BY "PEACE" IS NOTHING MORE THAN THE ENDLESS REPETITION OF HUMAN FOLLY.
I WAS GIVEN THIS POWER IN ORDER TO PUT AN END TO THAT FOLLY.

I AM BEHOLDEN TO NONE BUT THE SMALL MOTHER WHO GAVE BIRTH TO ME, LED ME, AND GAVE ME MY NAME.

YOUR "SMALL MOTHER"!?

カァ
ANSWER ME, OCCUPANTS OF THE CRYPT!! NO WORDS NOR MATTER CAN ESCAPE MY LIGHT!!

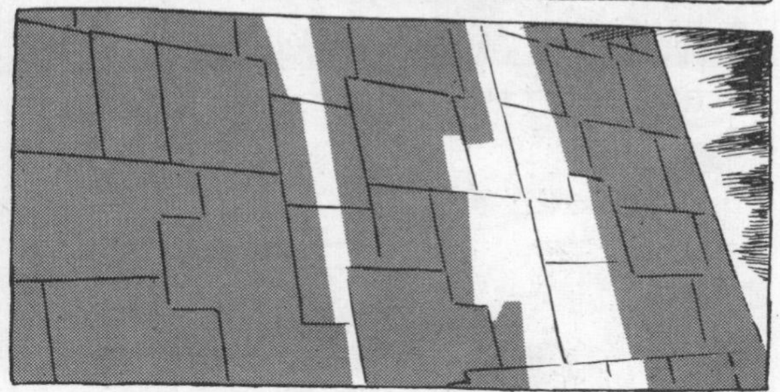

カタ

IT MOVED !?

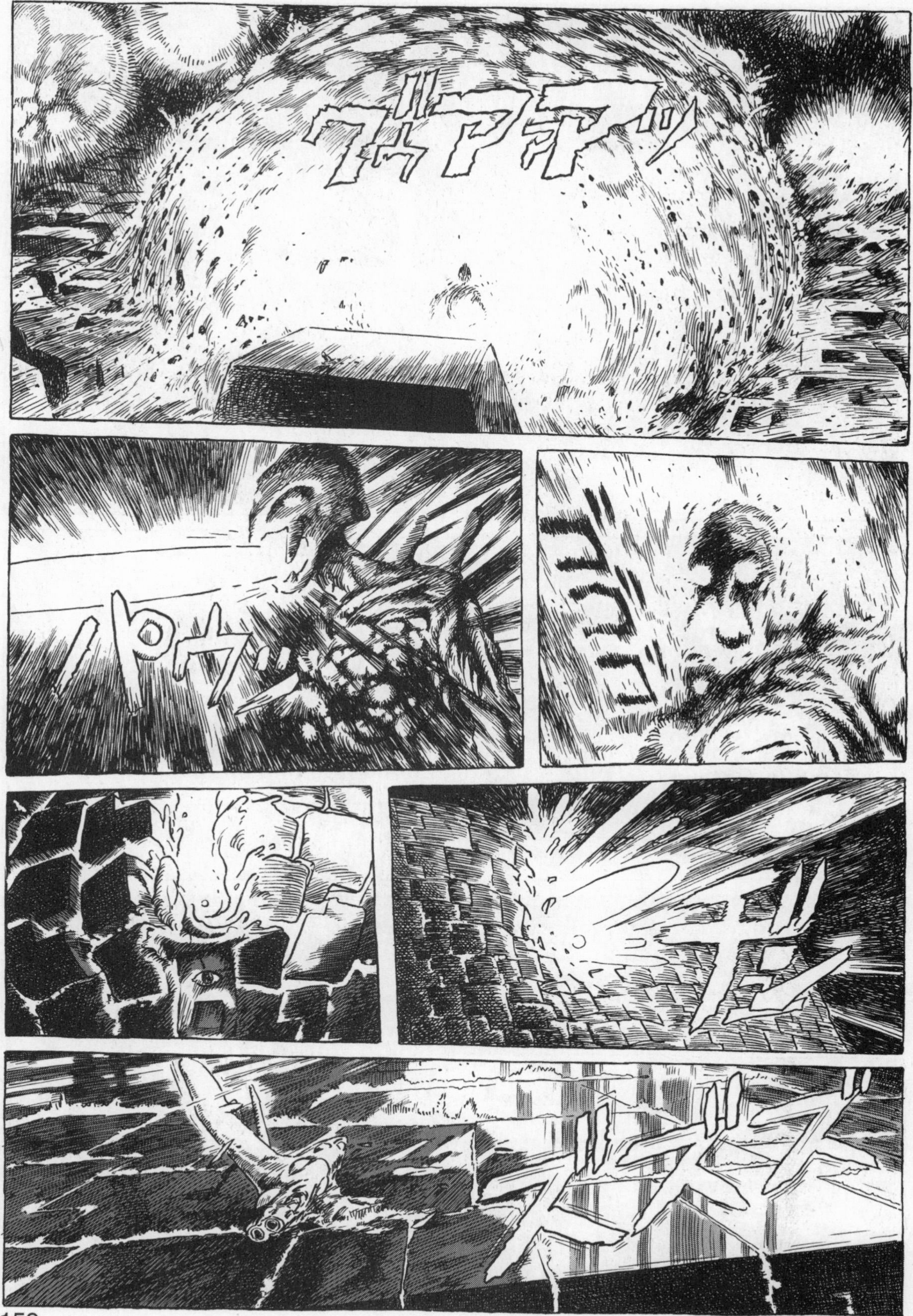
ヷアァアッ
パウッ
ヂン
ズズズ

ギャオオオ

ゴゴゴゴゴ

IT'S THE FIRE OF HEAVEN.
THIS ONE'S EVEN BIGGER THAN THE LAST.
GET DOWN!! A SHOCK WAVE IS COMING!!
ドーン
ゴオオオオオオ

AH ...

THE BLOCK IS GONE SUDDENLY. I CAN HEAR AGAIN.

THE AIR IS FILLED WITH SCREAMS.

...MO...

MO... THER...
OHMA'S VOICE !!

OHMA! IT'S ME!! WHERE ARE YOU!?

WHAT'S HAPPENED, OHMA !?
... MOTHER ...

THERE'S AN ENORMOUS CRACK IN IT. DID YOU DO THAT, OHMA!?
OHMA IS SENDING ME AN IMAGE OF THE CRYPT!!
THE CRYPT... IS STILL... ALIVE...

OHMA !!

ドン
グラ
ハァハァ
……

A SHIP!!
オオオー

ウオオオ

A TORU-MEKIAN SHIP!!
THE OTHER ONE IS CRASHING TOO!!

AH!

ガガーン

YAHOO!!

SPLIT THE BOOTY!!

STOP !!

ボウウウーム
ワー
ワー
WHAT INCREDIBLE LUCK!!
HURRY, BEFORE EVERYTHING BURNS UP !!

FIRST WE'VE GOT TO SEARCH FOR SURVIVORS !!

NAUSICAÄ IS ANGRY. WHY?
I DON'T KNOW. SHE FRIGHTENS ME.

ヂルヂルヂル

ゴー…!
ジュ ジュー

THEY WERE DEAD BEFORE THEY CRASHED.

THEY TRIED TO ESCAPE FROM THE FIRE.

STOP THAT AT ONCE! YOU MUSTN'T STEAL FROM THE DEAD!!
DEAD OR NOT, THEY MUSTN'T BE SHAMED LIKE THIS !!

I HAVE NO RIGHT TO BE ANGRY.
I'M SORRY.

AH ...

THESE ARE ALL FOR YOU, NAUSICAÄ.
P-PLEASE DON'T BE ANGRY.

THIS IS HOW THESE PEOPLE HAVE LIVED FOR HUNDREDS OF YEARS.

YOU CAN HAVE THEM ALL.
TAKE THESE, TOO!

AREN'T THEY PRETTY? IF YOU WEAR THEM ON YOUR CAP, THEY'LL KEEP THE FOREST DEVILS AWAY.

ASHES ...
THIS MUST BE WHAT IT WAS LIKE AFTER THE SEVEN DAYS OF FIRE.

THERE IS SO MUCH WE NEED TO LEARN.

NAUSICAÄ IS ANGRY.
NO, I'M NOT ANGRY ...
BUT NEVER MIND THAT. I THINK WE'D BETTER NOT INHALE TOO MUCH OF THIS ASH.

LET'S TAKE A LITTLE REST. WE'VE ALL RUN A LONG WAY.

MEN ...

LET'S EAT A BIT OF THE FOOD WE PREPARED.

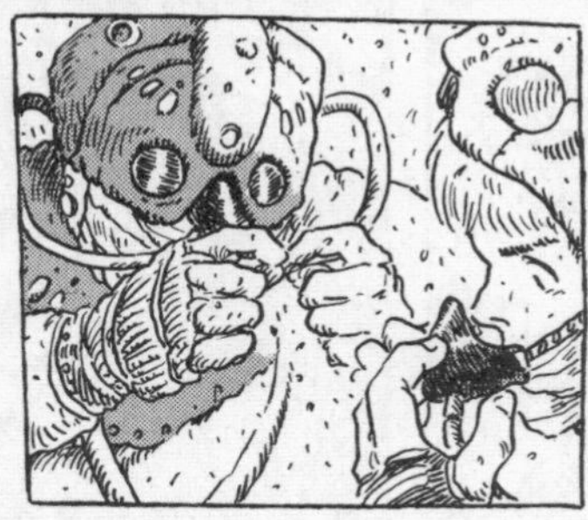

PUT ON YOUR MASKS.
ビリッ!!

I STILL HAVEN'T TOLD YOU ALL WHY WE'RE GOING TO SHUWA, HAVE I?
WHAT I'M GOING TO TELL YOU NOW, I WANT YOU TO TELL TO YOUR OWN CLANS WHEN YOU'VE ALL RETURNED HOME.

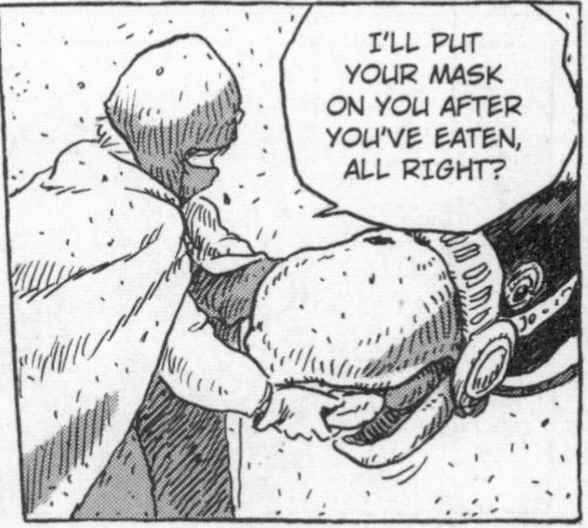
I'LL PUT YOUR MASK ON YOU AFTER YOU'VE EATEN, ALL RIGHT?

DO YOU KNOW WHY THE SEA OF CORRUPTION CAME INTO BEING?
YES, AN ELDER ONCE TOLD ME. GOD PUNISHED HUMANITY FOR POLLUTING THE WORLD.

YES, THAT'S WHAT WE'VE ALWAYS BELIEVED.
BUT THAT'S WRONG. IF ANYTHING, THE REVERSE IS TRUE.

AS THE TREES OF THE FOREST AGE, THEY TURN TO STONE AND EVENTUALLY DISINTEGRATE INTO SAND, WHICH COLLECTS ON THE FOREST FLOOR.
THAT SAND IS THE CRYSTALLIZED AND HARMLESS FORM OF THE VARIOUS POISONS THAT POLLUTE OUR SOIL, AIR AND WATER.
THE FOREST GIVES OFF A BIT OF POISON IN THE FORM OF THE MIASMA, BUT IN FACT IT IS MAKING THIS WORLD CLEAN.

YOU MEAN ...

... THE WORLD WILL SOMEDAY BE CLEAN AGAIN?
WHEN!? WHEN!?

I'M AFRAID I DON'T KNOW WHEN... BUT THAT DAY WILL COME, OF THAT I AM CERTAIN.
EVEN AS I SPEAK, THE SEA OF CORRUPTION IS HARD AT WORK. AS LONG AS WE DO NOT DESTROY OURSELVES, A BRIGHT NEW WORLD WILL ONE DAY WELCOME US WITH OPEN ARMS.

THIS IS WONDERFUL! WHAT A WONDERFUL THING WE'VE HEARD!!
WE MUST TELL OUR PEOPLE.
WE DON'T MIND LIVING WITH THE FOREST IN THE MEANTIME!

IF THAT'S THE CASE, SHOULDN'T WE TRIGGER AS MANY DAIKAISHO* AS WE CAN IN ORDER TO SPREAD THE FOREST MORE QUICKLY !?
NO, WE MUSTN'T DO THAT.

*DAIKAISHO: THE "GREAT TIDAL WAVE," IN WHICH HORDES OF INSECTS FLOOD OUT FROM THE SEA OF CORRUPTION, OVERRUNNING CITIES WHICH ARE THEN ENGULFED BY THE FOREST.

IT WAS JUST A QUESTION!
HAH, HAH. THAT'S BECAUSE YOU'RE AN IDIOT.
ONLY THE PEOPLE OF THE FOREST CAN LIVE ON THEIR OWN.

CAN YOUR PEOPLE SURVIVE IN THE DEPTHS OF THE FOREST WITHOUT TRADE WITH THE TOWNSPEOPLE?
OH, I HADN'T THOUGHT ABOUT THAT.

HUMAN BEINGS TRANS-FORMED THE HUMAN BODY TO SUIT A POLLUTED WORLD.
BUT WHAT GOOD CAN COME OF MAKING THAT KNOWN? AND BESIDES ...

SELM, I'VE TOLD A LIE. AND I'LL GO ON TELLING THIS LIE.

... SOMETHING INSIDE ME CALLS OUT PASSIONATELY TO THE LANDSCAPE I SAW ...
... THE END OF THE SEA OF CORRUP-TION TO WHICH YOU LED ME.

THE WORLD IS BEGINNING TO BE REBORN.
EVEN IF OUR BODIES CANNOT TOLERATE THAT PURITY...

...JUST AS THE BIRDS MIGRATE ACROSS THE LAND, WE SHALL LIVE, AND LIVE AGAIN.
...EVEN IF THE MOMENT WE ARE EXPOSED TO IT, WE SPEW BLOOD FROM OUR LUNGS...

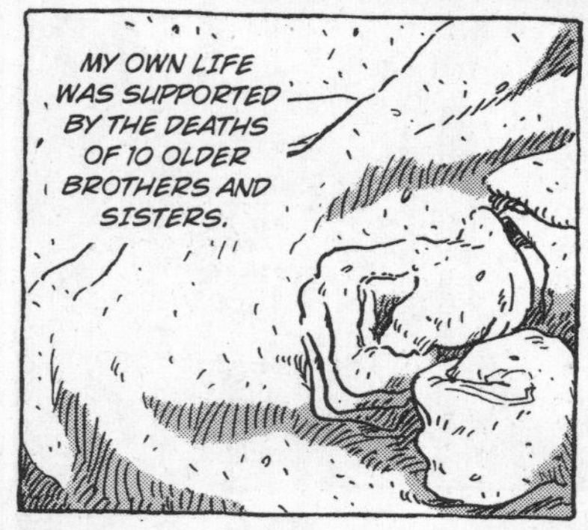

MY OWN LIFE WAS SUPPORTED BY THE DEATHS OF 10 OLDER BROTHERS AND SISTERS.

FOR THE SAKE OF A SINGLE SPROUT, COUNT-LESS FOREST SPORES RAIN DOWN AGAIN AND AGAIN, DYING A USE-LESS DEATH.

SOMETHING INSIDE IS TELLING ME PASSIONATELY THAT THAT ISN'T TRUE.
I DON'T THINK SO.

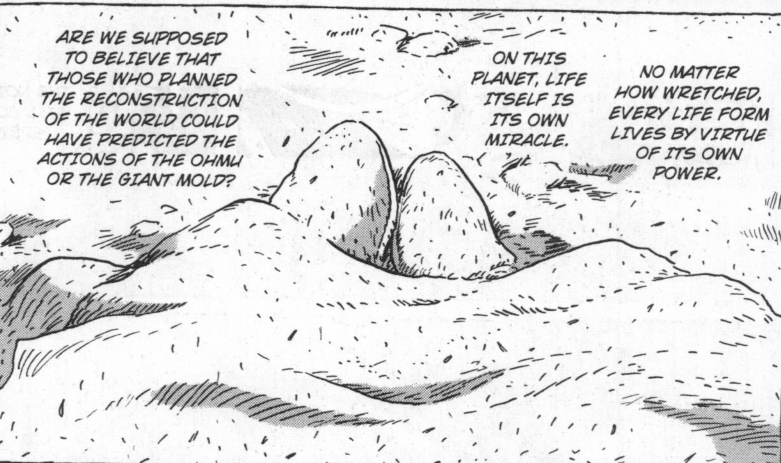

ARE WE SUPPOSED TO BELIEVE THAT THOSE WHO PLANNED THE RECONSTRUCTION OF THE WORLD COULD HAVE PREDICTED THE ACTIONS OF THE OHMU OR THE GIANT MOLD?
ON THIS PLANET, LIFE ITSELF IS ITS OWN MIRACLE.
NO MATTER HOW WRETCHED, EVERY LIFE FORM LIVES BY VIRTUE OF ITS OWN POWER.

I SUPPOSE THOSE MEN LEFT THAT BLACK THING TO BE THE KERNEL OF THE RECON-STRUCTION...

I HAVE MADE A LONG JOURNEY TO DISCOVER THE SECRET OF THE WORLD.
I'M ALL RIGHT.

NAUSICAÄ ...?
...AND IT NEVER OCCURRED TO THEM THAT THAT ITSELF WAS THE ULTIMATE DEMON-STRATION OF CONTEMPT FOR LIFE.

I'VE RUSHED TOWARD MY GOAL, LEAVING MANY DEAD BEHIND ME.

THOSE WHO PROTECTED ME, THOSE WHO LED ME, DEAR FRIENDS-- AND ENEMIES AS WELL... LEFT THEM WITHOUT SO MUCH AS A BURIAL.
SO PLEASE... LET US NEVER FORGET THE DEAD.

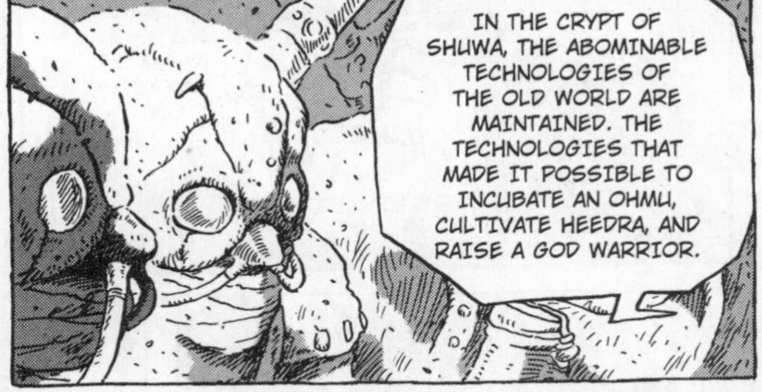
IN THE CRYPT OF SHUWA, THE ABOMINABLE TECHNOLOGIES OF THE OLD WORLD ARE MAINTAINED. THE TECHNOLOGIES THAT MADE IT POSSIBLE TO INCUBATE AN OHMU, CULTIVATE HEEDRA, AND RAISE A GOD WARRIOR.

AND SO ...

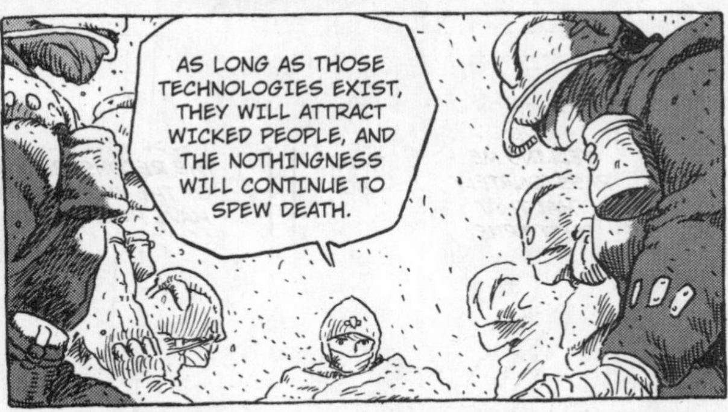
AS LONG AS THOSE TECHNOLOGIES EXIST, THEY WILL ATTRACT WICKED PEOPLE, AND THE NOTHINGNESS WILL CONTINUE TO SPEW DEATH.

...I SENT MY OWN CHILD.
THE FIRE OF HEAVEN WE SAW EARLIER WAS HIS.

I HAVE AGAIN UNLEASHED THE FIRE THAT ONCE DESTROYED THE WORLD.

OHMA WAS A KIND AND GENTLE CHILD. HE PROBABLY PERISHED IN THAT FIRE.

PLEASE, WHEN YOU HAVE RETURNED SAFELY HOME, TELL ALL THE PEOPLE OF THE WORLD WHAT I HAVE TOLD YOU AND WHAT YOU WILL WITNESS IN SHUWA.

LET'S GO, NAUSICAÄ.
YES.

WE WILL TAKE OHMA'S PLACE AS YOUR CHILDREN!
DON'T CRY, NAUSICAÄ! WE'LL TELL EVERYONE!
WE WON'T TAKE FROM THE DEAD ANYMORE! WE'LL TELL EVERYONE!

SELM ...
I WILL BE WITH YOU WHEREVER YOU GO.

PHEW. IT'S HOT AND IT STINKS.
モゾモゾ

WELL. EVERYTHING'S BEEN SWEPT AWAY NICELY, HASN'T IT?

UMPH.

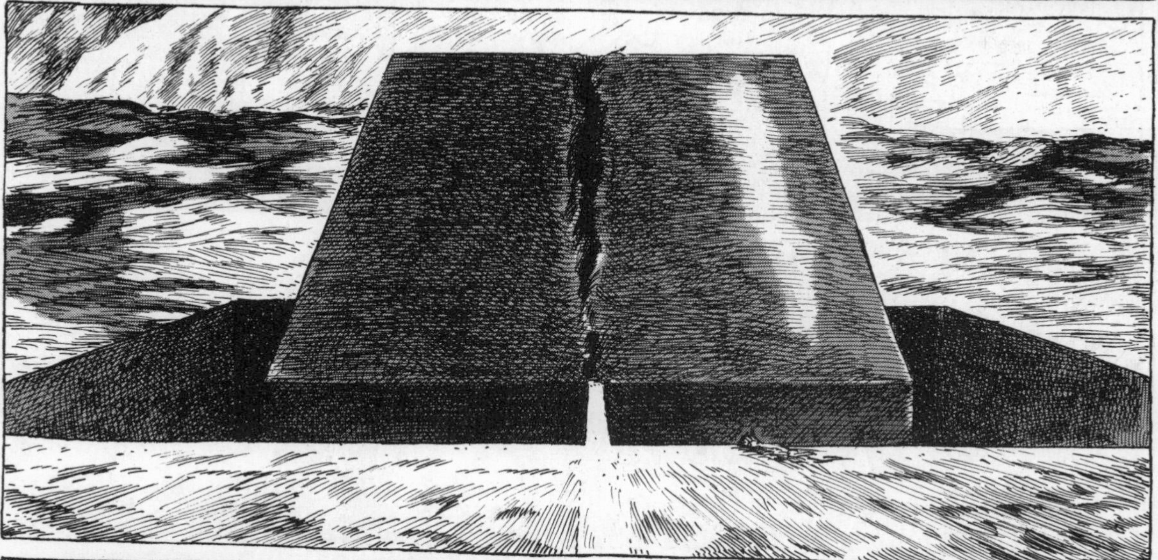

......
.....

IN EFFECT, WHOEVER'S IN THE CRYPT HAS CLEANED HOUSE, RETURNING EVERYTHING TO ITS ORIGINAL STATE.

.....
.....
WHAT IS THAT SOUND?

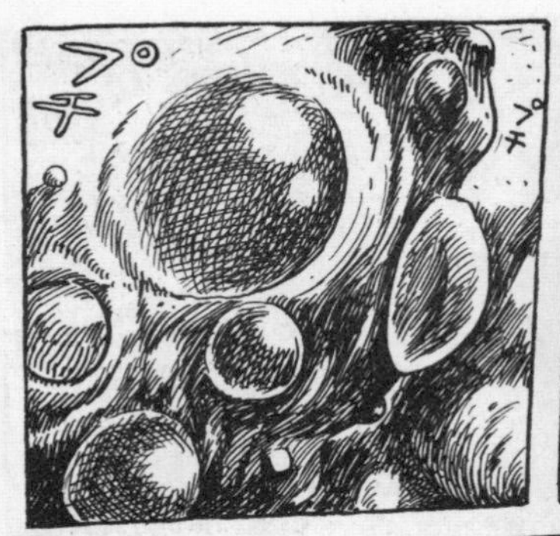
プチ
プチ

IS THIS A TRICK OF THE LIGHT? IT SEEMS AS IF THE EDGES OF THE GASH ARE MOVING.

MASTER !!
チリーン
チリリーン

STILL ALIVE, ARE YOU, FOOL? JUDGING FROM THE FACT THAT YOU'RE WANDERING AROUND ALONE, I TAKE IT OUR TROOPS HAVE BEEN OBLITERATED?
A BRILLIANT DEDUCTION.

THE TORUMEKIAN ARMY ISN'T WHAT IT USED TO BE. THEY PANICKED AT THE FIRST EXPLOSION.

I ASSUME THE SHIPS THAT WERE ABLE TO TAKE OFF WERE DESTROYED BY THE SECOND FLASH.

WHEN I PEEKED OUT FROM THE CRATE IN WHICH I'D BEEN HIDING, ALL I COULD HEAR WAS THE MOANS OF THE DYING.

I MUST SAY, I'M RELIEVED TO FIND YOU.
I HATE THE IDEA OF DYING ALONE.

HAH! WHAT YOU REALLY MEAN IS THAT YOU WANT TO BE THERE WHEN I DIE.
ANOTHER BRILLIANT DEDU--!?
!?

HEE, HEE. HERE THEY COME, HERE THEY COME.

......

HUMAN BEINGS ARE CRAWLING OUT.

OUR BLOOD IS UNFATHOMABLY ANCIENT, YET FOREVER NEW.
WE ARE THE ONE TRUE AND UNQUESTIONED SUCCESSOR TO THE THRONE.

MIND YOUR MANNERS, CHURL.

YOU ARE THE NEW KING?

WE HAVE COME TO LEAD YOU TO THE MASTER OF THE CRYPT. WE SHALL SEE IF YOU ARE INDEED FIT TO BE KING.
HMPH. ARROGANT WORDS FOR ONE WHO HAS COME CRAWLING OUT OF A TORN HOLE. WHY DIDN'T YOU OPEN THE DOOR EARLIER?

HEE, HEE, HEE. THE VIPER OF VIPERS, THE TRULY COLD-BLOODED KING OF KINGS.

SO YOU LIKE TO HAVE THINGS YOUR OWN WAY, EH? YOU'RE THE SCHOLARS WHO SERVED THE DOROK COUNCIL OF PRIESTS, ARE YOU NOT? WHY DO YOU NOW OPEN YOUR DOOR TO A TORUMEKIAN EMPEROR?

WE ARE SUBJECT TO NO OUTSIDE AUTHORITY. WE GUIDE YOU NOW ONLY BECAUSE YOU HAVE LOST ALL YOUR MILITARY POWER.

OH-H, SO YOU'RE PARASITES!!
THE BUGS CLING TO THE CRYPT, THE FOOL CLINGS TO THE KING!!

OUR RELIGIOUS ORDER IS COMPRISED OF THOSE FEW WHO HAVE BEEN SELECTED TO LIVE INSIDE THE CRYPT AS SERVANTS TO THE MASTER OF THE CRYPT.
THE "SCHOLARS" YOU REFER TO ARE NOTHING MORE THAN THE UNDERLINGS OUR ORDER TRAINED AND PROVIDED TO THE COUNCIL OF PRIESTS IN ACCORDANCE WITH THE AGREEMENT BETWEEN THE MASTER AND THE EMPEROR.
NOW THAT THE DOROK EMPIRE HAS CEASED TO BE, THE ORDER REQUIRES THE COOPERATION OF ANOTHER OUTSIDE FORCE.

WE'RE BOTH PARASITES--LET'S BE PALS!

SINCE LONG BEFORE THE HOLY EMPEROR AND BEFORE THE DOROK KING WHO PRECEDED HIM.
YET IN COMPARISON TO THE WISDOM OF THE MASTER, I AM BUT A CHILD.

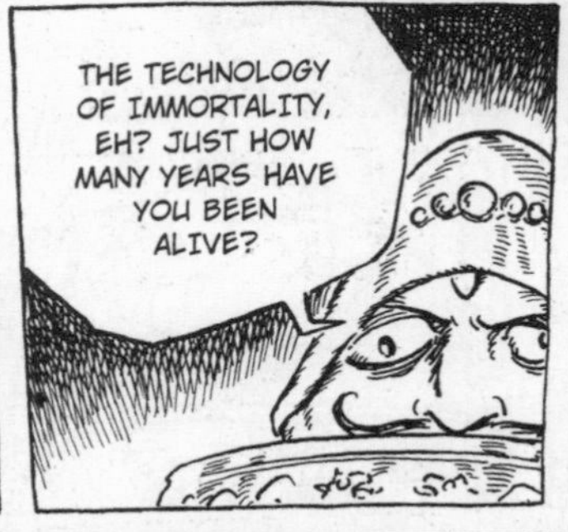
THE TECHNOLOGY OF IMMORTALITY, EH? JUST HOW MANY YEARS HAVE YOU BEEN ALIVE?

WAWAWAH! OH, JOY! I'VE FINALLY MET SOMEONE UGLIER THAN MYSELF!!

THE INSIDE OF THE CRYPT WAS SLIGHTLY INJURED BY THE BATTLE, BUT IT SHALL BE RESTORED SHORTLY. COME WITH ME.

I'LL MEET THIS "MASTER OF THE CRYPT," OR WHATEVER YOU CALL HIM. LEAD THE WAY, MONSTER.

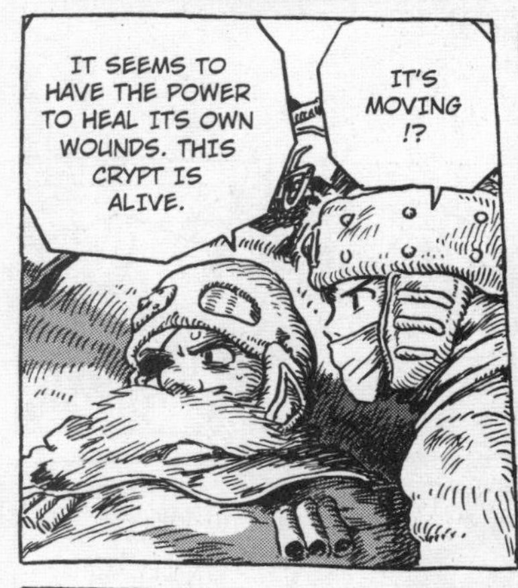
IT'S MOVING !?
IT SEEMS TO HAVE THE POWER TO HEAL ITS OWN WOUNDS. THIS CRYPT IS ALIVE.

ASBEL, LOOK YONDER.
THE VAI EMPEROR JUST WENT IN.
THERE ARE PEOPLE INSIDE.

IT'S A GOOD THING OUR PRINCESS WASN'T HERE. ASBEL, GO INSIDE AND SEE WHAT YOU CAN SEE. YOU SHOULD BE ABLE TO GET IN NOW.

ALL RIGHT, ALL RIGHT, BUT...
GIVE THE PRINCESS A MESSAGE FOR ME... NO MATTER WHAT HAPPENS, *JUST STAY ALIVE.*

SINCE THIS JOURNEY BEGAN, THIS HAND'S GOTTEN STIFFER AND STIFFER.

DON'T WORRY ABOUT ME. THE HARDENING DISEASE WAS BEGINNING TO GET ME ANYWAY.

IT'S WARM, LIKE FLESH.

HA, HA. DON'T LET THE BLOOD OF PEJITEI DIE OUT, ASBEL.

...LET'S JUST SAY WHICHEVER OF US SURVIVES WILL GIVE HER THAT MESSAGE.

NOW THEN... MAY AS WELL TRY TO MAKE MYSELF USEFUL.

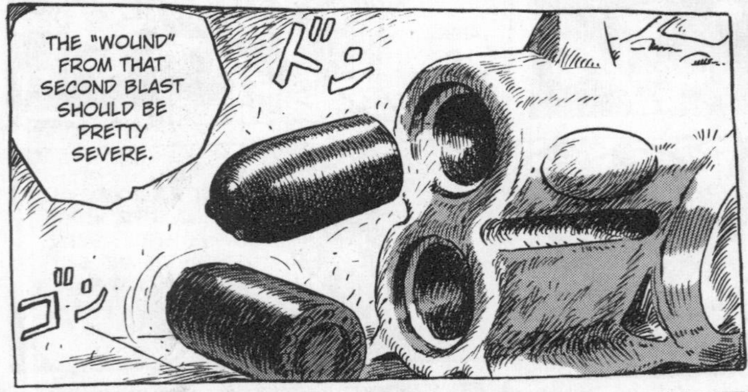
THE "WOUND" FROM THAT SECOND BLAST SHOULD BE PRETTY SEVERE.
ドン
ゴン

IF IT'S TRUE THAT THIS STRUCTURE IS ALIVE, THEN THAT GIVES US SOMETHING TO WORK WITH.
OUCH.

HERE WE GO. *UMPH!*

LET'S STICK THIS THING IN THE WOUND.

UNH.

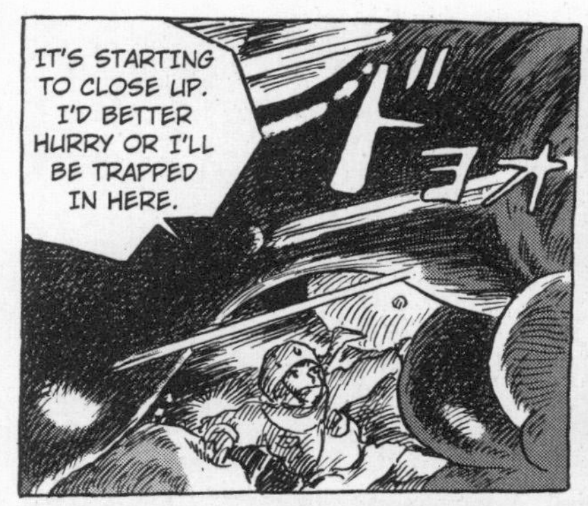
IT'S STARTING TO CLOSE UP. I'D BETTER HURRY OR I'LL BE TRAPPED IN HERE.
ドョオ

ヌウウウ
ウオオオオオ

IT'S LIKE A PARASITE'S NEST.

THIS MUST BE A TOWN BUILT BY THE PEOPLE WHO LIVE IN THE CRYPT! IT'S BUILT OF COMPLETELY DIFFERENT MATERIALS THAN THE CRYPT ITSELF.

THIS LOOKS LIKE A PRIEST'S LIVING QUARTERS IN A MONASTERY.

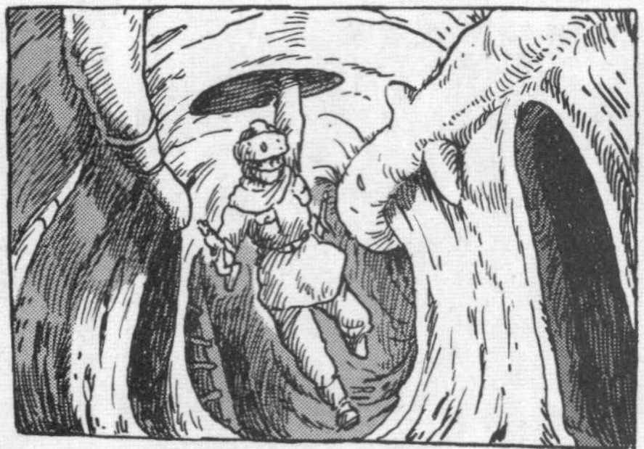

WHAT IS THIS? I'VE NEVER SEEN SUCH AN ALPHABET.

THEY'RE MOVING!? ARE THESE THINGS HEEDRA!?

A THIEF, EH? COME TO STEAL OUR RESEARCH SECRETS, HAVE YOU!?
H-HAS ANYONE SEEN MY BODY!?

MY BODY'S GONE!?
<WHO ARE YOU!?>

THIS IS LIKE THE INSIDE OF A STOMACH!!
CORPSES !?
WAH !!

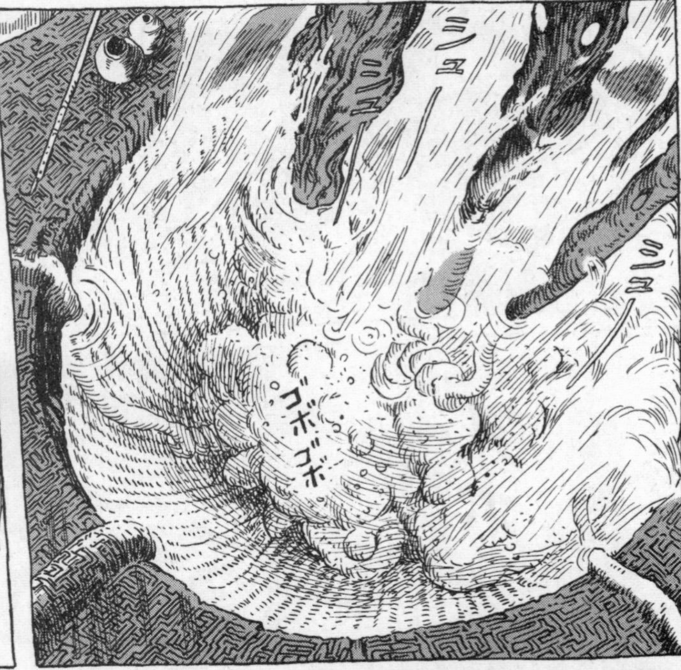
シュー
シュー
ゴボゴボ

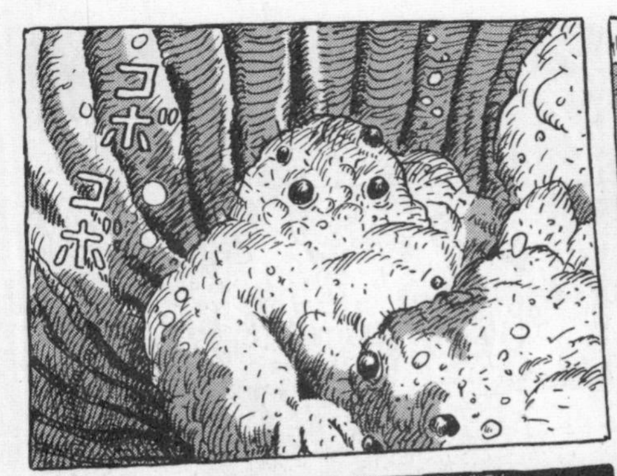
コポコポ

A HEEDRA INCUBATOR !?

THEY FEED THEM WITH DEAD BODIES !?
グシュ

ガ!

ギャャアア

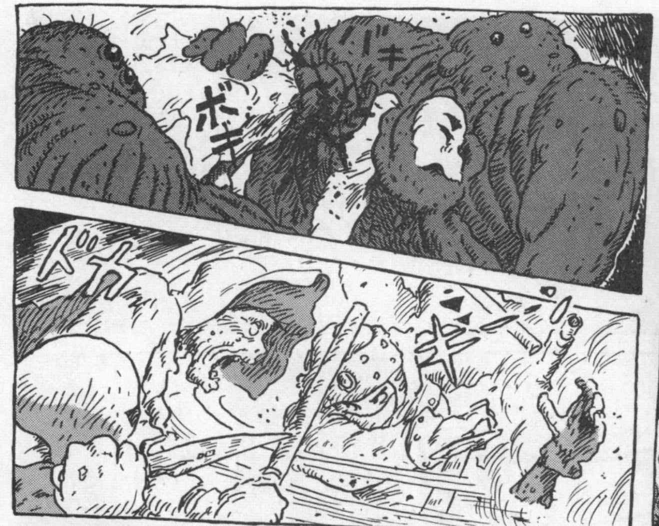
バキ
ボキ
ドカ
ギー

卵を見!!

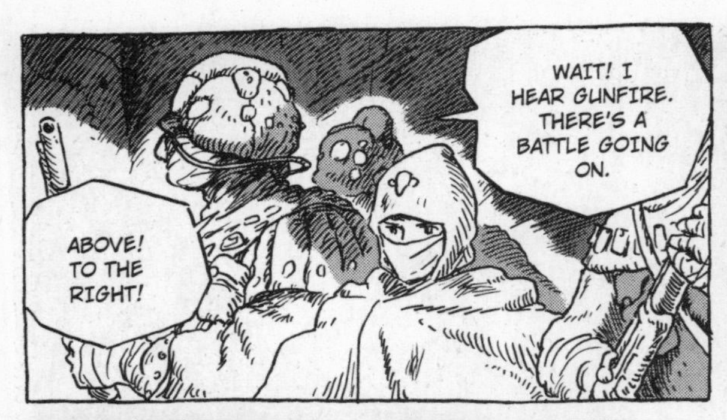
WAIT! I HEAR GUNFIRE. THERE'S A BATTLE GOING ON.
ABOVE! TO THE RIGHT!

THERE'S A SHAFT AHEAD.
NOT HERE. FARTHER DOWN.

PAY NO ATTENTION. LET'S MOVE ON.

<NONE BUT A KING MAY PROCEED BEYOND THIS POINT.>

.....

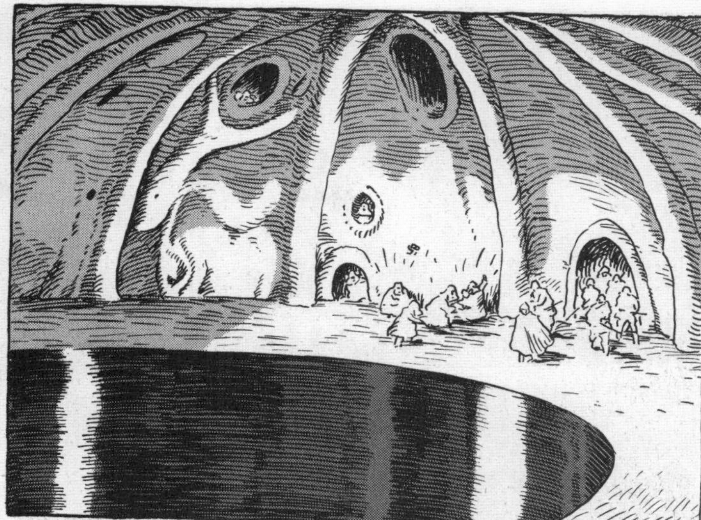

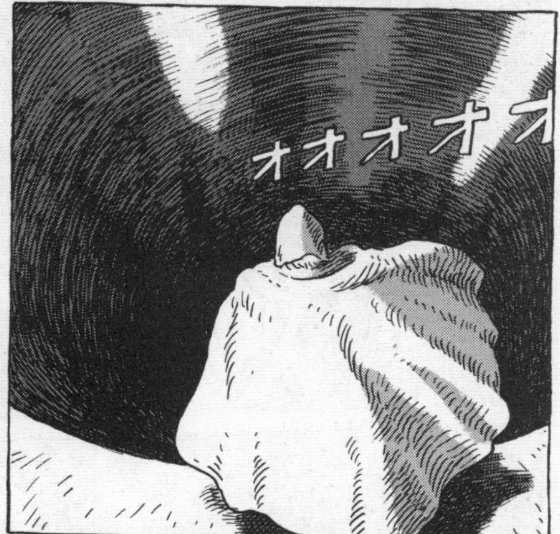
オオオオオ

IT'S DOWN HERE.

YOU ARE THE LEADER HERE, AREN'T YOU?
<H-- HOW DID YOU KNOW ...?>

TAKE ME DOWN.

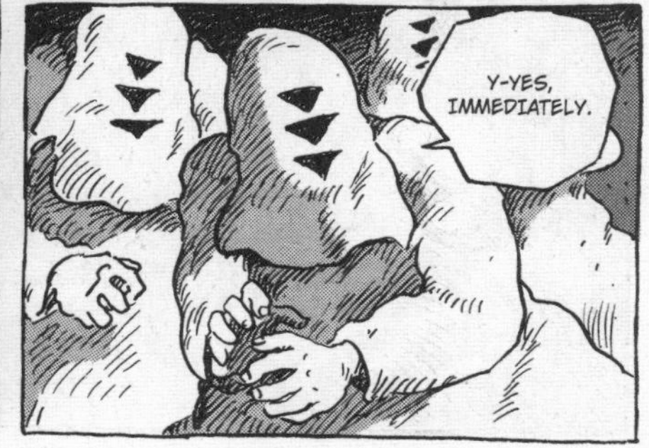
Y-YES, IMMEDIATELY.

MOTHER ...

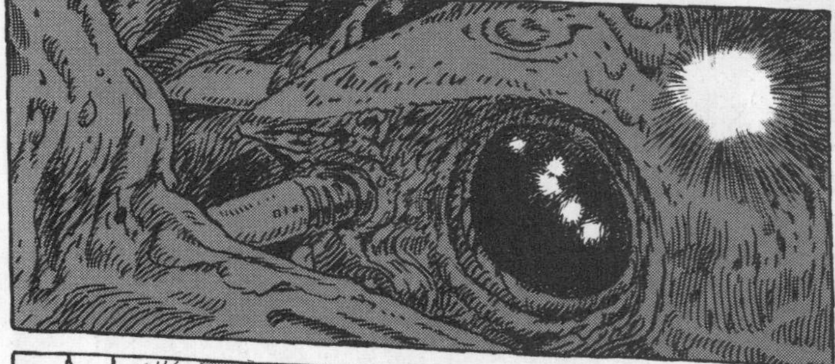

MOTHER
...

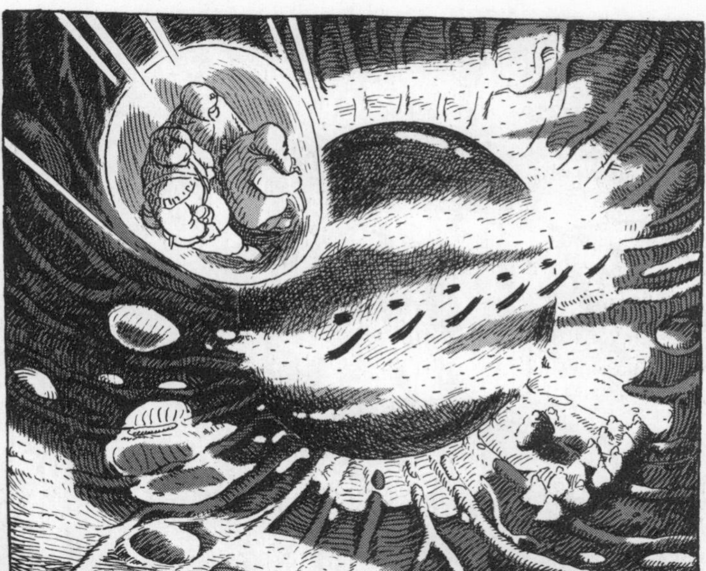
ンンンンンンン

シンン
オンンンン

オンンンンンン
ンンンンンン

DO YOU TAKE ME FOR A FOOL!? YOU MEAN TO SAY THIS WILL CHOOSE A HUMAN KING !?
YOU'RE TELLING ME THIS LUMP OF FLESH COVERED WITH SCRIBBLING IS THE MASTER OF THE CRYPT?
ドンドン

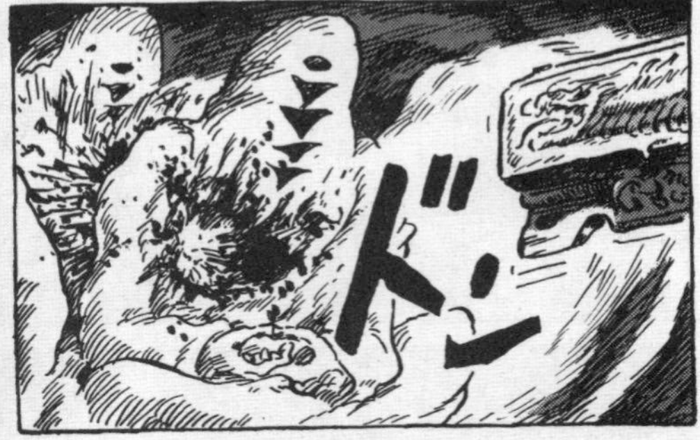
ドン

ドンドン
TELL THE TRUTH! YOU'RE JUST TRYING TO KEEP THE TECHNOLOGIES OF THE ANCIENT WORLD FOR YOURSELVES!!

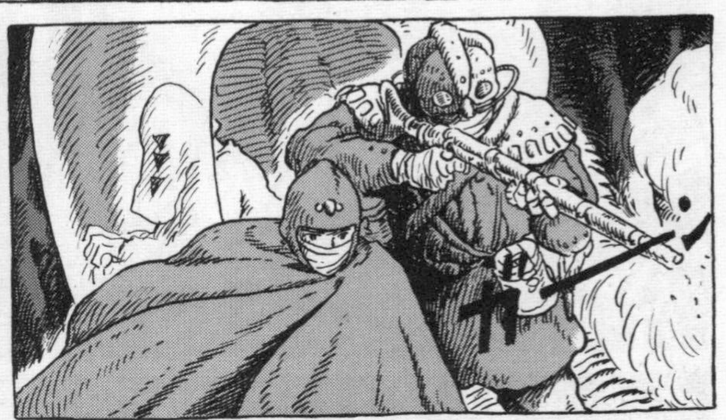

YOU'RE NOT DOROK. WHO ARE YOU?

UH-OH! IT'S ANOTHER NEW KING. AND A WOMAN, TO BOOT!!

AN ANCIENT WRITING SYSTEM FROM THE OLD WORLD. THE DOROK EMPEROR'S UNUSUALLY LONG LIFESPAN AND THE COUNCIL OF PRIESTS' EVIL TECHNOLOGIES... THEY RESULTED FROM THE DECIPHERING OF THIS TEXT!

THEY'RE PULSING. THESE CHARACTERS ARE ALIVE.

NO, WE ARE A RELIGIOUS ORDER THAT DEDICATE OUR BEINGS TO THE DECIPHERING AND VERIFICATION OF THE HOLY TEXT.
EACH WINTER AND SUMMER SOLSTICE, A SINGLE NEW LINE OF THE HOLY TEXT COMES INTO BEING.

LOOK! MONSTERS WHO DON'T EVEN KNOW HOW TO DIE.
THE CRYPT'S PET HEEDRA.

HMPH.
THE TEXT IS NOT FINISHED. WE HAVE AS MUCH WORK AHEAD OF US AS WE DO BEHIND US. WE REQUIRE THE COOPERATION OF AN OUTSIDE FORCE.

YET EVEN THAT SINGLE LINE IS SO CHALLENGING THAT THE COMBINED EFFORTS OF OUR ENTIRE ORDER ARE INSUFFICIENT TO KEEP PACE.
THE TEXT ELUCIDATES THE ORGANIZATION OF THE WORLD AND THE SECRETS OF LIFE!

DO PRIESTS SPEAK THE SAME RUBBISH EVERYWHERE?
PITEOUS DWARF, THE MASTER OF THE CRYPT IS THE SOLE RAY OF LIGHT IN THIS WORLD OF DARKNESS. HE IS THE CRYSTALLIZATION OF ALL THE WISDOM OF THE AGES.

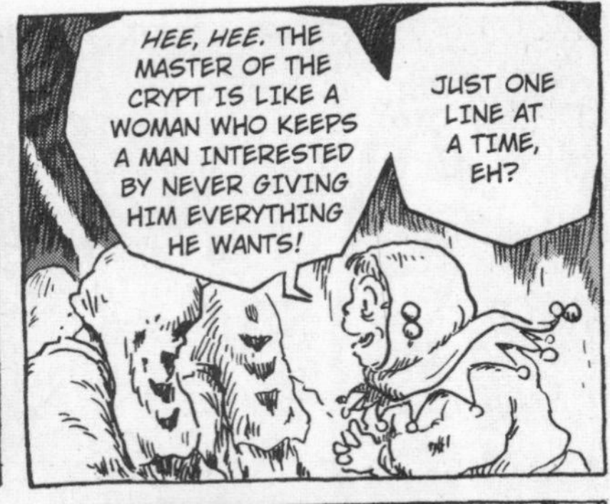
HEE, HEE. THE MASTER OF THE CRYPT IS LIKE A WOMAN WHO KEEPS A MAN INTERESTED BY NEVER GIVING HIM EVERYTHING HE WANTS!
JUST ONE LINE AT A TIME, EH?

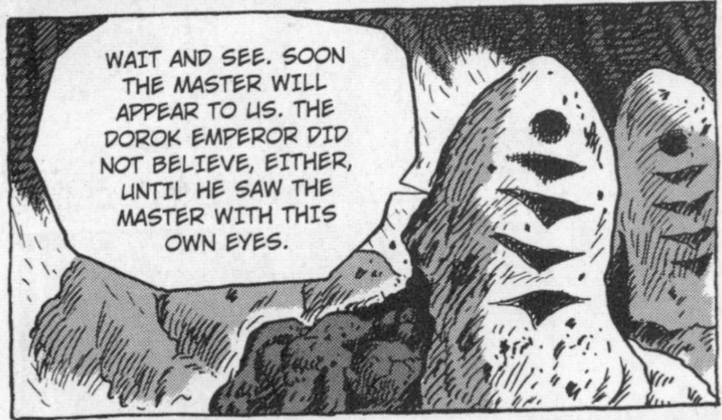
WAIT AND SEE. SOON THE MASTER WILL APPEAR TO US. THE DOROK EMPEROR DID NOT BELIEVE, EITHER, UNTIL HE SAW THE MASTER WITH THIS OWN EYES.

"WE'LL GIVE YOU IMMORTALITY AND HEEDRA, SO TAKE CARE OF US." THAT'S YOUR BOTTOM LINE, ISN'T IT!?
THERE IS NOTHING FOR US TO LEARN FROM YOU.

AS LONG AS THE NEW KING PROVIDES OUR ORDER WITH PROTECTION, WE PROVIDE HIM WITH WHATEVER AID WE CAN.

AND THAT'S HOW YOU BRING IN A NEW KING ONCE THE OLD ONE'S LOST HIS USEFULNESS, IS IT!?

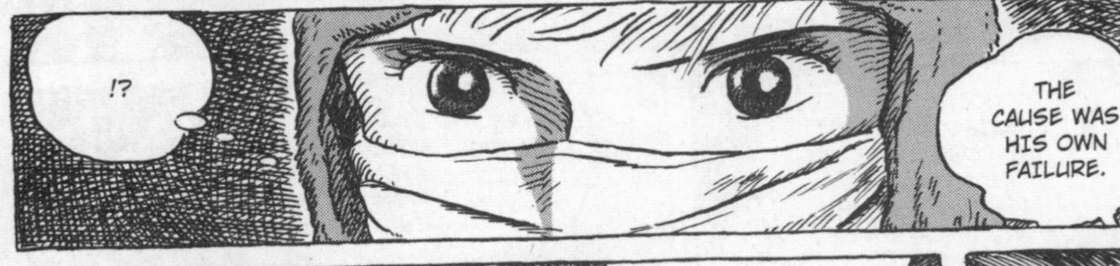
!?
THEN ANSWER ME THIS-- WHY DID YOUR FORMER PROTECTOR, THE DOROK EMPEROR, FALL FROM POWER!?
THE CAUSE WAS HIS OWN FAILURE.

ARE YOU LISTENING, MASTER OF THE CRYPT!? IF YOU WANT A KING, MAKE A MORE APPEALING OFFER!!

FAILURE IS THE ESSENCE OF POLITICS!!
ENOUGH OF YOUR BABBLE!! BRING OUT THIS MASTER OF YOURS!!
ドガッ

AH!! THE MASTER HAS REGAINED HIS LIGHT! THE WOUND HAS BEEN CLOSED!
THE NEW KING SHALL BE CHOSEN!!

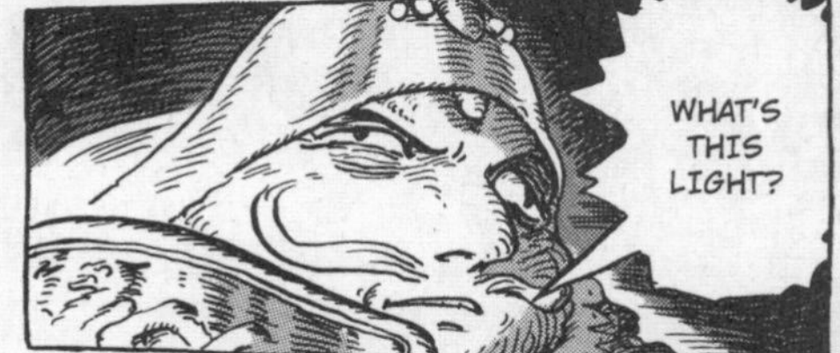
WHAT'S THIS LIGHT?

オオオオオオオ

キィン

IF IT MEANS TO SQUEEZE THEM OUT, I'LL JUST HAVE TO DETONATE THEM WITH A FUSE.

クオオオオオ
DAMN! IT SAW THROUGH MY SCHEME.

ギシ ギシ

IT'S CLOSING !!

<BEGONE SINNER!! YOU POLLUTE OUR SANCTUARY!!>
OUT OF THE WAY!!

<THE MASTER HAS REJUVE-NATED HIMSELF.>
<AH!! THE WOUND IS CLOSING!!>

オオオ
WE'RE GOING TO BE LOCKED IN!!
I'LL TELL NAUSICAÄ!

イイイイイイ

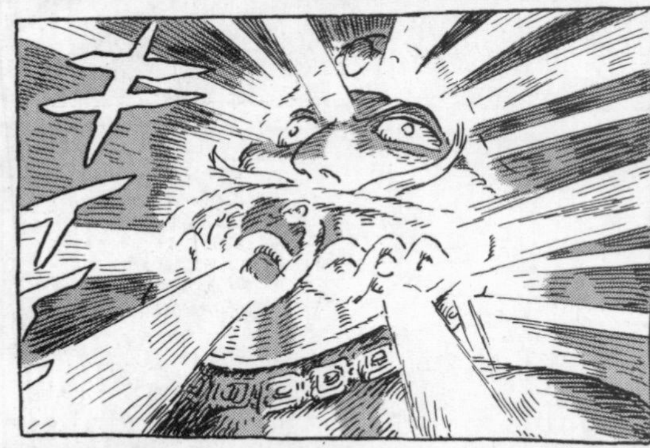

イイイイイイー
IT'S SEARCHING MY MIND.

ギイイイイイイ

M-MY HEAD'S GOING TO BURST!!

IT IS IMPORTANT THAT WE SPEAK TO YOU IN PEACE, AND TO THAT END WE HAVE DISARMED YOU.

FORGIVE OUR ROUGH WELCOME.
CHILDREN.

WE SPEAK TO YOU AS REPRESENTATIVES OF THE GREAT MANY WHO DIED MEANINGLESS DEATHS BECAUSE OF THEIR OWN FOLLY. YOU ARE LIVING IN THE LONG PERIOD OF PURIFICATION.
BUT THE DAY SHALL COME WHEN THE SEA OF CORRUPTION CEASES TO BE, AND A GREEN, PURE LAND IS REBORN.

...THAT WE MIGHT LEND A HAND IN THE REBUILDING OF THE WORLD WHEN THAT MORNING COMES.
CHILDREN, WE GATHERED ALL HUMAN WISDOM AND BUILT THIS CRYPT IN AN AGE OF DESPAIR AND BEWILDERMENT...

THE GREAT SUFFERING OF THE PURIFICATION IS OUR ATONEMENT. THAT GLORIOUS MORNING OF THE DAY OF RECONSTRUCTION SHALL SURELY COME.

READ THE WORDS THAT APPEAR ON OUR BODY, AND PASS ON THE TECHNOLOGY YOU FIND THERE. WHEN THE TEXT AT LONG LAST APPEARS IN ITS ENTIRETY, THEN THAT DAY SHALL COME...

...THE DAY THE SUFFERING ENDS.

CHILDREN, GIVE US YOUR HELP, THAT THIS LIGHT SHOULD NOT GO OUT.

NAY !!

YOU ARE NOTHING BUT SHADOWS !!

ダーン

フワッ

WHY DO YOU NOT SPEAK THE TRUTH!? THE TRUTH ABOUT YOUR PLAN TO COMPLETELY REPLACE THE POLLUTED LAND AND ALL LIVING THINGS!!

SH-SHE HAS SULLIED THE LIGHT!!

ARE THOSE SHADOWS WE SAW THE MEN AND WOMEN WHO CREATED THE SEA OF CORRUPTION IN ORDER TO SLOWLY DESTROY THE OLD WORLD!?

ジジジジ
ジジジジ
ジジジジ

TH-THE MASTER IS ANGRY!
WAIT! DON'T LEAVE ME BEHIND!

バチ
DO YOU INTEND TO GO ON DECEIVING US UNTIL THE VERY DAY YOU PLAN TO DESTROY US!?
WHY!? BECAUSE NO MATTER HOW MUCH KNOWLEDGE AND TECHNOLOGY YOU HAVE, YOU WILL STILL NEED SLAVES TO DO THE WORK FOR YOU ON THE MORNING YOU REPLACE THE WORLD!?
ジジジ…

ギ
OUR BODIES MAY HAVE BEEN ARTIFICIALLY TRANSFORMED, BUT OUR LIVES WILL ALWAYS BE OUR OWN! LIFE SURVIVES BY THE POWER OF LIFE.

IF SUCH A MORNING IS TO COME, THEN WE SHALL LIVE TO FACE THAT MORNING!

オオオ…オオ
WE ARE BIRDS WHO, THOUGH WE MAY SPIT UP BLOOD, WILL GO ON FLYING BEYOND THAT MORNING, ON AND ON!!
ジジジジジ

TO LIVE IS TO CHANGE. THE OHMU, THE MOLD, THE GRASSES AND TREES, WE HUMAN BEINGS... WE WILL ALL GO ON CHANGING. AND THE SEA OF CORRUPTION WILL LIVE ON WITH US.

SPEAK THE TRUTH! WE HAVE NO NEED FOR YOU.

BUT ***YOU*** CANNOT CHANGE. YOU HAVE ONLY THE PLAN THAT WAS BUILT INTO YOU. BECAUSE YOU DENY DEATH.

YOU THERE!! STOP!!

WHICH TRUTH?

FOOL !?
M-MY MOUTH IS MOVING BY ITSELF...

Y-YOU WANT ME TO SPEAK THE TRUTH?

POISONED AIR. PUNISHING SUNLIGHT. PARCHED EARTH. NEW ILLNESSES COMING INTO BEING EVERY DAY. DEATH WAS EVERYWHERE.

HAVE YOU EVER TRIED TO IMAGINE THE DEGREE OF HATE AND DESPAIR THAT FILLED THE WORLD IN THOSE DAYS?
IT WAS A WORLD IN WHICH TENS OF BILLIONS OF HUMAN BEINGS WOULD DO ANYTHING TO SURVIVE.

OUR CHOICES WERE LIMITED.
ALL KINDS OF RELIGIONS, ALL VERSION OF JUSTICE, EVERY PARTY WITH A DIFFERENT INTEREST... WE CREATED A GOD TO ARBITRATE.

WE EVEN HAVE THE TECHNOLOGY TO RESTORE THE BODIES OF YOU WHO HAVE BEEN ADAPTED TO A POLLUTED WORLD, SO THAT ALL MAY LIVE IN THE NEWLY PURIFIED WORLD.
THIS IS THE GRAVE MARKER OF THE OLD WORLD, BUT IT IS ALSO THE HOPE FOR A NEW WORLD.

WE HAD NO TIME. WE DECIDED TO ENTRUST EVERYTHING TO THE FUTURE.

THE TRANSITION SHOULD BE A SMOOTH ONE. WHEN THE LONG PERIOD OF PURIFICATION IS OVER, THE HUMAN RACE SHALL BECOME A PEACEFUL PART OF THE NEW WORLD.

WHEN OUR KNOWLEDGE AND TECHNOLOGY HAVE SERVED THEIR PURPOSE, IT SHALL SURELY BE MUSIC AND POETRY THAT HUMANITY TREASURES ABOVE ALL ELSE.

IN SHORT, YOU ARE A GOD. ONE OF THE MANY GODS CREATED A MILLENNIUM AGO.
AND OVER THAT MILLENNIUM YOU HAVE BECOME COVERED WITH SARCOMATA AND FILTH.

I DO NOT DOUBT THAT YOU WERE CREATED OUT OF IDEALISM AND A SENSE OF PURPOSE IN AN AGE OF DESPAIR.

WHY DIDN'T THOSE MEN AND WOMEN REALIZE THAT BOTH PURITY AND CORRUPTION ARE THE VERY STUFF OF LIFE?

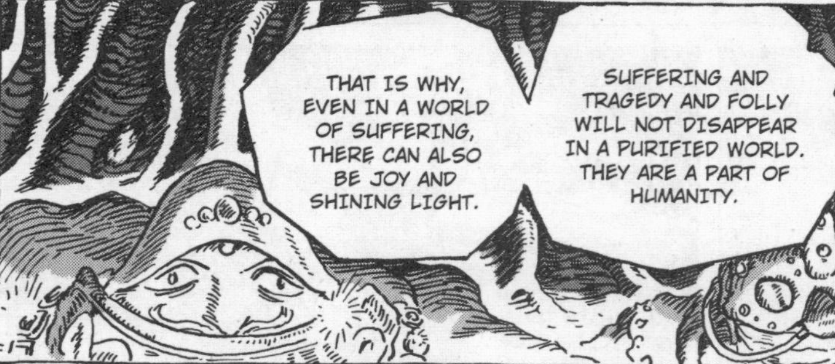
SUFFERING AND TRAGEDY AND FOLLY WILL NOT DISAPPEAR IN A PURIFIED WORLD. THEY ARE A PART OF HUMANITY.
THAT IS WHY, EVEN IN A WORLD OF SUFFERING, THERE CAN ALSO BE JOY AND SHINING LIGHT.

PITIABLE HEEDRA. EVEN *THEY* ARE LIVING THINGS.
BECAUSE YOU WERE CREATED AS AN ARTIFICIAL GOD OF PURITY, YOU HAVE BECOME THE UGLIEST CREATURE OF ALL, NEVER KNOWING WHAT IT MEANS TO BE ALIVE.

THE POSSIBILITY OF VARIOUS UNEXPECTED PROBLEMS WAS ACCOUNTED FOR WHEN THE PLAN WAS MADE.
I AM THE SOLE LIGHT THAT REMAINS IN THE DARKNESS.

YOU CARRY THE SCENT OF AN INDECENT DARKNESS.

YOUR QUESTION IS LAUGHABLE. WE HAVE LIVED ALL THESE CENTURIES WITH THE SEA OF CORRUPTION.
EXTINCTION HAS LONG SINCE BECOME A PART OF OUR LIVES.

GIRL, ARE YOU SAYING THAT EFFORTS TO REBUILD THE WORLD SHOULD BE ABANDONED, AND HUMANITY LEFT TO BECOME EXTINCT?

WITHOUT ME, HUMANITY SHALL SURELY BECOME EXTINCT.
YOU CANNOT LIVE BEYOND THAT MORNING.

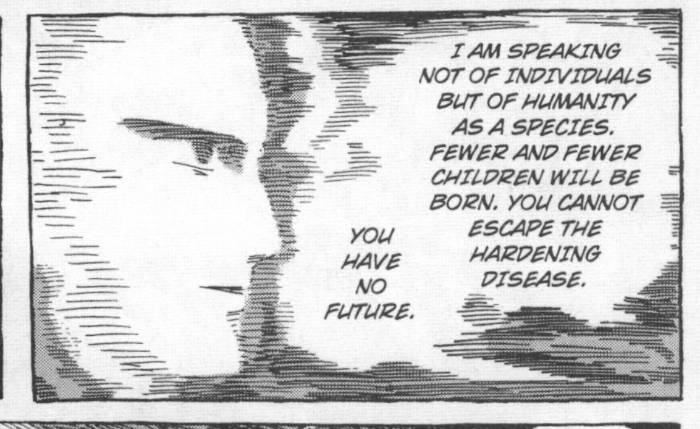
I AM SPEAKING NOT OF INDIVIDUALS BUT OF HUMANITY AS A SPECIES. FEWER AND FEWER CHILDREN WILL BE BORN. YOU CANNOT ESCAPE THE HARDENING DISEASE.
YOU HAVE NO FUTURE.

YOU ARE WRONG. LIFE IS THE LIGHT THAT SHINES IN THE DARKNESS!!

THAT IS NIHILISM!! NOTHING-NESS!!
THAT IS FOR THIS PLANET TO DECIDE.

YOU ARE A DANGEROUS DARKNESS. LIFE IS LIGHT!!

THE SYMPATHY AND LOVE OF THE OHMU WERE BORN FROM THE DEPTHS OF NOTHINGNESS.

ALL THINGS ARE BORN FROM DARKNESS AND ALL THINGS RETURN TO DARKNESS.
AND NOW IT IS TIME FOR YOU TO RETURN TO DARKNESS!!

HEE, HEE, HEE. THIS GIRL'S A DELIGHT!!

WE SHALL NOT BECOME THE GUARDIAN OF THE TOMB!
WE SHALL NOT SERVE YOU!! WE SHALL DECIDE OUR FATE FOR OURSELVES.

YOU ARE THE ENEMIES OF HOPE.

HO-HO! HE'S ANGRY NOW. HE CLOSED UP THE HOLE.
F-FORGIVE US, MASTER...

ジンジンジン
DAMN, THAT'S HOT! THIS LOUSY TOMB THINKS IT IS GOD!!

ズズズ

!? IT'S STARTING TO MOVE.

DON'T LET ME DOWN!!

NAUSICAÄ!!

ヒィィィィィィィー
HANG ON!! IT'LL DESTROY YOUR MIND.
CALL OHMA. HURRY!!
ゴォオオ
キィィィィィィィ

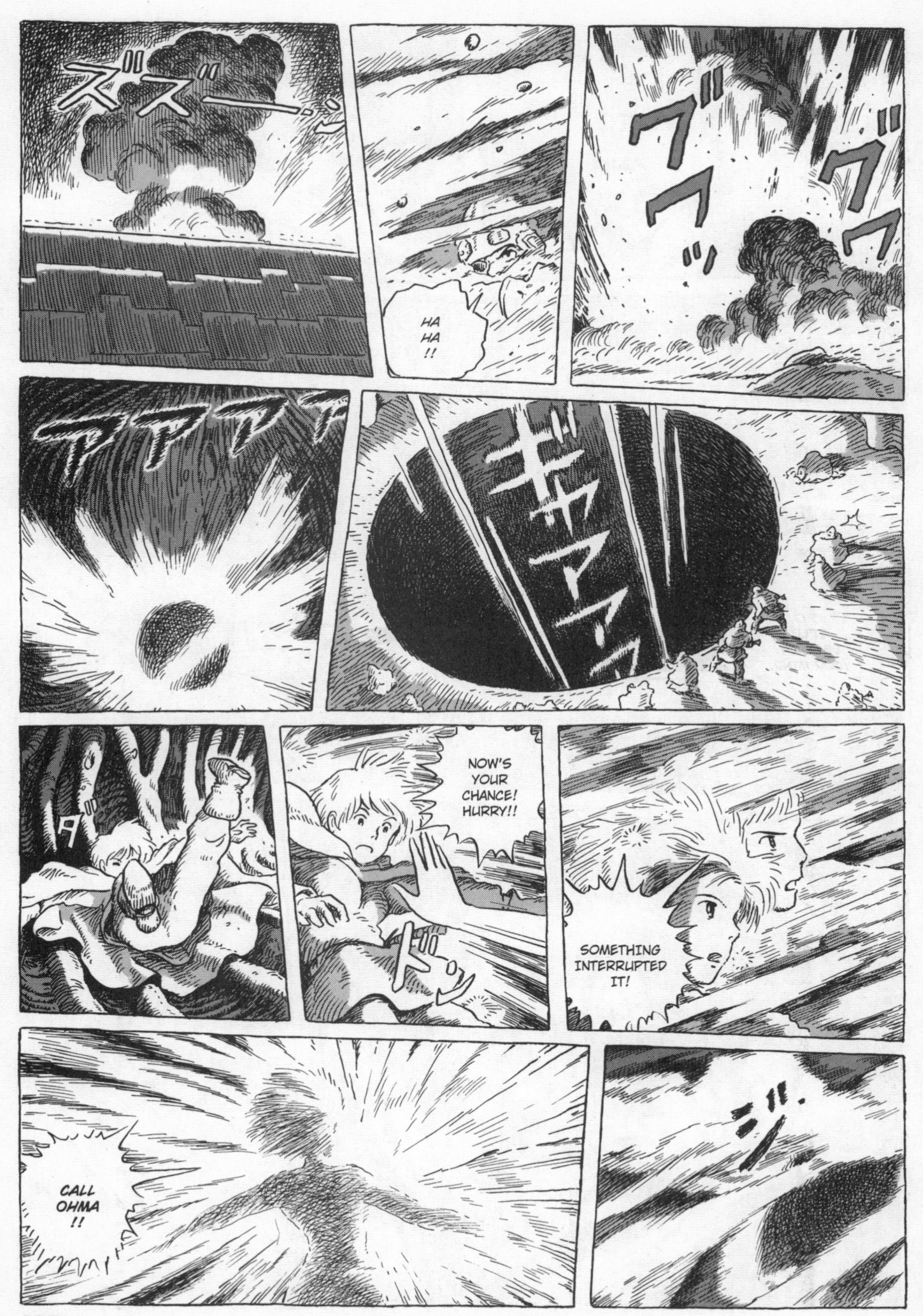

HA HA!!
SOMETHING INTERRUPTED IT!
NOW'S YOUR CHANCE! HURRY!!
CALL OHMA!!

HURRY, NAUSICAÄ !!

OHMA!! COME TO ME!!

OHMA!

OHMA !!

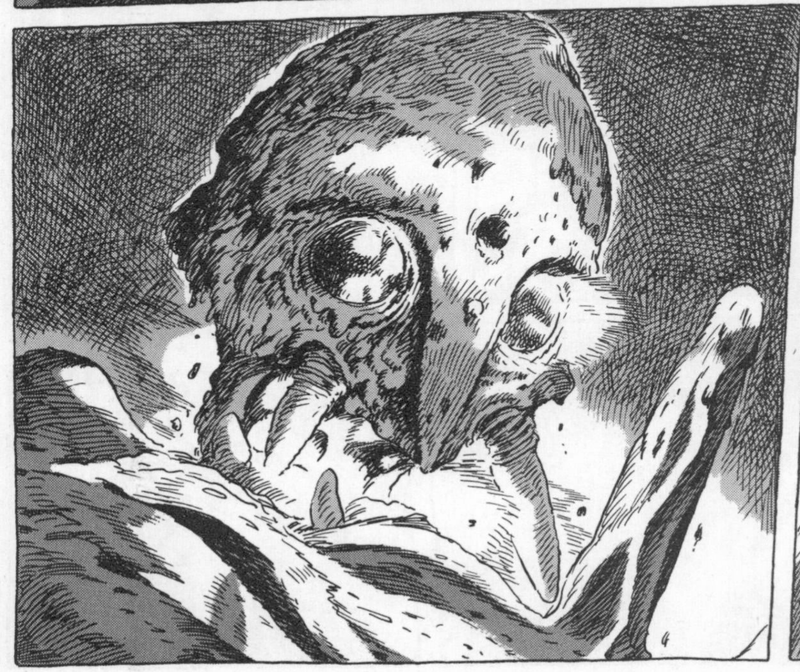

ギュン

THE CRYPT IS MOANING!!
THE WOUND HAS BURST OPEN!!

!? IT'S CEASED ITS ATTACK!

G-GAHHH! DO NOT CALL FORTH THE MONSTER THAT DESTROYED THE WORLD!!
CEASE, CHILD OF DARKNESS !!

I DON'T CARE. IF YOU ARE LIGHT, THEN WE DO NOT NEED LIGHT.

HISTORY SHALL REMEMBER YOU AS A DEVIL. THE ONE WHO DESTROYED THE LIGHT OF HOPE!

BECAUSE *OUR* GOD INHABITS EVEN A SINGLE LEAF AND THE SMALLEST INSECTS.
WE CAN KNOW THE BEAUTY AND CRUELTY OF THE WORLD WITHOUT THE HELP OF A GIANT TOMB AND ITS SERVANTS.

カア

OHMA, FORGET ABOUT US. SEND YOUR LIGHT TO THIS PLACE!!

THE MASTER'S BLOOD !!

グイ

ミシミシ

ブチ

MOTHER
...

ズリ
ズリ

ウオン
ウオン

ウオ
THE LIGHT'S GONE OUT. IT'S IN PAIN.

IT'S CRYING.
IT'S SAYING THAT ITS EGGS ARE DYING.
ウオン

EGGS!? YOU MEAN THE EGGS OF THE HUMANS WHO WERE TO REPLACE US ONCE THE WORLD HAD BEEN PURIFIED?
ウオン

I SHUDDER AT THE DEPTH OF MY SIN.
THEY WERE TO HAVE BEEN A PEACEFUL, INTELLIGENT PEOPLE. NOT VIOLENT LIKE US.
ウオオオン

HAH! CAN SUCH A CREATURE BE CALLED A HUMAN BEING...!?

OHMA! RETURN THIS BEING TO DARKNESS!!

TH-THE LIGHT...

IT'S GOING TO BURST!!

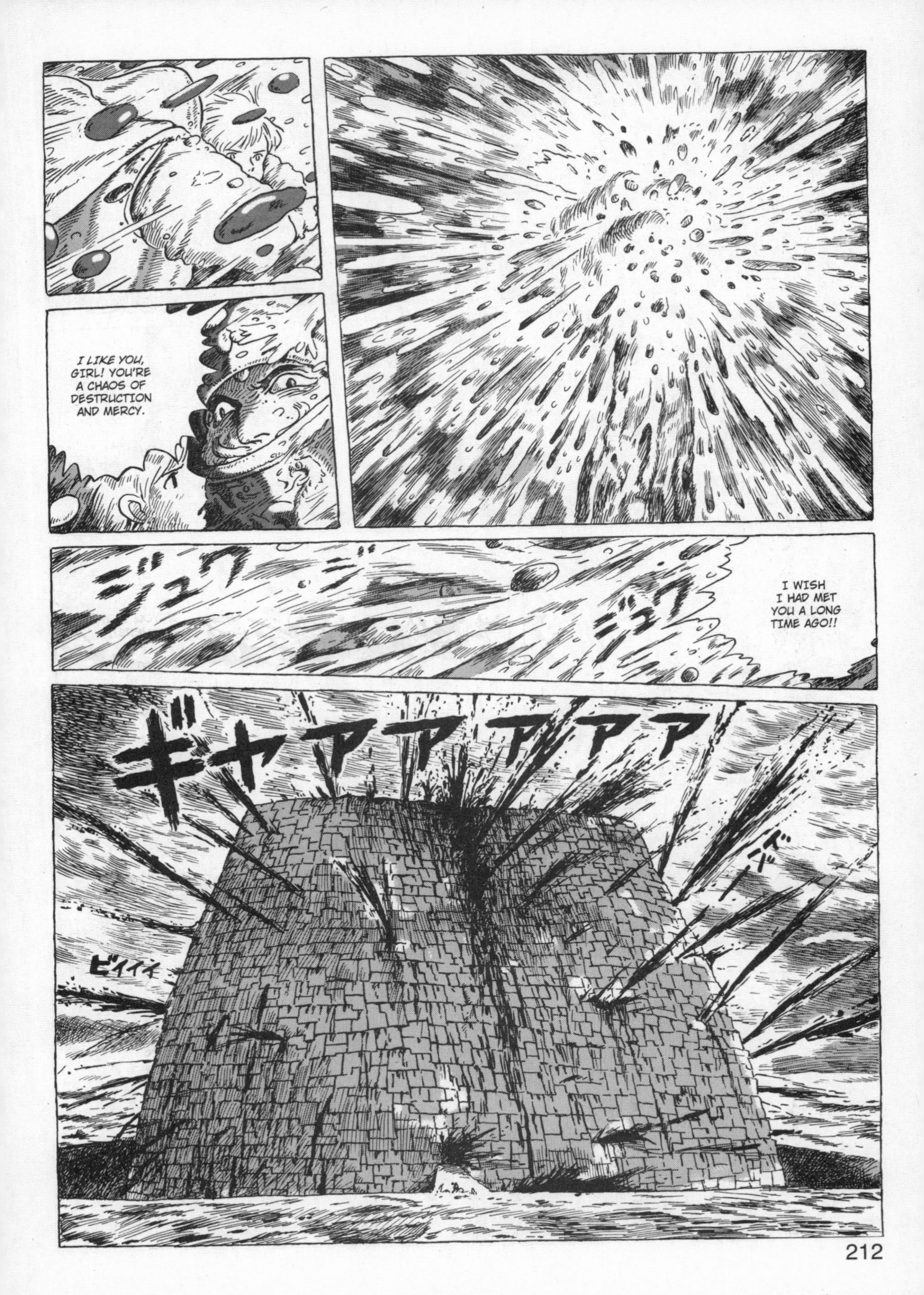
I LIKE YOU, GIRL! YOU'RE A CHAOS OF DESTRUCTION AND MERCY.
I WISH I HAD MET YOU A LONG TIME AGO!!
ジュウ
ジ
ジュウ
ギャアアアアア
ビィイイ

ドドドーン
ゴゴゴゴ

アアアアア
バキ

GET OUTSIDE! YOU'LL DIE IF YOU STAY IN HERE!!
NO! WE SHALL STAY WITH OUR MASTER!
ゴオオオ

THE WORM-HANDLERS !?
ASBEL !!

NAUSICAÄ WENT DOWN!?
SHE HASN'T RETURNED. WE'RE WORRIED.
I'LL GO. OUT OF MY WAY!

YOU MEN GO ON AHEAD.
B-BUT, ASBEL--
GO! YOU HAVE TO TELL THOSE OUTSIDE WHAT HAPPENED HERE.

チカ
チカ
ゴオオオー
オオオーーン
ENTERING SHUWA VALLEY! ALL SHIPS REDUCE SPEED!
ゴオーーンゴオーーン

THIS IS THE DOING OF THAT MUSHROOM CLOUD WE SAW.
ゴオオオーー

IT'S SHUWA! WE'VE ARRIVED IN SHUWA.
WHERE!? I CAN'T SEE A THING!

キラッ

THE GUNSHIP! ATOP THE CRYPT!!

THE HOLY CITY HAS COMPLETELY VANISHED.

NOTIFY ALL SHIPS. WE'RE GOING TO LAND.
I'LL GO WITH YOU.
LET'S GO!!
ルルル

THE CRYPT IS SPEWING BLOOD.
オオオオ
I'LL GO ON AHEAD. LET ME BORROW ONE OF YOUR FLYING JARS.

... AH!

ドオオドオオ

ジュル
ドオドオドオ
OHMA ...

MOTHER ...

ジュルルルル
ジュー
ドオオオオ

MOTHER. I WANT TO SEE YOU, BUT MY EYES...
I'M JUST HAPPY THAT YOU ARE WELL.

I'M UNSURE, MOTHER. HAVE I BECOME A GOOD PERSON?

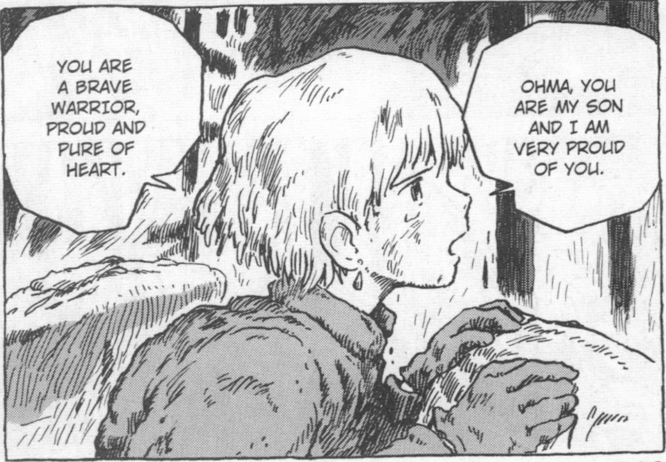
OHMA, YOU ARE MY SON AND I AM VERY PROUD OF YOU.
YOU ARE A BRAVE WARRIOR, PROUD AND PURE OF HEART.

AND ...
... YOU ARE SO GENTLE.

ズ

...
MOTHER...
DON'T...
CR...
ゴブグク

NAUSICAÄ
!!

CLIMB
ON! IT'S
GOING
TO GO!

ドオオオ
NAUSICAÄ
!!

HEY!
IT'S THE
OLD GUY.
ドロドロドロドロドロ
ルルルルル
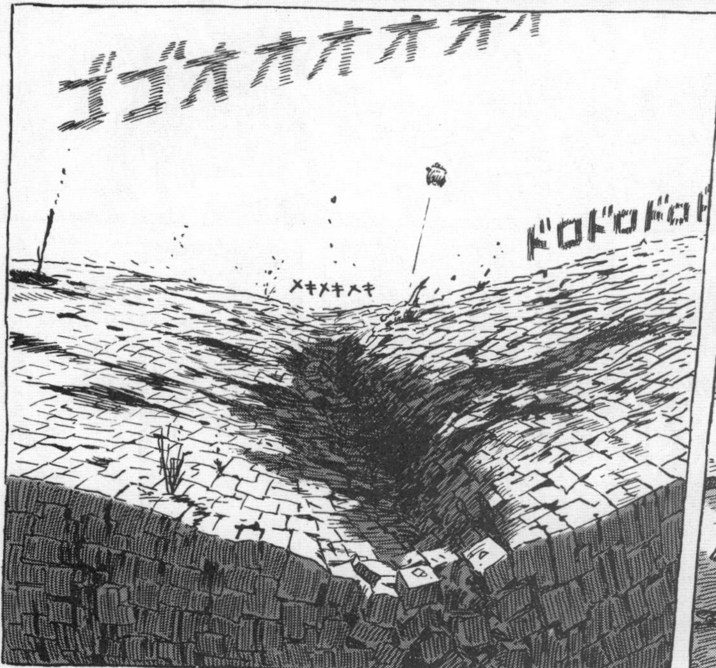
ゴゴオオオオオオ
ドロドロドロド
メキメキメキ

WHAT KIND
OF GREETING
IS THAT!?
CAN'T YOU BE
A BIT MORE
GRACIOUS?
OH,
IT'S
YOU.

グラ
グラ
UH-OH,
BETTER
HURRY.
イテテ

ベキベキ

ゴゴゴゴ

ドロドロドロドロ

ドロドロドロドロドロ
ズズズズ

ゴゴゴゴゴーゴー

H-HOW CAN YOU TELL!? I CAN'T SEE--
NO DOUBT ABOUT IT. I CAN *FEEL* HER.

IT'S NAUSICAÄ! SHE'S ALIVE!!

NAUSICAÄ HAS RETURNED!
SHE'S COME BACK FROM THE LAND OF THE DEAD!

I'M SO GLAD! WE WERE ALL WORRIED ABOUT YOU!

NAUSICAÄ !!

HER CLOTHES ...!?

THE SCORCHED EARTH GLOWS GOLD IN THE LIGHT OF THE SETTING SUN.

EVEN BLUER THAN THE BLOOD OF THE OHMU.

THE WORM-HANDLERS ARE DANCING THE DANCE OF REBIRTH.

OH... OH...
CHARUKA. ARE WE DREAMING?

FORGIVE ME, NAUSICAÄ. MASTER YUPA DIED FOR MY SAKE.
DON'T APOLOGIZE. DON'T SAY A THING.

SEE, CHARUKA? IT'S JUST AS CHIKUKU SAID, ISN'T IT?

WE HAVE ALL LOST FAR TOO MUCH.

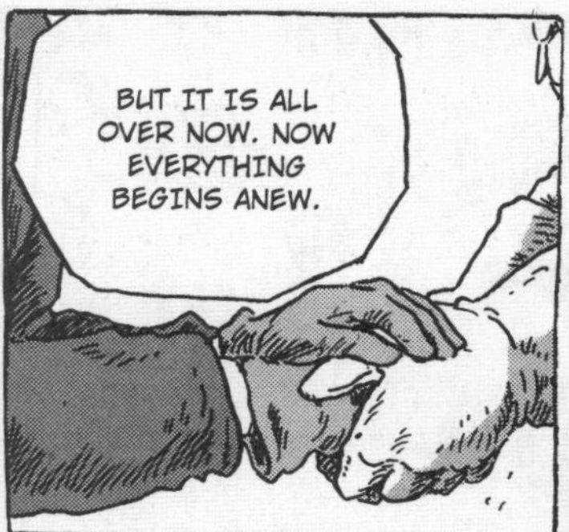
BUT IT IS ALL OVER NOW. NOW EVERYTHING BEGINS ANEW.

THERE'S SOMEONE I WANT YOU TO SEE.

YOUR FATHER. HE PROTECTED ME AND TOOK THE FULL FORCE OF THE CRYPT'S LAST LIGHT HIMSELF.

IT SEEMS THE CRYPT'S LIGHT HAS DRAINED THE VENOM OUT OF ME.

KUSHANA! COME CLOSER. IT PAINS ME TO SPEAK.

I NEVER LEARNED TO LIKE YOU, BUT I GIVE YOU THE THRONE.
AS THE TRUE SUCCESSOR TO THE THRONE OF THE KINGDOM OF TORUMEKIA, YOU MUST REBUILD OUR IMPOVERISHED COUNTRY.
FOOL, YOU ARE WITNESS TO MY FINAL WORDS.
Y-YES, SIR.

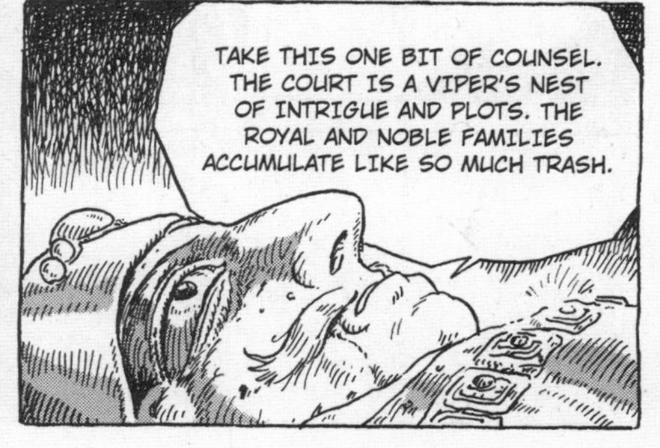
TAKE THIS ONE BIT OF COUNSEL. THE COURT IS A VIPER'S NEST OF INTRIGUE AND PLOTS. THE ROYAL AND NOBLE FAMILIES ACCUMULATE LIKE SO MUCH TRASH.

BUT DO NOT KILL EVEN ONE OF THEM.
KILL A SINGLE ONE AND YOU WILL END UP AS I DID, KILLING AND KILLING AGAIN.
HE CERTAINLY SPEAKS FROM EXPERIENCE!

THE KING IS DEAD!!
THE VIPER'S FANGS HAVE BEEN BROKEN!

IT WAS A MOST INTERESTING END TO AN INTERESTING LIFE. THAT GIRL ...

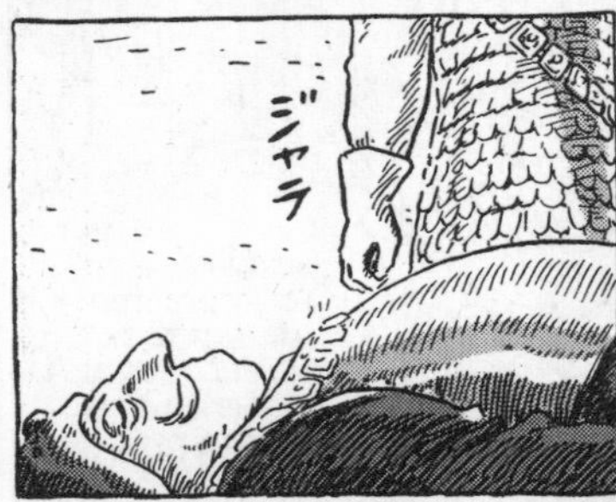
ジャラ

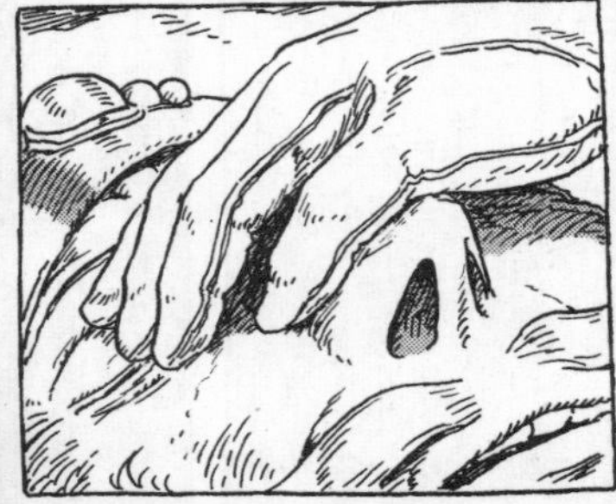

WE SHALL CLOTHE THE KING'S BODY IN BATTLE DRESS AND BURY HIM ON THIS SPOT.
BUT LET US GO HOME TO PAVE A PATH OF JUSTICE FOR THAT KING!!

I SHALL NOT BECOME KING. I ALREADY AWAIT A NEW KING.

THE BLOOD OF THE OHMU AND THE BLOOD OF THE CRYPT ARE THE SAME...

AND US, TOO! I'LL NEVER WASH THESE CLOTHES AGAIN!
LOOK, I'M NOT AS BLUE AS YOU, BUT I GUESS THESE SPOTS MAKE ME SOMETHING OF A "BLUE-CLAD ONE" MYSELF.

MITO, THANK GOODNESS YOU'RE SAFE.
HA, HA, HA. I'VE DEFIED FATE AGAIN.

NAUSICAÄ.

TOGETHER.
LET US LIVE, ENTRUSTING EVERYTHING TO THIS PLANET.

LET US KEEP THAT OUR LITTLE SECRET.

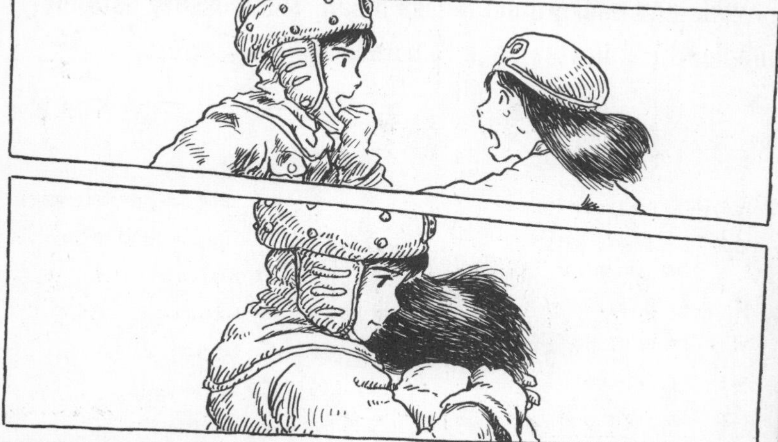

EVERYONE.
LET US DEPART. NO MATTER HOW DIFFICULT IT IS...

YES.

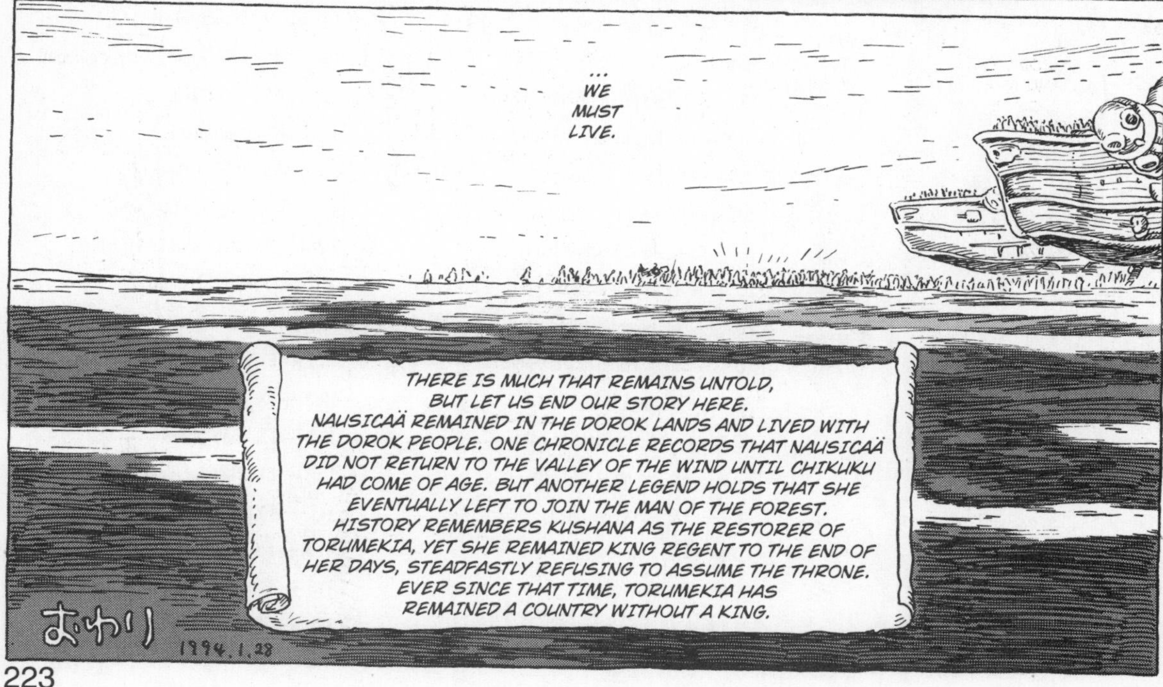
... WE MUST LIVE.
THERE IS MUCH THAT REMAINS UNTOLD, BUT LET US END OUR STORY HERE. NAUSICAÄ REMAINED IN THE DOROK LANDS AND LIVED WITH THE DOROK PEOPLE. ONE CHRONICLE RECORDS THAT NAUSICAÄ DID NOT RETURN TO THE VALLEY OF THE WIND UNTIL CHIKUKU HAD COME OF AGE. BUT ANOTHER LEGEND HOLDS THAT SHE EVENTUALLY LEFT TO JOIN THE MAN OF THE FOREST. HISTORY REMEMBERS KUSHANA AS THE RESTORER OF TORUMEKIA, YET SHE REMAINED KING REGENT TO THE END OF HER DAYS, STEADFASTLY REFUSING TO ASSUME THE THRONE. EVER SINCE THAT TIME, TORUMEKIA HAS REMAINED A COUNTRY WITHOUT A KING.
おわり
1994.1.28

Nausicaä of the Valley of the Wind Guide to Sound Effects

VIZ has left the sound effects in *Nausicaä of the Valley of the Wind* as Hayao Miyazaki originally created them – in Japanese. Use this glossary to decipher, page-by-page and panel-by-panel, what all those foreign words and background noises mean. The glossary lists the page number then panel. For example, 6.1 indicates page 6, panel 1.

22.3—FX: Gachi gachi (shiver shiver)
23.3—FX: Kata kata (tremble tremble)
23.4—FX: Gugu (gwah)
23.7—FX: Gugu (gwah)
24.5—FX: Suuu haaa (shwooh fwooh)
24.7—FX: Uooon (wroom)
24.8—FX: Ooon (ooohn)
24.9—FX: Oooo (wrooooh)
24.10—FX: Uwaaaan (wraaaan)
24.10—FX: Daan dan (bang bang)
25.1—FX: Gaaaa (gwooom)
25.2—FX: Guwaaan (gaboom)
25.3—FX: Waa waa (aaah aaah)
25.7—FX: Suu (shwooh)
25.9—FX: Shuu shuu (fshh fshhaa)
26.1—FX: Jyuuu jyu jyu shuu jyuu jyuu (sizzle sizzle zshh fshhhooo sizzle zshh)
26.3—FX: Ha ha (huff huff)
26.5—FX: Bali (crunch)
27.2—FX: Gugu (grrh)
28.2—FX: Shuu shuu shuu (fshhhoo fshh fshh)
28.3—FX: Shuu shuu (fshh fshh)
28.4—FX: Ka (kraah)
28.7—FX: Don (dwom)
28.8—FX: Gaan (boom)
28.9—FX: Chun (bea)
28.10—FX: Ji (vshh)
29.1—FX: Jyu (vshh)
29.4—FX: Chun chun (vwip vwip)
29.5—FX: Waaa (aaaugh)
29.5—FX: Ji ji (vsh vsh)
29.5—FX: Dadada (bwatata)

12.5—FX: Kaa (glow)
13.2—FX: Jin jin jin jijiji jiji (zzn zwnzwn zzn)
14.1—FX: Uooon (wrooom)
14.4—FX: Ba (fling)
14.6—FX: Pa (grab)
14.9—FX: Suu (shwoooh)
15.3—FX: Ka (flash)
15.4—FX: Su (shwoosh)
16.2—FX: Vuiiiiii (vwreeeen)
16.3—FX: Bilibili (rattle rattle)
16.4—FX: Bibi (shake)
16.5—FX: Pili pili bili bili (rattle rattle shudder shake)
17.6—FX: Dokuun dokuuun (baduump baduuump)
18.7—FX: Jijiji (vibrating light)
18.8—FX: Hyuuu (hwooh)
18.9—FX: Zulu (zwich)
19.1—FX: Ha ha (huff huff)
19.8—FX: Kila (glint)
20.1—FX: Fuwa (float)
20.2—FX: Jyuuu (sizzle)
———FX: Jiji (vibrating light)
20.3—FX: Jyulululu (sizzle)
20.4—FX: Jyuuu (sizzle)
20.4—FX: Jyulululululu (fzzzshhh)
20.4—FX: Jyuu (fshhh)
20.4—FX: Jijiji (vibrating light)
20.6—FX: Ha ha (huff huff)
20.7—FX: Gula (wobble)
20.8—FX: Dou (dwonk)
20.9—FX: Dan (thud)
21.5—FX: Yoro (stumble)

4.4—FX: Gooon goon (gwoom gwoom)
5.1—FX: Piku piku (twitch twitch)
5.2—FX: Gobo (gack)
5.3—FX: Gui (wrench)
5.5—FX: Buchi (vwrok)
5.5—FX: Dolo (drip)
5.6—FX: Zulu (slip)
5.6—FX: Bata bata (jerk thrash)
5.9—FX: Oooon (wrooon)
6.1—FX: Goon goon (gwoom gwoom)
6.2—FX: Bata bata (flap flap)
6.6—FX: Uooon (vwooom)
6.7—FX: Oooo (wrooooh)
7.1—FX: Kaaa (kraaah)
7.3—FX: Oooo (wroooh)
7.5—FX: Jun (vweeh)
7.6—FX: Shun (fwish)
8.6—FX: Goon goon (gwoom gwoom)
9.1—FX: Kaaa (kraaah)
9.2—FX: Pau (pow)
9.4—FX: Gooo (gwoooh)
9.6—FX: Zuzuuun (kaboom)
9.7—FX: Shuu shuu (fshh fshh)
9.8—FX: Shuu (fshhh)
10.1—FX: Ki (screech)
10.2—FX: Wahahaha hahaha (laughter)
10.3—FX: Hehehe (laughter)
10.5—FX: Dan (thonk)
10.6—FX: Hehehe (laughter)
11.1—FX: Bata bata (fwap fwap)
11.5—FX: Pyoko (bounce)
12.1—FX: Gooo (gwoooh)
12.2—FX: Goon goon (gwoom gwoom)

73.10—FX: Pili (pang)
74.4—FX: Gooo (gwoooh)
76.1—FX: Za (zish)
76.5—FX: Za za (zish zish)
76.7—FX: Ta (tump)
78.7—FX: Dada (dash)
79.2—FX: Za (zwosh)
79.4—FX: Doka doka (dwak dwak)
82.1—FX: Oooo (wrooooh)
85.1—FX: Uoooo (wrooooh)
85.3—FX: Gu mili mishi (grip crack crush)
85.5—FX: Biii biii (beeep beeeep)
———FX: Ooo (wroooh)
85.7—FX: Gula (stumble)
85.8—FX: Ba (bwah)
86.2—FX: Bata bata (rattle rattle)
86.3—FX: Bata bata (flutter flutter)
86.4—FX: Bata bata (rattle rattle)
86.5—FX: Oooo (wroooh)
87.4—FX: Koku (nod)
87.6—FX: Gui (grak)
88.2—FX: Chika chika (flash flash)
88.5—FX: Pow (pwoof)
88.6—FX: Kuwa (kaboom)
89.1—FX: Gogogo (gghoooh)
89.1—FX: Uoooo kuwaaa (wrooooh kwoom)
90.4—FX: Shuu shuu (fshh fshh)
———FX: Jiji (vibrating light)
90.5—FX: Bota bota (blap shlip)
93.3—FX: Gyu (clench)
93.4—FX: Ji (pulsing light)
94.2—FX: Busu busu (sizzle sizzle)
94.4—FX: Jiji (pulsing energy)
96.2—FX: Shuu shuu (fshh fshh)
96.7—FX: Gulali (wobble)
96.8—FX: Zuzuuun (zadmmm)
97.3—FX: Zei zei zei ha
(wheeze rasp pant pant)
97.5—FX: Geho (gack)
97.6—FX: Zei zei (huff huff)
97.9—FX: Hiii (eeek)
97.10—FX: Zei zei (wheeze wheeze)
97.11—FX: Uuuu (ngh gghh)

48.7—FX: Uoooon (vwrooom)
48.8—FX: Oooon (wrooom)
49.2—FX: Fuu fuu (hiss hiss)
49.3—FX: Kiii (screech)
49.3—FX: Shi shi (shoo shoo)
51.1—FX: Uooo (wroooh)
52.1—FX: Vuolololo (vwmvwmvwm)
52.5—FX: Gagaga (ggsh)
53.3—FX: Zolo (huddle)
53.7—FX: Da (dash)
53.7—FX: Walawala (rush)
54.1—FX: Yoisho (oomph)
54.2—FX: Yokora (alley oop)
54.5—FX: Suli (shif)
54.7—FX: Waaa (waagh)
54.8—FX: Hiii gyaaa (hiyaaah gaaaa)
54.8—FX: Dosu dosu (stab stab)
54.9—FX: Gusa gusa (jab stab)
54.10—FX: Dosu dosu (stab stab)
55.3—FX: Gasha gasa (clatter rustle)
55.4—FX: Doka doka zan dosa
(donk donk zash thud)
56.3—FX: Ooo ooo oo (moaning)
56.5—FX: Waa ooo (yeaaaah eayaaa)
56.9—FX: Gugu (ggish)
57.2—FX: Hiiii (hweeeh)
57.3—FX: Vuololololo (vwrvwroom)
57.7—FX: Gagaga (ggshaaa)
57.8—FX: Uoooon (wrooom)
64.3—FX: Gi (creak)
65.2—FX: Sawa (murmur)
67.5—FX: Za (zish)
68.7—FX: Zawazawa (yammer yammer)
69.3—FX: Za (zish)
70.2—FX: Za (zgash)
70.9—FX: Tatata (dash)
71.1—FX: Ga (whack)
71.2—FX: Don (thud)
71.4—FX: Sa (swish)
72.5—FX: Vomuu (vwom)
72.7—FX: Nnn nnn (bmmmm)
73.1—FX: Uoooo (wrooom)
73.8—FX: Oooo (oooom)

29.7—FX: Ba (bwah)
29.11—FX: Shuuu shuu shuu
(fshh fshh fshh)
30.1—FX: Ta (dash)
30.3—FX: Busu busu (crackle sizzle)
30.6—FX: Aa (moan)
30.10—FX: Gashi (grasp)
31.1—FX: Gugu (gurgle)
31.1—FX: Buchi (yank)
31.2—FX: Gaku (thump)
31.4—FX: Yolo (wobble)
31.8—FX: Ha ha (huff huff)
32.6—FX: Zulu (zlorp)
32.9—FX: Doon (crash)
34.3—FX: Guwa (gleam)
34.4—FX: Jin jin (vibrating light)
36.10—FX: Uoooon (wroooom)
37.1—FX: Gooo (gwhooh)
38.2—FX: Uooon (wrooom)
38.3—FX: Zaza (zzshaa)
38.4—FX: Zuzu (zgshh)
39.3—FX: Jyuuu (sizzle)
39.4—FX: Jiji (vibrating light)
43.3—FX: Ha ha (huff huff)
43.5—FX: Kuta (stumble)
43.7—FX: Bata (thud)
43.9—FX: Waaa (waaaaugh)
44.1—FX: Kuwaaa (roar)
44.2—FX: Zun (slamm)
44.3—FX: Jijiji (vibrating light)
44.5—FX: Waaa (waaaugh)
44.5—FX: Nuu (nwooh)
44.6—FX: Jiji (jgshh)
45.1—FX: Goso (rustle)
45.6—FX: Shuu shuu (fshh fshh)
45.7—FX: Shuu shuu (fshh fshh)
46.1—FX: Shuu (fshh)
46.3—FX: Goku (gulp)
47.4—FX: Shuu (fshh)
47.7—FX: Ka (flash)
47.9—FX: Jin jin jiji (pulsing light)
48.2—FX: Bota bota (blop plop)
48.6—FX: Gogogogo (gggwhooh)

98.2—FX: Toko toko (plod plod)

98.3—FX: Hyoi (lift)

98.4—FX: Toko (plod)

98.6—FX: Shuu shuu (fshh fshh)

99.2—FX: Hyoi (hwoink)

100.4—FX: Giii (creeeak)

102.2—FX: Chichi (chirp chirp)

102.6—FX: Koto (katunk)

103.1 —FX: Fuuu (whew)

103.6—FX: Za (splash)

104.1 —FX: Ki (squeak)

108.6—FX: Zawa zawa (jitter jitter)

110.4—FX: Da (grasp)

110.7—FX: Tan (tump)

110.8—FX: Zaza (rush)

111.9—FX: Baba (flutter)

113.1—FX: Ba (bwah)

113.5—FX: Yulaa (waver)

113.8—FX: Fu (fwoh)

114.1—FX: Suuu (shwooh)

114.5—FX: Gula gula (wobble wobble)

115.4—FX: Tan (clack)

115.5—FX: Bauuu (wwoosh)

115.6—FX: Guuun guuun (gwmm gwmm)

115.6—FX: Ha ha (huff huff)

115.7—FX: Za (zash)

116.4—FX: Sa (sha)

116.5—FX: Ba (dash)

116.8—FX: Pa (pop)

117.5 —FX: Biku (jolt)

120.2—FX: Suuu (swooh)

123.1 —FX: Uiii (vweeeeh)

124.1 —FX: Zuuun (boom)

124.2—FX: Oooo (wrooom)

124.6—FX: Uiiii (vweeeeh)

125.2—FX: Ki (squeak)

125.8—FX: Fu (fwah)

126.4—FX: Su (shwa)

128.4—FX: Sa (clasp)

130.6—FX: Suu (shwa)

133.10–FX: Zawa zawa (murmur murmur)

136.9—FX: Kuuu (coo

137.1—FX: Da (dash)

137.2—FX: Tatata (dart)

137.3—FX: Kuu (coo)

137.5—FX: Kuu (coo)

137.7—FX: Waa waa (yaaah yaaah)

137.11 –FX: Waa (yaaah)

140.2—FX: Pa pa (pat pat)

140.4—FX: Gyu (grip)

141.2—FX: Kuwa (coo)

141.6—FX: Oooh (yaaaah)

142.2—FX: Za za (zsh zsh)

142.3—FX: Ta ta (tmp tmp)

142.4—FX: Za za (zsh zsh)

142.6—FX: Za za (zsh zsh)

143.6—FX: Ha ha ha ha (huff huff huff huff)

143.7—FX: Shuu (fshh)

143.8—FX: Jiji (sizzle)

144.3—FX: Dolodolodolo (dwmdwmdwm)

144.5—FX: Kuuu (coo)

144.6—FX: Do (dash)

144.6—FX: Ooo (yeaaah)

144.9—FX: Doon zuzuun zuun doon
(boom zaboom dgmm boom)

145.1 —FX: Zugaan dan gaan
(daboom bang boom)

145.2—FX: Zuun zuuun (zmm zmm)

146.1 —FX: Zuuun zuzuuun (boom kaboom)

146.3—FX: Zuun zuzuun (zaboom boom)

146.3—FX: Kuwa (krack)

146.3—FX: Ka (flash)

146.3—FX: Gaaan zuzuun (gaboom kaboom)

146.3—FX: Dadadada (bwatatata)

146.4—FX: Gaaan (boom)

146.5—FX: Gau (gwoom)

146.6—FX: Kiiin kiin (klaang klank)

146.7—FX: Giiin (klang)

147.1 —FX: Dan dadan dan dan
(dabom bom bombom)

147.2—FX: Uiiii (vweeeeh)

147.3—FX: Kuwa (kaboom)

147.4—FX: Guwa guwa guwa
(gaboom boom boom)

147.5—FX: Da (dash)

147.6—FX: Mouwaaa (fwooh)

147.8—FX: Chika (flash)

147.9—FX: Jyu (vish)

148.1 —FX: Tata (dash)

148.5—FX: Jyun (vsh)

148.6—FX: Guwaaan (kaboom)

148.9—FX: Kuli (clik)

148.10–FX: Ui (vwip)

149.1 —FX: Jyun (vsh)

149.1 —FX: Ga (gaboom)

149.2—FX: Jyulululu (vwrrrsh)

149.3—FX: Zuzuun (zgrmmm)

149.3—FX: Gon (gonk)

149.4—FX: Gooo (gwhooh)

149.6—FX: Doon dodon doon
(boom bo-boom boom)

149.7—FX: Guwaan zuzuun
(gwoom zzboom)

149.8—FX: Doon dolodolodolodolo
(booom dwmdwmdwmdwm)

150.1 —FX: Waa waa waa
(aagh aaah aaah)

150.2—FX: Waa waa (aah waagh)

150.2—FX: Shuu shuu (fshh fshh)

150.3—FX: Shuu shuu (fshh fshh)

150.3—FX: Zulu (zlorp)

150.6—FX: Uoooon (wrooom)

151.2—FX: Gaan doon (baang boom)

151.3—FX: Guwaan (kaboom)

151.4—FX: Hii (eeek)

151.5—FX: Gaan (boom)

151.6—FX: Gau (gabom)

151.7—FX: Kaaa (kraaah)

151.9—FX: Pau (pow)

152.2—FX: Ha ha (huff huff)

152.6—FX: Goooo (gwhoooh)

152.9—FX: Ga (scrape)

152.10–FX: Ha ha (huff huff)

152.10–FX: Zuuun (zaboom)

153.1 —FX: Dolodolodolodolodolo
(dwmdwmdwmdwmdwm)

153.2—FX: Ha ha ha ha (huff huff huff huff)

153.2—FX: Yoro (falter)

153.4—FX: Ha ha (huff huff)

154.1 —FX: Gooo gogogogo gogogogogo
gooooo (gwhoooh gwmgwmgwm
gwhoooh rumble rumble)

154.2—FX: Goooo (gwhooh)

154.2—FX: Shuu shuu shuu shuu
(fshh fshh fshh fshh)

190.2—FX: Don (bang)
190.3—FX: Don don (bang bang)
190.4—FX: Don don (bang bang)
190.5—FX: Gaan (gabang)
190.6—FX: Giin (gonk)
190.7—FX: Dobo (splosh)
191.2—FX: Munnnn (hum)
192.7—FX: Doka (dwack)
192.9—FX: Ji (jus)
193.1—FX: Ba (beam)
193.4—FX: Kiin (vweeh)
193.6—FX: Oooo (wroooom)
193.7—FX: Gishi gishi (gwsh gwsh)
193.8—FX: Oooo (wrooooh)
193.9—FX: Tsu (tsk)
194.1—FX: Ooo (ooohn)
194.4—FX: Iiii (eeeeehn)
194.5—FX: Iiii (eeeeehn)
194.6—FX: Kii (keeeeeh)
195.8—FX: Giiii (gweeeeeh)
196.8—FX: Da (dash)
197.2—FX: Dan (bam)
197.3—FX: Fuwa (fwoh)
197.7—FX: Jijijiji jinjin jijijiji (vibrate sizzle)
198.1—FX: Bachi (crackle)
198.1—FX: Jijiji (vibrating pulse)
198.2—FX: Ji (pulse)
198.4—FX: Oooooo (hum)
198.4—FX: Jijijiji (pulse)
198.7—FX: Bali bali (crackle crackle)
199.1—FX: U (fw)
199.2—FX: Ooooo (hum)
199.3—FX: Lililin chilili (jingle ji-jingle)
201.1—FX: Jiji (pulse)
202.2—FX: Wahahahaha (guffaw)
202.6—FX: Lilin (jingle)
202.6—FX: Kuta (fwump)
202.7—FX: Kaaa (flaaash)
202.8—FX: Goheeee (gwooough)
202.9—FX: Baki baki gyuuu
(crunch crunch squeeze)
203.1—FX: Jin jin jin (pulsing)
203.2—FX: Zuzuzu (zgshh)
———FX: Dolodolodolo (rumble)

171.3—FX: Hahaha (laughter)
174.6—FX: Mozo mozo (squirm wiggle)
176.3—FX: Puchi (pwop)
176.5—FX: Chiliin chililiin (jingle jingle)
176.7—FX: Waa waa waa (aah aah aaah)
179.3—FX: Ta (dash)
179.6—FX: Puchi (pwip)
180.3—FX: Pu Puchi puchi (squich pop pop)
180.4—FX: Funyu (mwush)
180.10—FX: Don gon (dunk gonk)
181.1—FX: Nuuu (nwroh)
181.1—FX: Uoooo (wroooh)
181.2—FX: Guuu (gnnnh)
181.3—FX: Doyoo (dwuch)
181.7—FX: Ton (tump)
182.7—FX: Piku (twitch)
182.7—FX: Goto (glonk)
182.7—FX: Pukun (pwoink)
182.9—FX: Kyolo (glance)
182.10—FX: Goto goto (gatunk gatunk)
182.11—FX: Golo dosu dosa (roll donk thud)
183.1—FX: Da (dash)
183.5—FX: Zubo (zabosh)
183.6—FX: Zu zu zu (zgh zgh gsh)
183.7—FX: Gushu gushu (mush mush)
183.9—FX: Gushu gushu (gsh gsh)
184.1—FX: Shuu shuu shuu (fshh fsh fshh)
184.1—FX: Gobogobo (glub glub)
184.2—FX: Gobogobo (glub glub)
184.4—FX: Gushu (squish)
184.8—FX: Gaaan (bang)
185.1—FX: Gyaaa (aaagh)
185.2—FX: Baki boki (crack snap)
185.3—FX: Kiin doka (clang thwack)
187.3—FX: Ooooo (chant)
188.1—FX: Fuwa (float)
188.3—FX: Nnnnn oonnnnn (chant)
188.7—FX: Oooo (chant)
188.8—FX: Onnnn onnnnn nnnn (chant)
186.1—FX: Nnnnn (chant)
189.2—FX: Nnn onnnnn (chant)
189.3—FX: Onnnnn nnnnn (chant)
189.4—FX: Unnn (wrnnn)

155.5—FX: Gooo gooo (gwhooh gwhooh)
157.1—FX: Jiji (pulsing light)
157.4—FX: Ka (flash)
157.6—FX: Kata (katunk)
157.8—FX: Pau (pwoh)
159.1—FX: Guaaaa (graboom)
159.2—FX: Gogogo (ggshhh)
159.3—FX: Pau (pow)
159.4—FX: Jyun (sear)
159.6—FX: Zuzuzu (scrape)
160.1—FX: Gyaaaaaa (scream)
160.4—FX: Gogogogogo (gwooooohm)
161.1—FX: Dolodolodolodo (rumble)
161.5—FX: Dooon (booom)
161.7—FX: Gooooo (gwhoooooh)
162.1—FX: Dolodolodolodo (rumble)
162.9—FX: Jyuuu ji jilujilujilu (sizzle jwrrrl)
163.8—FX: Jyuu jyuu jyuu (sizzle sizzle sizzle)
———FX: Zululi (zlrp)
164.1—FX: Don (thud)
164.2—FX: Gula (wobble)
164.5—FX: Fu (fwoh)
164.8—FX: Ha ha (huff huff)
165.1—FX: Ooon (wrooom)
165.2—FX: Ba (bzap)
165.3—FX: Uoooon (wrooom)
165.4—FX: Kaaa (kshaa)
165.4—FX: Gogogo (gwhooh)
165.5—FX: Gogogo (ggwhooh)
165.6—FX: Beki (crack)
165.6—FX: Gagaaan (graboom)
165.7—FX: Waa (whoaa)
166.1—FX: Bouuum (bwooom)
166.1—FX: Waa waa (yaah yaaah)
167.1—FX: Juuu juuu (sizzle sizzle)
167.1—FX: Goo (gwhooh)
167.2—FX: Jilu jilu jilu (sizzle burn)
168.4—FX: Koso koso (whisper whisper)
168.5—FX: Jala (chlink)
168.7—FX: Kila (gleam)
169.4—FX: Bili (rip)
170.7—FX: Hahaha hahaha (laughter)
171.2—FX: Hahaha (laughter)

217.8—FX: Gula gula (wobble)

217.9—FX: Goooo (gwhoooh)

217.9—FX: Dolodolodolodolo (rumble rumble rumble rumble)

218.1—FX: Meki meki meki (crack crack crack)

218.1—FX: Beki beki (crumble crash)

218.2—FX: Gogogogogo (gggwhooh)

218.3—FX: Dolodolodolodolo (crumble crumble)

218.4—FX: Dolodolodolodolodolo (rumble rumble)

218.4—FX: Pyoooo pyuuu (spuuurt spray)

218.4—FX: Zuzuzuzu (rumble)

218.5—FX: Gogoggogogogo (rumble crumble)

219.1—FX: Kila (gleam)

219.3—FX: Waa waa (yaay yaaay)

219.4—FX: Waa waa (yaay yaaay)

219.5—FX: Waa waa waa (yaay yaaay yaaah)

219.5—FX: Dolo dolo dolo dolo (rumble rumble rumble rumble)

219.6—FX: Lulululululu (whir)

219.9—FX: Saaa (shwaaaah)

222.5—FX: Jala (rattle)

210.10—FX: Uon uon uo (moan)

211.1—FX: Uon uon (moan)

211.2—FX: Uon uon (moan)

211.3—FX: Uon (moan)

211.4—FX: Dodo (dagom)

211.5—FX: Guwa (grwoosh)

211.5—FX: Zaba (zaploosh)

211.7—FX: Giligili (crrruush)

212.4—FX: Jyuwa ji jyuwa (hiss sizzle)

212.5—FX: Gyaaaaa (gaaaaaaaagh)

212.5—FX: Dobaaa biii (sploosh spew)

213.1—FX: Aaaaa (aaaaah)

213.1—FX: Waa waa (aagh gaah)

213.1—FX: Baki beki (bwak crack)

213.2—FX: Dodooon gogogogo (crumble crumble)

213.3—FX: Gooo (crumble)

213.4—FX: Zuzu (zghh)

213.6—FX: Zuzun (zgmm)

214.1—FX: Chikachika (flash flash)

214.1—FX: Goooo oooon goon goon (gwooo wrooom gwroom gwoom)

214.4—FX: Gooon (gwoom)

214.6—FX: Kila (glint)

214.7—FX: Ooo (ooohn)

214.8—FX: Lululu (whir)

215.1—FX: Dolodolo (dwoooosh)

215.1—FX: Doooo (bl-blooorsh)

215.4—FX: Do do do (dwoosh)

215.4—FX: Jyululu (hisssss)

215.4—FX: Jyuuu (hiss)

215.6—FX: Dobo (splosh)

215.7—FX: Nouu (nwooh)

216.1—FX: Jyulululululu (fshhh)

216.1—FX: Jyuuu (ssssszzzz)

216.1—FX: Doooo (bl-bloooorsh)

216.4—FX: Dodooo (dvoooosh)

217.1—FX: Buku buku (glub glub)

217.2—FX: Zu (zlsh)

217.2—FX: Dodo (dwshhh)

217.3—FX: Doooo (dwoooooosh)

217.6—FX: Lulululu (whir)

217.6—FX: Dolo dolo dolo dolo (rumble rumble rumble rumble)

203.5—FX: Shupaa (swhoooh)

203.6—FX: Bali bali (crackle crackle)

203.7—FX: Bali bali (crackle crackle)

203.8—FX: Zun (zaboom)

204.1—FX: Hiii (hweeeeh)

204.2—FX: Iiii (eeeh)

204.3—FX: Iiii (eeeh)

204.7—FX: Kiiii (keeeeeh)

204.8—FX: Goooo (gwoooh)

205.1—FX: Guwa guwa (blam blam)

205.3—FX: Zuzuuun (kaboom)

205.4—FX: Gyaaa (gaaaaagh)

205.5—FX: Aaaa (aaaagh)

205.7—FX: Don (shove)

205.8—FX: Da (slide)

205.9—FX: Ji (pulse)

206.6—FX: Jiji (pulse)

207.1—FX: Gugu (tug)

207.2—FX: Guu (strain)

207.2—FX: Shuu shuu (fshh fshh)

207.4—FX: Jun (vweem)

207.5—FX: Kuwa (kraack)

207.6—FX: Babababababa bachi bachi (bzzzzap crackle crackle)

207.7—FX: Oooo (hum)

207.8—FX: Ooooo (hum)

208.1—FX: Gyaaa (aaagh)

208.7—FX: Kaa (kraaah)

208.8—FX: Pau (pwooh)

209.1—FX: Dowaa (dawoom)

209.2—FX: Gyaaa (gyaaaaagh)

209.3—FX: Dobaa (splash)

209.4—FX: Gooo (gwhoooh)

209.5—FX: Zuzu (zzllrrp)

209.6—FX: Shuu shuu shuu (fshh fshh fshh)

210.1—FX: Gui (heave)

210.2—FX: Mishimishi mili (rrrip crack)

210.3—FX: Buchi (vwitch)

210.4—FX: Zulu (zlach)

210.5—FX: Shuu (fshh)

210.6—FX: Zuli zuli (drag drag)

210.7—FX: Buchi (squish)

210.7—FX: Beki beki (crack crack)

210.9—FX: Uon uon (moan)